Mirandi Riwoe is the author of the novella *The Fish Girl*, which won Seizure's Viva la Novella V and was shortlisted for the Stella Prize and the Queensland Literary Awards' UQ Fiction Prize. Her work has appeared in *Best Australian Stories*, *Meanjin*, *Review of Australian Fiction*, *Griffith Review* and *Best Summer Stories*. Mirandi has a PhD in Creative Writing and Literary Studies and lives in Brisbane.

Book club notes are available at www.uqp.com.au

Praise for *Stone Sky Gold Mountain*

'Fresh and vivid, absorbing and tragic. Written with great sensitivity for those on the margins of our violent past.' CARRIE TIFFANY

'A staggering re-creation of an Australian history too few of us know, and a heart-bruising testament of resilience and love. You'll be gripped – and moved – from the first page.' BENJAMIN LAW

'This book is a triumph. An eloquent and moving reminder of a half-forgotten history, the casual cruelties of colonisation and exile, the tenderness of connection. Beautifully observed.' KRISTINA OLSSON

'In *Stone Sky Gold Mountain*, Mirandi Riwoe has resurrected a lost world and woven a tale unlike any I have read before. I recognise this place – the smells, the flora, the fauna – but it has been crafted anew, in rich and glorious detail. Just as she did in *The Fish Girl*, Riwoe forces us to change our long-held focus, and the result is one of revelation. Every Australian, indeed everyone, should read this groundbreaking book.' MELANIE CHENG

'This is a wonderful novel. A compelling story of tenderness and brutality, so lightly told, yet deeply felt.' JOSEPHINE WILSON

'Beautiful and true. Broke open an all-too-forgotten history of Australia I needed to know about. Then it broke open my heart.' TRENT DALTON

STONE SKY GOLD MOUNTAIN

MIRANDI RIWOE

UQP

First published 2020 by University of Queensland Press
PO Box 6042, St Lucia, Queensland 4067 Australia
uqp.com.au
uqp@uqp.uq.edu.au

Cover design by Sandy Cull
Cover images: Letters from Shutterstock/Veris Studio;
Crow courtesy of the Graphics Fairy
Author photograph by Red Boots Photographic
Typeset in 12/17 pt Bembo Std Regular by Post Pre-press Group, Brisbane
Printed in Australia by McPherson's Printing Group

This project was supported by Asialink Arts, the Queensland
Government through Arts Queensland, and a gift to the
memory of Masa Hiraoka and Setsu Hiraoka and Yasuko
Hiraoka Myer.

The University of Queensland Press and this
project have been assisted by the Australian
Government through the Australia Council,
its arts funding and advisory body.

A catalogue record for this book is available from the National Library of Australia

ISBN 978 0 7022 6273 9 (pbk)
ISBN 978 0 7022 6389 7 (epdf)
ISBN 978 0 7022 6390 3 (epub)
ISBN 978 0 7022 6391 0 (kindle)

University of Queensland Press uses papers that are natural, renewable and
recyclable products made from wood grown in well-managed forests. The logging
and manufacturing processes conform to the environmental regulations of the
country of origin.

MIX
Paper from
responsible sources
FSC
www.fsc.org   FSC® C001695

For Papa

To search for gold was like trying to catch the moon
at the bottom of the sea.

TAAM SZE PUI

I wish to inform you that they are only strangers
in this land themselves. Many of them have only been here a few moons,
and none for more than one or two generations.

JAN CHIN

FROM A LETTER TO HIS FATHER IN SHANGHAI, *THE SYDNEY MORNING HERALD*, 1858

PALMER RIVER,
NORTH QUEENSLAND,
AUSTRALIA

1877

1

Ying dreams of her little brother, Lai Cheng. His dark hair shorn so close to his skull it is merely a field of prickles across his head. Up close, his scalp gleams through, the colour of a boiled duck egg. His eyes are puffy. The birthmark, mulberry red, in the shape of a stork in flight, cups his left eyebrow. Over his grimy shirt he wears a vest, the tattered wool much too thin to guard his sparrow chest from the wind's bite. He holds a rice bowl in one hand, and he wipes his nose along his sleeve, smearing a snail-line of snot. He's still crying, and their sister, Su, shorter than he is, slaps his flat cheek.

A tuft of Su's thick hair rises like a wave in a sleek, black ocean from where she has slept on it. The sleeves of her jacket reach only mid-wrist. For two winters now it has been small for her. Her red slippers – once Ying's – are faded, and Ying can see the soybean stain on the left toe from the time Su dropped her bowl of noodles.

When Ying wakes, her chest quakes as though she's still weeping. Pressing her eyes shut against their instinctive flutter, she tries to hold on to the last memory she has of her family, standing in the muddy lane, the branches of the large magnolia creaking with the breeze. When she finally opens her eyes, she stares at the familiar pattern of mould that blotches the canvas wall.

Voices rumble through the torn fabric, the sound almost drowned out by the sharp beat of pickaxes pounding rocks.

She lies on her side and sweat pools in the hollow between her collarbone and throat. The bedding beneath her, and the dirt beneath that, is as warm as heated brick. Perspiration beads her brow, heats her marrow, as if she has a fever. She rolls onto her back and stares up at the sagging roof, wondering where Lai Yue might be.

'Brother?' she calls softly.

Climbing to her feet, she lifts the flap that serves as the door to their hut and takes in the makeshift shanty town: a huddle of lean-to buildings erected upon the ruins of the last shanty town. A group of men tramps past, shovels resting on their shoulders, pigtails swinging. Their neighbour, Chee Fatt, slurps rice porridge from a bowl. Ying's stomach stretches, as empty as a hollowed gourd.

She sidles past, dodging other improvised shacks made from timber debris and sacking, hessian and tin, and crosses a shallow clearing that's been pitted and ravaged by those feverishly hunting for gold. She makes her way as far into the bush as she dares, to crouch by a shrub at the very edge of the foul-smelling copse. As she relieves herself, a bird stares down at her from a high branch, its breast as yellow as the Qing porcelain bowl her father once prized – the one with the elegant pheasant painted across its surface. The bird tweets at Ying three times while the feathery grass whispers against her bottom.

Returning to her tent, she passes Chee Fatt once again. Her mouth waters as she watches him drink the last of his soup. She'll sip some water – that often works, for a short period at least, to soothe the familiar pangs that warble their hungry notes in her stomach. As she looks around for her older brother, hoping he's managed to beg some porridge for their morning meal, her left hand slips into her pocket, feels for the preserved plum she's saved there. A small prize she found lying on the path to the other side of the camp three days ago. Her fingers rub its pruned skin, find the ridges from where her teeth have nibbled a hole in its flesh. Her tongue clenches at her throat, but she's not hungry enough yet. Not so starving that her hands tremble and her heartbeat trips. Her pocket food is for such a time. Until then it rests, waiting for her.

'How is the porridge?' she asks Chee Fatt, politely.

He burps. 'Is good,' he replies in English. Nods at her. 'Say English. *Is good.*'

Ying repeats what she hears. Chee Fatt's a neat little man with the cheekbones of a squirrel. He hasn't stepped straight off a boat like Ying and Lai Yue. He wears a felt hat with a wide brim like the white men, and his shiny coat – long-sleeved with white peonies embroidered upon it – is even fancier than the headman's. It's similar to the one her grandfather wore on market days when he was still alive. But that was sold long ago, after the second thirsty summer when the mulberry leaves drooped on the trees, and the green fruit remained hard and bristled.

Chee Fatt has been in this southern land for many years, knows the language, can comprehend the white people. He arrived at their dig site three days after Ying and her brother and he works for the Sip Yee tong, as they all do. But he isn't beholden to the syndicate's supply of food and water like the others. He already has copper and silver coins of his own. While the rest of the diggers wait for their porridge and watery tea, he eats well, buying the odd cabbage and piece of meat from the pedlars who pick their way through the camp every few days.

3

The first time Ying saw Chee Fatt, she felt a pinch of alarm because he smoked from a pipe – carved rosewood, with a bronze tip and ebony stem – that reminded her of the pipe smoked by the magistrate's taxman. The taxman was tall, with features as hard and unforgiving as a jagged slate outcrop, and when he last visited her mother, not that long before Ying fled with her brother, he carried away the last of their silk thread, four fine ceramic bowls and a sack of rice. But he'd missed her grandmother's large mortar and pestle, made from swollen stone the colour of sand. It was too heavy to lug across the seas, so Ying had left it hidden from the taxman behind the broken tub, although she'd managed to tuck the smaller set – the wooden one with the ceramic pestle – into her sack.

When Ying was little, her grandmother let her open and close the many drawers of her medicine cabinet, which was made of a wood so old the tree was now extinct. Of course, the cabinet is long gone, sold to pay gambling debts. Before it was taken away, Ying deposited what medicinal ingredients she could – cardamom, silkworm droppings, ginkgo nuts and more – into fabric pockets tied with string. Only four kinds of herbs and seeds remain. By the time they reached dry land, most of her belongings were covered in mildew, and her sack was soiled with vomit and salt water.

Ying stands by the side of the river, a little downstream from the camp. She gazes at her countrymen who step through the water, crouching low over their pans. Clusters of straw hats bob in and out of view far up the riverbed until, in the distance, she can see a group of white men at their own derelict camp. The sounds of rock scraping tin, the slough of wet dirt, and the low murmur

4

of Ah Kee's singing are punctuated by the raucous caw of the large grey birds that bicker among the branches of the ironbarks. The heat from the sun is implacable, and most of the lean men have taken off their shirts. Wah Sing's face is flushed red as he bends over the splintered cradle he purchased from a departing miner, while the skin on Poh's back peels away in blowsy, dirty flakes.

When she and Lai Yue first arrived at this site five weeks ago, after those terrible, relentless months of trudging from the coast, Ying cut the sleeves from her blue shirt, and on days like today, when the fabric is wrung through with sweat, she waits for – prays for – the occasional breath of air to fan her body. Ying wishes her dig site was in the water instead of this area of rubble she's been assigned. The best she can do to cool down is to tramp through the shallows. She's also learnt to soak a cloth in the water, place it over her head beneath her straw hat, and wait for the exquisite trickle down her neck and back.

The river is the colour of her mother's pork and lettuce soup, but it smells of mud and decaying tea tree leaves. Chee Fatt says that originally the water was clear, full of fish. A week ago her brother caught a long, spangled fish; simply reached into the murky water beyond his pan and grabbed it by the tail. Once they'd shared out the roasted flesh among some of their friends, Ying ate her ration of four pale slivers one at a time, savouring its muddy taste, not even wishing there was some soy sauce to splash across the dish.

Ying's eyes search the trees that rustle at the edge of the camp. She looks across the river to the other side, past the brown grass and shrubs that shimmer in the blaze of the sun. But no dark figures stir in the shadows of the gums. Beneath the fear that rests inside her, she wonders. She wonders if they miss their fish.

'Ying, found any gold?'

She looks up at her brother, who's holding out a small bowl to her. She swats a fly from where it's trying to sup on the perspiration that forms at her hairline.

Shaking her head, she says, 'Nothing today', and stares down into the cold porridge he's given her. Barely enough to fill a teacup. 'Remember the porridge Mother made us when we were ill, Brother?' The sprinkle of spring onions across the top, pink pickles, sometimes sausage. Steam rising in the winter air. So much porridge it would make her stomach as tight and distended as a drum. A single tear drops onto the thumb that holds her bowl.

'I dreamt of when they were taken away,' she tells him. Her siblings so young, neither of them reached Ying's shoulder. Much too young to be sold. Bargained down to the best price so the family could repay the loan their father failed to honour. 'What do you think happened to them? Do you think we'll see them again?'

She and Lai Yue had hidden behind a crate of geese, close enough to see the planes of their mother's face – cheeks collapsed in on missing molars, a veil of misery glazing her eyes. Even when a pedlar ran past, pulling a cart piled high with radishes, their mother didn't blink away the dust that rose in the air, or step back from its trundling wheels. She didn't flinch, either, when the broker hammered the sign into the dirt that advertised Ying's siblings for sale.

Lai Yue scowls. 'Ying, wipe your face. It will look strange if the others see tears in your eyes. They will wonder what sort of man weeps.'

'I'm not sure we did the right thing, running away so far. We should have found work closer to home. Closer to Mother.'

'And be slaves ourselves, Ying? I've told you many times: Mother didn't understand that this is the fastest way to regain what Father lost. The farm. Our grain. All the silk.'

'And the children?'

'Yes,' he says, through clenched jaw. He sets a stool on the ground.

Ying sips the porridge from the lip of the bowl. She glimpses something black in the rice and, pressing her eyes shut, she takes another mouthful, imagining that it's a cube of preserved duck egg. She can almost feel its jelly melting on her tongue. Only three more mouthfuls – painstakingly measured mouthfuls – and the porridge is finished.

Lowering herself onto the stool in front of her brother, she lifts the straw hat from her head. She holds her plait in her right hand and leans her head back towards him. The metal of the razor scrapes across her scalp, as warm as blood.

When Lai Yue is finished, Ying runs her hand over the bald front-half of her head. Her fingertips search out the line that divides the skin of her scalp from where her queue begins.

She turns to glare at Lai Yue. 'You always take too much off. It looks ugly.' She unravels the plait so she can free the shaved hair that hangs loose from her scalp.

Her brother shrugs. 'I have to make it straight. Sometimes I shave too closely in one place, and then I have to straighten up the rest. And anyway, you're supposed to look like an ugly boy. You're not a pretty girl here, Ying.'

She breathes in, feeling the band tight about her chest. Her breasts are no bigger than shrimp dumplings, but still she has to hide them. She's seen the look in the eyes of some of the men when they catch sight of the white women in town. She doesn't want to see that look directed at her. Not here. Not where lust will be mixed with fury at her trickery.

A grin lifts Lai Yue's lips. 'Not that you were ever a pretty girl, Ying, even in China.'

His words sting, yet she's pleased to see that smile. She can't remember the last time he looked happy. He's only nineteen years years old, but there are creases in his forehead that weren't there before they came to this place, and the skin under his eyes is pale, baggy. The bruise on his cheek has faded a little, is no longer the livid purple of an eggplant, and the cut above his lip has nearly healed and looks like nothing more than one of the many other wrinkles or creases scored into his skin by this land's cruel sun.

They weren't quick enough the last time a rowdy bunch of white fellows descended upon them. Didn't hear the drunken cries of 'Roll up! Roll up!' in time to save their two pickaxes, the sturdy metal pan they'd traded Ying's winter coat for, and the last of the rice they'd hidden deep in the soil. One man – as gingery as a fox, with thick, shaggy eyebrows – swung the spade against Lai Yue's head and called out something in his devil tongue before chasing after the others. Their camp, nearly sixty Chinese men, had scattered in all directions like a swarm of locusts shaken violently from a tree.

Ying is learning their white language swiftly, but not quickly enough to catch words shouted in anger, in threat.

The sun is directly above, baking Ying's straw hat. She pauses for a moment and leans on her long-handled shovel. She feels dizzy and when she glances up her vision is sepia-tinted. Water. She needs water. Her tongue runs across her cracked bottom lip. Her legs are wobbly as she makes her way to the jam jar full of water she's left by the stacked dirt. Her hand trembles as she lifts the glass to her lips, so that some water dribbles down her chin. She thinks of the preserved plum nestled in her pocket, imagines rolling its sweetness in her mouth. Her stomach shifts, but she decides not to eat it. It won't be too long until their next bowl of porridge. She can wait, just as she's waited every other day, her stomach shrinking against her backbone like a starving beast. She runs her fingers over the preserved fruit. Lifting her fingertips to her nose as though she's swiping a fly away, she sniffs the aniseed fragrance that lingers there. It's almost as pleasurable as tasting the plum. Almost.

The men are quieter now in the stark heat of the day, as they hack rock and toss dirt across their wash dishes. Even Ah Kee doesn't sing anymore. He hunches over his cradle, rocking it back and forth. Ying has tried using a cradle only once. There's a knack to it that she just couldn't master, so the headman moved her to the dry plots where gravel islands wait for the younger men — boys — to bring their buckets of water to wash through the soil.

Ying moves to the space beside the plot she's worked all morning, slicing the earth with her shovel. Luckily the dirt is rubbly, easily dug, almost like the red soil of home, where her family's orchard once flourished. When she has a substantial heap of paydirt, she falls to her knees and rummages through it, picking out shards of broken whisky bottles. Her palms have taken on the colour of the soil, darker at the creases. Even when she soaks her hands in the river water, she's unable to rinse away all the dirt. She thinks that maybe she will be stained by this riverbed for the rest of her life.

Handful by handful, she deposits the dirt into her pan, jiggles it around, searches out some colour. But the only thing that glimmers is a drop of her sweat that dashes against the dull metal of the pan. The tip of her third finger catches the jagged edge of a tin lid, splitting flesh and nail. For the rest of the afternoon she digs with her injured finger held aloft. By the time the sun is to the west, she's stacked the dirt into a fresh gravel island.

A flicker – so tiny Ying wonders if it's merely a quiver of sweat marring her vision – catches her attention as she shovels away some earth from the side of the hole. She drops to her knees and scrabbles through the dirt, ignoring the sharp pangs that travel up her forearm from her injured fingertip. Her insides clench with excitement, but she is patient, her tongue pressed between her lips as she sifts through the clumps in her pan. She presses the soil between her fingers until it crumbles into granules. By the fourth handful, a speck the size of a satiated flea glitters against the skin of her palm. She grins. Feels as proud, as happy, as when she'd trapped seven sparrows for her mother's soup last winter. She stands and looks around for Lai Yue, but she can't see him. The other diggers gathered close by, mesmerised by the heat and their own pack-animal rhythms, pay her no attention. Lai Yue likes her to keep their finds secret, until he's seen what she's uncovered. Gulping down the last of her water, she gently flicks the crumb of gold into the bottom of her jam jar.

By the time the men wander off from their plots to seek their evening porridge, Ying has found nine gold fragments. Three of them are even as big as grains of rice. She wonders if she should stay throughout the night, guarding her site, or if she should continue digging by the light of a lantern. But she knows that would make others curious; they might take over her plot and she wants to be the one to unearth whatever riches she's discovered. She will return to her panning in the morning, just as she normally would.

With the jam jar tucked under her arm, she walks towards her side of the camp.

She approaches her tent, passing Chee Fatt, who's roasting a large chunk of bullock meat over an open fire.

'How are you?' she asks him in English, averting her eyes from his meal. But the aroma of the smoke and the charred meat are almost too much for her. It feels as though there are glass beads in her stomach, slipping and rearranging themselves. Her fingertips find the preserved plum.

'Much better,' he says. Nods at her. '*Better.*'

'Better,' she repeats.

When he first came to their camp, Chee Fatt remained aloof from his countrymen. He worked his allotted areas and then returned to his hut and fire, only ever speaking with the headman. One morning, though, Ying heard terrible retching coming from outside their tent. She found Chee Fatt next to his barren fire, curled into himself like a sleeping pangolin. Vomit covered his shirt, and a milky trail of diarrhoea seeped into the ground. Ying still smiles to think of Lai Yue's gagging as they pulled Chee Fatt's inert body into his shelter. She'd relished the opportunity to use her grandmother's herbs, to sort through the bark that looked like woodchips, to grind them until they were as loose and fine as silt. They begged salt from Poh, and Ying made a paste from two caterpillar mushrooms – her last two – eventually leaving Chee Fatt to sip rice water left over from the cook. Each day for eight days, Chee Fatt paid for her care with a piece of gold the size of an oatmeal flake. And now he teaches her the white man's tongue.

She's placing the jam jar on the floor of the tent she shares with Lai Yue when the sound of raised voices reaches her. Her heartbeat picks up pace. Not another attack, please. She stands on her tiptoes to peer over the men who dip in and out of her field of vision, as Chee Fatt remains seated, just glancing over his shoulder.

A group of white men, perhaps nine or ten of them, cleaves a path through the crowd. Ying hears someone mutter 'barbarians', and Wah Sing spits in the dirt.

Lai Yue appears at her side. 'They've come to check we have our digging licences.'

Ying thinks of the two government notes hidden away in the secret pocket of Lai Yue's belt; of how their price of twenty shillings has forced them further into debt to the syndicate.

The white man who leads the posse holds his hand up, forcing those behind him to halt. A rifle is cradled in his left arm. His mouth widens into a smile as his gaze takes in the Chinese crowd. He's slighter than his men, and clean-shaven. Ying's shoulders relax. He seems friendly. Reasonable.

The man speaks loudly to make himself heard. Ying recognises some of his English words, like 'warden', 'licence', 'pay' and 'Maytown'.

The headman of their dig pushes forward. He exchanges a few words with the warden and then indicates to his people that they must line up, present their papers. As the Chinese diggers gather, a commotion by the riverbed catches their attention. One of the warden's men returns, grasping a Chinese youth by the upper arm. She thinks the boy's name is Jian. He's skinny, his blue shirt tattered, and he is no taller than the white man's shoulder. He's protesting, trying to pull away. His captor says something to the warden, shaking his head. No licence.

The warden shrugs and calls to his men in the rear. Two burly men lead a chestnut packhorse forward. With much ceremony

12

and some jangling, they unfurl a lengthy chain. Tens upon tens of metal pendants dangle from the links.

Jian howls and scrapes his heels through the dirt as they tug him towards the horse. Ying holds her breath and watches in horror as the tall men circle the boy. She can't see what they're doing. When they finally step back, their captive is manacled to the chain. Nearly another hundred handcuffs swing free.

The warden smiles pleasantly at the line of Chinese men, gesturing for them to move forward, show their licences. Each time he checks a slip of paper, he tips his hat and says, 'Thank you, John Chinaman.'

Ying's about sixth in line now, behind her brother. She tries to concentrate on the sound of the dry leaves rustling above her, the shuffle of feet across the scrubby ground. Anything to drown out Jian's shrieks, and the loud, pleading voices of those who join him on that long, thin chain. The warden's men laugh, cup their hands to their ears as though they can't hear, can't understand.

When Lai Yue hands over their licences to the warden, Ying wonders if her brother's fingers are trembling, or if it's the slight breeze that ruffles the paper. The warden reads the slips of paper, glances up at their faces. He still smiles, but his eyes are as blank as sea-polished pebbles. He folds the licences over and returns them. 'Thank you, John Chinamen.' As they make their way to their tent, one of the warden's men shoulders past them, heading straight for Chee Fatt, who remains seated by his fire. With their faces obscured behind shaggy facial hair, and their pink skin florid from the sun, Ying finds it difficult to tell the white men apart, but the man who pushes past them, who stands over Chee Fatt, has thick whiskers, and his skin is as pockmarked and dirty as a yam wrenched straight from the earth.

13

Chee Fatt nods, places the pronged bullock meat on a boulder. He says something in English and tries to stand, but the other man pushes him down, so that Chee Fatt nearly rocks off his stool. Ying thinks the warden's man is talking in English but she can't understand the rolls of his tongue, how the words growl from his mouth.

Chee Fatt looks up at the white man, puzzled, repeats himself. 'Yes,' Ying hears. 'I will get now.'

He stands and moves to his hut, the other man inches behind. Chee Fatt tries to smile reassuringly at Ying, says, 'I was waiting for the end of the line. I was waiting for my meat to cook.' He returns with a neat leather satchel. Sliding his slender fingers into the opening, he digs around. He frowns. Pulling the satchel open wider, he peers inside. Rummages some more.

The white man shouts something, and Ying clutches the hem of her tunic. She feels faint.

'I have it.' Chee Fatt repeats this three times, once in English, as he sets the satchel on the ground, emptying its contents of tobacco, pumpkin seeds and one folded newspaper. 'My money? My licence?'

Others press forward, and the fire's smoke, mixed with curdled sweat and something like the gamey stench of fear, starts to make Ying feel sick.

Chee Fatt rests back on his heels, his eyes wide, as he stares at the satchel. Sweat peppers his forehead. He holds his hands open, palms up. 'Where is it?'

'Another one,' the pockmarked man calls out to his boss, grasping Chee Fatt by the elbow. Chee Fatt doesn't resist, doesn't protest. It's like all energy has been shocked out of him. He only has time to gather together his satchel before he is dragged from his camp.

The Chinese headman moves forward to intercede, but he's pushed aside. The warden gazes at Chee Fatt, looks almost sympathetic, and then nods his head towards the chain. Chee Fatt stares at the dozen men already shackled and shakes his head from side to side, his arms tightly folded around his satchel. He tries to escape the other's grasp, takes three running steps towards the bush. With a whoop, the pockmarked man grabs Chee Fatt's queue. He hauls him by the hair across the clearing, as though Chee Fatt is a yoked goat. Chee Fatt falls to his knees in the dust, and Ying has to look away, can't stand to see his shame. It's then that she notices that Chee Fatt's bullock meat, blackened at the edges, has rolled into the dirt.

Chee Fatt is out of sight now. She can only hear the clanging of the chain and the harsh voices of the white men.

The warden's horse snorts, and the warden strokes its nose, says, 'Not long.'

As Lai Yue and others crane forward to watch what's happening, Ying takes a few steps towards the meat. An ant has already found it, cuts a quick route across the grains of the flesh. A few seconds later, another ant joins the first. Eventually, five ants dart around in circles, surveying their find.

The warden finishes checking licences, tethering those who cannot pay the fine. His men gather up their captives in a long line and prepare to leave. Glancing up, Ying thinks she recognises the back of Chee Fatt's neat, bare head as they're led away. Through her despair her stomach constricts with hunger.

A tin cup arcs through the air, ricocheting off the warden's hat. He takes the hat from his head, and his fingers smooth the felt. He says, 'You Chinkies have to learn there is no cheating our laws', and turns to follow his men through a grove of bloodwood, his rifle slung over his shoulder.

Ying's countrymen throng together in a group murmuring to each other.

White devils.

Evil dogs.

One man, hunched, head bowed, weeps into the muddy river water.

Nobody looks Ying's way.

Swiftly, she bends down and swoops up the bullock meat and slips it into her pocket.

2

Lai Yue jerks awake like a hooked fish yanked from the sea. He blinks twice, but it's so dark in the tent that he might as well be blind. His shirt is drenched in sweat; his heart hammers in his chest. His startled mind can't grasp what he fears, can't gather the strands of confused colours and feelings together. As his heartbeat steadies and he remembers where he is, who he is, a sadness settles in. It's a familiar weight, saturating his bones.

The chirring call of an owl pierces the silence. Lai Yue is not sure what time it is, but it must be very late because he can no longer hear men squabbling over their game of fantan, cannot smell tobacco smoke or the sweet reek of opium. Everyone must have retired for the night.

Lai Yue wrenches himself onto his side, away from Ying. The flap to their tent is down, shutting out mosquitos and the light of the moon, but his eyes still manage to take in Shan: the rash of freckles across her nose and wide cheeks, the angle of her hip jutting from her thin frame.

He feels a surge of anxiety, a rising swell slapping his ribs like waves breaking against the sides of a ship. He's alert, as much awake as he was adrift just moments before. Vigilantly evading sleep, for he's wary of the fears that haunt his sleeping mind. It's during these dark hours that he enjoys talking with Shan, even though he's not convinced it's helpful.

'My love, you must work harder so we can return to our own land,' she murmurs to him. 'You have to hurry.' She reaches out, and her hand hovers over his face, almost touches him.

'I know. I know,' he whispers. He thinks of his mother, wonders how she reacted when she realised that he and Ying had fled the day his siblings were sold at the markets. Was she so angry that a tincture of blood reddened her neck, like the time he broke the neighbour's window to steal a coin left on the sill? Or did she collapse in a heap on the timber floors, wailing at their desertion? Maybe his mother didn't react at all. Maybe she stared ahead, blinded, as she did when that man led their younger siblings away.

'If you gather enough gold you can buy back your brother and sister, too,' Shan says. 'Who knows where they have been taken?'

'I know. I know.'

Lai Yue wonders whether his brother remains near their village, or if he was taken a great distance by ship. When Lai Yue was a boy, his family had a servant who had thin whip-lines scored into his palms. He said it was from his time far, far away, when he had to clear sharp stalks of sugarcane. Does Lai Cheng now have the same scars etched into his hands? And what of little Su? He pictures her scrubbing a slate floor, pushing a grubby wet rag back and forth. Down on her knees. A flush to her cheeks, an angry cast to her young mouth. There's a prickling under his skin, behind his ears, on his throat.

Months, he and Ying have been absent from home. He hopes it will only be a matter of a few weeks before they are able to pay out the syndicate for their travel and licences. But he can't be sure. He hasn't found any gold in three days and the crumbs Ying uncovered barely paid for their food and lodging. He thinks of the gold he's secreted – six sizeable pieces and that one nugget, as gnarled as a knuckle of ginger. Perhaps even as much as seven or eight candareens. They're hidden in his belt, which never leaves his body, not even when he washes. Rubbing its pattern into his flesh. He's hoarding the gold in case they're moved on before he can repay their debt to the syndicate. Before he has found enough gold. He's saving the stash for later, for when they can finally board a ship for home. The gold is to save his brother and sister. To buy back all of his mother's belongings. He knows that only when these deeds are done will he be a whole man again.

He gazes into Shan's eyes, which gleam amber in the shadows. 'Won't be long now.'

'Did you say something, Brother?' Ying asks, her voice sleepy.

'What? No,' he replies, irritated. He can feel the heat from his sister's body, tries to shift further away from her towards the side of their tent. Once more his skin prickles, like ants picking their way across his flesh.

He places his arm over his head, the crook of his elbow resting against his ear. He peers into the darkness. Shan has vanished.

It was only once they were betrothed that Lai Yue met Shan. She'd come from another village to live with her uncle after her parents had passed away. A dreary little thing, he thought her. So tiny, her limp hair drawn flat to her scalp. It had rained for twenty-three straight days by then, and the grey light cast shadows under her eyes, around the pucker of her lips. That's how he remembers that time. Everything wet and cold. Mud smeared across the stone floor, discontent heavy on his mind.

The villagers had never seen a mudslide like the one that year. It engulfed the hillside, gorged on the trees and homes by the river, a crescendo that out-roared the sound of the downpour. He'd been on his way to meet Shan one last time before their wedding and could only watch as mud, rainwater, five people, countless chickens, one goat and the wreckage of several houses hurtled down the hill. He ran to the edge of the river as the debris slid into the brown water, a swirl of sticks, shattered timber, whole saplings crashing downstream, caught on a swift current. Three people emerged from the swill, staggering to their feet, struggling towards the cane poles held out by their rescuers. They stretched out their arms longingly, as though they were separated lovers. They were caked in mud like something risen from the earth; so much so, it was difficult to tell if they were male or female.

But Shan didn't rise from under the water. Lai Yue imagines that this is why her skin looks so clean, so luminous, so much prettier than when she was alive. She didn't surface in a sheen of clay like the survivors did. Her body wasn't found for four days, and by then the river had calmed, washed clean by the incessant rain.

After the funeral, sitting among the offerings of tea, boiled eggs and sliced oranges, Lai Yue noticed his mother having a whispered conversation with Shan's uncle. At one stage she clasped her hand to her forehead, squeezed the skin between her brows.

'What were you two talking about?' he asked his mother, as they picked their way home across the wet cobblestones.

She glanced up at him, worried. Tiny raindrops splattered her face. 'Shan's uncle told me that she was very determined to marry. He thinks … he thinks …'

A spot behind Lai Yue's ribs swelled. 'He thinks what?'

'That you are in danger. That she will try to reach you from where she is. Take you to her.'

They walked in silence. Steam billowed from the windows of

the noodle house, and a rickshaw's wheels splashed water onto the hem of his trousers.

When they finally reached their home, he touched his hand to her shoulder. 'You mean ...'

Again, she covered her face with one hand, the other resting on the gate's latch. She shook her head, muttering, 'How much more? How much more?'

His mother found a woman in a nearby mountain village who could offer blessings to help Shan on her way. To release Lai Yue from peril. But her fee was steep, and Shan's uncle lost interest in paying out anything more for the girl, and Lai Yue's mother no longer had anything of worth to sell. Even the jade chopsticks, in their family for eight generations, had been sold to pay for their winter firewood.

So Shan has remained with him. He feels her presence, carries her like a sack on his back. Not too heavy, but there. It's not all bad. Sometimes, on nights such as this, when sleep's treachery is something to be avoided, Lai Yue appreciates the company. And she hasn't managed to take him yet.

3

Pain slices through the muscles at the back of Meriem's arms as she drags a sheet from the hot water.

For her grandmother, every Monday was what she called 'wash day'. But most days are wash day for Meriem; Sophie likes fresh sheets when she finally manages to go to sleep.

Meriem heaves the wet sheet from the washing tub into an empty tub. Water splashes Tinker, the black mongrel they acquired with the house, and she smiles as he skedaddles. In sections, she wrings the water from the linen's length, draping the drier areas of fabric over the side of the tub so that it rests on the benchtop. Her shoulders strain and her jaw tenses as she twists the sheet, again and again, until the drizzle of water turns to a drip. She pauses to catch her breath, thinks of the wringer Sophie has promised her when the carriers next reach town. Won't be too soon.

The water in the washtub is grey. Meriem's fingers edge across the top of the bench until they close over the cake of soap. She dips it into the water, lathers it between her hands, before replacing it.

Already moisture dampens her armpits. Although still early, heat suffuses the air of Maytown, even in her dark washing room with the tin roof. Lucky, they were, to rent this house from Maggie Gilhooley. The other two rooms even have timber floorboards, not just a dirt floor like most of the other houses in town. Midas touch, is what they say about Maggie, but Maggie's business is in girls not gold.

Meriem dunks another sheet into the water and stirs it around with the dolly stick. After she's swirled it, rubbed it, wrung it as dry as possible, she lifts her apron to wipe her face, neck, and up behind her ears too, where a line of perspiration runs down her back. The heat that rises from the hot water is suffocating, and droplets of condensation dribble down the walls. She closes her eyes, and tries to conjure up a winter morning in Queanbeyan, where the air was so cold it hurt her lungs to breathe in, and the frost on the grass crunched underfoot. She remembers the time they'd all laughed when Boney, the spaniel her mother named after Napoleon, puzzled over his bowl of water that had frozen during the night.

Meriem presses her spongy fingertips to her cheeks, knows the skin on her hands is pruned and white. Between her teeth, she catches a corner of skin, numb now, and nibbles it away.

With the sheets over her left forearm, Meriem steps out into daylight and blinks. She pulls her glasses from where they're tucked into her bodice and places them on her nose. She always takes them off when washing because the glass fogs up, makes it even more difficult for her to see what she's doing.

Her eyesight is deteriorating. She's sure of it. It's been two years since she first noticed the spots in her vision. They looked no worse than the small dots of rust on a copper teapot, but, over time, the spots had widened, converged, melted together like bits of butter in a pan, until now she can't see anything in the middle of her right eye besides what looks like a burnt piece of biscuit.

She tilts her head so she can catch sight of what is on the periphery of this biscuit shape – Tinker pissing on a shrub, two magpies hopping among the grass searching for grubs – and walks towards the wire that is strung up between two posts. Flinging one sheet then the other over the line, Meriem pegs them down with beefwood seeds. She can smell oats boiling in one of the shacks further down the dirt road, and the sweet odour of the manure that the Chink uses in his vegetable plot. She thinks of the plum tree in their garden back home in Queanbeyan. Her mother's jonquils that merrily appear each spring. The vine that encroaches upon her father's shed.

She walks around to the front of the house and, as she passes a side window, she's greeted by the sound of buttocks and thighs slapping against each other like raw fillets of chicken. Sophie's work day has begun.

Later in the morning, Meriem wipes down the booze cabinet, caressing kerosene into the oak. She glances over at Sophie, who's in between custom. Her long limbs are draped over the arm of the tapestry armchair as she reads one of the books she keeps in a valise.

The house they share is on the outskirts of the burgeoning township, which is how they managed to hire it for such a reasonable sum. Sophie prefers that it's out of the way. She says the menfolk always manage to find her anyway, sniff her out like an otter seeks a clam. Sophie often walks around the house naked, her damp skin cooling despite the humidity. Meriem admires Sophie's rounded bottom, and envies the woman her small, taut breasts so unlike Meriem's own pendulous bosom. But sometimes, when Meriem is serving Sophie her supper, or is awaiting her instructions, she wishes that Sophie would at least put on her silk dressing gown, the one with the swansdown collar that the neighbour's cat has chewed into stiff strands.

When she's finished with the housework Meriem walks to the main thoroughfare, dust from the dirt road billowing about her hem, the sun's heat on her skin as palpable as a woollen shawl. The dwellings and shops on High Street are crowded together higgledy-piggledy, like a row of uneven teeth. The stench of human waste and manure grows stronger, and smoke rises thick from makeshift chimneys. A woman, straight-backed and hatless, stands by a dray, and Meriem wonders how it's made its way across such rugged terrain. In the distance, towards the river, a shamble of bedding and canvas awnings bake in the midday sun. Hundreds of men – some very young, many who should know better, the educated and the street-smart – mill about, packing their tools and provisions, readying their horses or boots for travelling further afield in search of the colour. A temporary camp for most, last post for some.

Trudging towards Palmer Street, a seemingly endless snake of Chinese men file past Meriem, bamboo poles balanced across their shoulders. Shoulders hunched with the weight of the pails that hang from each end. So many Chinamen. At least they're attired in trousers like good Christian men, not those strange dresses she saw two old Chinese men wearing in the tea house.

Meriem comes to a tent, newly erected, on the corner of Leslie Street. A man stands out the front, pipe jammed in his mouth. He has on a brown waistcoat, unbuttoned over a filthy shirt, and a green and blue woollen cap pulled low over his curly black hair. Meriem can only imagine how smelly his hair must be under there. Two mongrels dance around his feet, holding their heads up to sniff the meat hanging from hooks: a large rack of ribs and a leg of something that Meriem can't place.

'Sure, ye'll find good bullock meat here, lass.' His Irish accent is thick. Sweat glimmers through his sideburns. 'An' a nice bit of kangaroo. A good price for ye.'

She smiles, says, 'I might pick some up on my way home.'

He turns away, but not before she sees his irritation. He kicks the larger dog's hindquarters, so that it yelps and scoots out of the way. She wants to say something, something sharp, something that will make him feel as small as a roach. But she also senses his brutishness, how his bulk overshadows her. So she remains silent, allows herself only a tight shake of the head.

She's careful of where she treads, what with horse manure and the oysters of phlegm the Chinks hawk up onto the road. She makes her way past four Chinese stores with their strange script painted across red banners that flicker in the breeze, three grog shanties, a blacksmith's shed, and a fellow selling all manner of rubbish – nails, rags, horse collars, lidless kettles, used tallow candles – until she stands in front of Cowper's General Merchandise. The store is housed in a handsome timber building, only slightly smaller than the Mayweather Hotel across the way. Its sturdy lines and elevated position lend it a more permanent air than the rickety constructions that surround it. Firewood is piled up against the outer walls, and the verandah is cluttered with buckets, rain capes, mining cradles and tools. A large sign across the doorway declares the sale of drugs and medicine, while scrawled on a board by the door is a list of the incidentals that can be found within.

Today is the day. Today Meriem will buy herself some of the peppermint humbugs she's craved for near on a fortnight.

She holds her breath as she climbs the shallow steps, tries to straighten her shoulders until she's stretched into a confident stature. The interior of the shop is dim, and it takes her weak eyes almost a minute to adjust. Slowly she makes out a pile of mats and rugs, while next to her, on a cabinet, lie comb and brush sets, bottles of eau-de-cologne and tooth powder. She's jostled as a group of women enters the store, so she moves further in, towards her right, and is startled as she runs into a slim man, realising a moment later that she's actually looking at a tall bolt of muslin.

She edges to the back of the shop, where bottles of pickles, sweets and cereals line the counter. Three women lean on the bench, chatting with Mrs Cowper.

'Do you think Mr Hoover will be at the dance, Margaret?' one of the women asks the proprietress.

'No doubt at all. He'll be looking forward to seeing your Kitty there.'

They titter and nudge the tallest woman in the group.

A young man rushes into the store, and slaps some coins down onto the countertop. 'Box of bullets, Mrs Cowper, please.'

The women exclaim, ask him questions about where and who, while Mrs Cowper rummages through cabinet drawers for the ammunition. Two more men, dusty and eager, enter the store, add a shovel and pitchfork to the order.

By the time their horses can be heard galloping off, the store is left with dried mud trailed across the floorboards and a whiff of unwashed bodies. The four women resume their chatter.

Meriem lingers by a basket of potatoes. She'll wait until the women have moved on before she approaches the counter. She's only tried to buy groceries at Cowper's once before. That time Mrs Cowper ignored her, just as she does when they pass each other at the prayer meeting each Sunday. But later, Meriem wondered if she imagined it. It was a busy morning and the shop was in a frenzy, with a new batch of hopefuls heading to the river, buying up provisions of flour, tobacco and pans. Finally, after waiting maybe twenty minutes, Meriem left empty-handed. And here she is again. Lured by the promise of sugar candy.

The large jar of humbugs is on a bench just behind Mrs Cowper. Even in the gloom of the shop, Meriem's poor eyesight picks up their striped lustre. Reminds her of that afternoon in the meadow with Ned. Ignoring the dip behind her heart, she recalls how the humbug clattered against her back teeth as she tried to suck its bulk. How they both laughed when she had to take it from her mouth so they could kiss. Him tasting of liquorice, her of mint.

'Move, for God's sake, miss,' someone grunts behind her.

Mr Cowper drops a full sack of wheat flour at her feet. She shifts so he can lug the sack behind the counter, and her hip bumps a shelf of condiments. The jars clink, and two of the women at the counter turn to look at her. Heat swamps her body, and a fresh rush of sweat slicks her underarms. She tries to draw herself inward. Take up less room. If she could blend into the shadows like one of them shiny brown lizards, she would.

She tries to catch the shopman's eye, hoping to trade with him so she needn't interrupt the women, but he heads straight out the doorway into the back room.

'She can wait.'

Meriem's gaze returns to the group of women. They stare at her. Mrs Cowper repeats, 'She can wait.'

The women huddle closer, lower their voices. Meriem pretends to read the advertisements on the shop's walls. She tries to maintain a calm expression, her jaw clenched tight.

Mr Cowper returns, carrying a wooden crate. She moves closer to the counter where he unpacks a pile of moleskins, folding them into a neat stack.

'Excuse …' she begins, but he just says, 'Sorry, miss', and tips his head towards Mrs Cowper. 'She'll help you.' After patting the last pair of trousers, he leaves with the empty crate.

Meriem steps away. A blush stings her neck.

One of the older women sighs loudly, looks over at Meriem, and says, 'Well, I suppose we'd better let you go, Margaret.'

'Yes, best get back to sorting out these goods.'

The women pass Meriem on their way out, circling her as though stepping around a cow pat.

Pasting a polite smile to her face Meriem steps forward. But Mrs Cowper turns away and noisily unpacks tins of sardines. Once the crate is empty, she reaches under the bench and brings out canisters of tea and stacks them on the shelf behind. When she is finished, she unties the apron from her waist and joins Mr Cowper in the back room, only half closing the door behind her.

Meriem hears her voice, low and sharp. 'I won't serve that girl. If she chooses to work in that woman's house, she chooses the consequences, thank you very much. You deal with her if you want her coin.'

Meriem can't hear Mr Cowper's mumbled reply. She moves backward, her eyes on the humbugs. What was she thinking? What a stupid idea to come into this store again. So much trouble over a bag of lollies.

As she leaves, she tells herself that she will just have to cook a batch of humbugs herself. That's what she'll do. But her mind betrays her with memories of her last attempt to make the lolly: burnt sugar in the air; the batter so sticky it had broken her fingernail when she pried it from the knife; Sophie's laughter ringing in her ears as she tried, so hard, to join her in making fun of the mess.

29

Meriem steps down to the road, the flimsy timber of the middle stair bowing under her weight, and she makes a low humming noise in her throat. Its vibration soothes the scorched feeling in her chest. She blinks against the sunlight.

She'll buy what she needs from Jimmy's shop, just as she always does. She turns right and strides along the dirt road, dust and gravel spraying her boots. That skinny fishwife, Mrs Cowper. Meriem's seen plenty of Maggie Gilhooley's 'dressed girls' in Cowper's store before. Mrs Cowper wasn't too grand to take their blunt, was she? But maybe she was as afraid of Maggie and her bully-boy as the rest of the township. It was very rare to see Maggie's girls with marks on their skin. Not like poor Sophie. Bruises discoloured the pale skin of her arms at times; once, a savage blow to the eye. She's so beautiful. So beautiful that Meriem suspects some men want to destroy her.

She wonders how Sophie would have taken Mrs Cowper's snub had she been there. Broken glass would be involved, for sure, and some choice words. A small smile lifts Meriem's lips, although it's not enough to balm the fiery shame. Her own mother would never have allowed a shop woman to speak to her like that. Never. Meriem's gait slows. But Meriem's mother was a good woman – well liked and respected. She was a dutiful wife, kept a clean house, tended her garden, cared for her seven children. Most of all, of course, she didn't work for a harlot. Meriem's smile is grim. What would her mother think of her now, if she knew? Meriem could almost be enticed to pen the letter herself. She adds the idea to her mental list of all the pinching ways she could punish her family.

Thinking of home used to sadden her, but now she's just left with a hard feeling. She passes a large white tent, the word *COFFEE* scrawled across its side. The old cow who serves the bitter brew looks at her askance, as she always does. Meriem returns her glare.

Making her way into Jimmy's weatherboard store, she pauses by the door to inhale the familiar smells: sawdust, soil, the sharp stench from the dried fish piled into a wooden pail. Once adjusted to the shadows, her eyes take in the profusion of crockery, buttons, bolts of silk, kitchen utensils, oilcloths and boots stuffed into every nook of the simple space. Meriem feels a little unsettled whenever she catches sight of Jimmy's heathen altar – its garish red colour and the sickly scent of the perpetually burning joss sticks – behind the rough slab of wood that serves as his front counter.

She picks up a cabbage and two dirt-encrusted carrots and places them in front of Jimmy. She watches his fluid movements as he pours two cups of sugar into a canister for her. His hair is black, as glossy as a gelding's summer coat, and his skin is smooth, unlike that of most of the fellows in town or at the diggings. His spectacles have round lenses like her own, but his frames are made from steel.

'Jimmy, do you have any sweets?'

He looks about the store, as if he's not quite sure where to find them. 'What sweets, Miss Merri?'

'Sweets? Like sugar candy? Any toffee? Humbugs?' She's hopeful, because Jimmy seems to have all sorts. Didn't he once, on querying, pull a vial of pink dye out of a drawer that time Sophie wanted to colour what she calls her 'Venus whiskers'? And Jimmy also kept Keen's Mustard and Parsons Rolled Oats and Empire flour, just like the Cowpers, but she can see that this time he doesn't know what she is talking about.

'No, miss,' he says, shaking his head. As he places the lid on the canister, his eyes light up. 'But this. I have this. It is sweet.' He hurries around his counter and lifts an earthenware jar out from a cabinet. Having taken the cork stopper from the top, he pokes out something soft and yellow with a fine wooden stick and holds it out to her. 'Try.'

Meriem studies it in the palm of her hand. She sniffs it. Pickled ginger. She knows she doesn't like ginger, doesn't enjoy the warm bite it leaves on her tongue. But Jimmy is smiling at her, eager for her to taste it. She licks it up and chews. Her eyes water as she says, 'Delicious. Thank you. No more. Oh, no. That's quite enough, thank you, Jimmy.'

He pulls a disappointed face and pops the other piece he's skewered into his own mouth. 'You bring me this – what did you call?'

'Toffee, Jimmy. Toffee. Or humbugs.'

'You bring and show Jimmy. I will get, yes?'

'Yes, of course.' But, of course, she can't. She appreciates his help, though, so she buys several pieces of the ginger for Sophie. It's just the kind of exotic taste she would find appealing.

Two diggers, virginal in their stiff clean moleskins, gain Jimmy's attention as Meriem reaches the entrance of the store. The half-caste boy who works for the blacksmith calls out to Jimmy from the doorstep. He holds up a bunch of maybe twelve frogs, hanging limp from twine that's tied firmly about the top of their thighs. Meriem thinks they're dead, until one long green leg yawns wide, its sticky, bulbous toes reaching for purchase against the boy's wrist. The boy shakes himself free from the frog's grip, and the frogs bump each other, twist and swing, their short arms flopping loose. Meriem puts her hand out to still them, the feel of their clammy skin reminding her of when she was young, how she caught a plump tree frog by the water pump, and pressed it to her cheek, savouring the cool dew of its skin.

She frowns at the lad. 'Don't be so cruel, boy. How would you like it if somebody strung you up like that?'

He draws away from her, as if she might strike. He dips his head in apology, points at Jimmy and says, 'He likes to eat 'em.'

Meriem glances back into the shop. She'll never understand his Chink ways. 'Yes, that might be so, but you still don't need to be cruel.' She shakes her head at the boy, allowing her lips to rise in a not-quite smile, and walks out into the brutal sunlight. She can't wait to get home. Out of this blasted heat, beyond the foul diggers swaggering down the dirt road.

It only takes her a few steps to realise she snapped at the boy because he's small, easily intimidated. Because she's irritated with Mrs Cowper, and irked by memories of her family, their backs turned to her. She presses her mouth into a dissatisfied line. Looking over her shoulder, she sees the boy's bare feet, soot black, and his dark hair snarled to his scalp like sheep's wool. She thinks of the man who kicked his dog earlier – wonders what she would have done if it were him holding the frogs. He could've swung them about his head and would she have done anything? Recalling his thick arms and scowling features, she thinks not.

Perhaps she should return to the boy and find something kind to say but, as she watches, he scurries around the side of the shop, out of view.

She crosses the road and enters the butcher shop she usually frequents. Three large carcasses, marbly red, are neatly strung up across the front of the shop like fleshy bunting. The butcher's boy waves a branch at the black flies that pepper and buzz around the meat. She'll purchase a couple of steaks, and then head home the long way, so she can avoid that hairy brute selling his kangaroo offcuts.

4

Despite the molten sunrise glinting through the paperbark leaves, Ying manages to find privacy in the shallows of the river. Three others crouch in the water too, further along. One of them washes his shirt, rubbing it between his hands, while the other – Poh, she thinks – performs his morning ablutions, water slick along his arms. He washes his face, blows his nose into his pinched fingers. She wonders if the third fellow, submerged in the water up to his waist, is relieving himself, contaminating their run-off water.

Ying squats so that her trousers become drenched and so the men can't see the small cloud of blood that billows from between her legs. She scrubs the loose fabric at her crotch between her hands and swishes the water, watching as the darkness dissipates. She imagines her blood flowing through the stream, washing over rocks, settling in the moss. Invisible, but there. Filtering in and out of gaping fish gills. Now a part of the river.

She hasn't bled since the sea voyage. She can't understand why. Luckily, on the steamer over she was wedged in the corner of a bunk with her brother, the cabin far too cramped with men and belongings to move far. The betrayal of her femaleness hidden in the shadows of the crossing.

Ying pulls herself to the bank and rests on her haunches, head lowered between her knees. Shivering, she thinks she'll never feel warm again. Yesterday, even when the furnace-like heat caused two men to crumple to the ground, Ying felt a wintry frost crackle over her bones, burrowing down into her very marrow.

The river seems icy, but it's not cold enough to numb the pain that judders through her injured fingertip. She holds her right hand up in front of her face. In the shadowy light she can just make out the flap of skin where the sardine tin sliced through flesh. She sees how red her finger has become; it feels taut, swollen, and when she places the wound against her cheek, she can feel its warmth.

Taking a square cloth from beneath her straw hat, she scoops three handfuls of dry, sandy earth into it, tying its ends into a tight knot. She draws in a long breath and looks over her shoulder to where their tent is located, three deep behind the others. She rests her head on her hand, already exhausted. But she has to get to the tent as soon as possible, so she can position the wad of sand in privacy.

Her knees are so weak as she stands that she keeps her fingers stretched towards the ground, in case she lurches forward. With slow careful steps she trudges to their tent. One hand clasps the sand padding, while her damaged hand rests on her thigh, where she can feel the sinewy strain of muscle beneath her thinning flesh.

By the time she crawls onto her bedding she's still shivering, but a light sheen of perspiration flushes her skin. She holds open the waistband of her trousers and shoves the padding in place, and then allows her arms to fall to her sides, spent. She's dizzy, has to close her eyes against the whirl of the canvas. Her throat is parched; her mouth dry, pasty. The jam jar of water is on the floor, not far from her right ear, and as soon as she's righted herself, as soon as her heart stops shuddering, she will reach over and take a sip. Soon.

Sometime later she opens her eyes, and sunlight glares through the tent's flap. She closes her eyes again, covers them with the crook of her arm. Beyond the clamour of pain arcing from the wound on her finger, she hears a group of men pass the tent, complaining about the stink of the privy grove. Further away, the sound of water, slapped and poured from panning dishes, shimmied through cradles. And underlying it all, like a velvet carpet, sensual and easily forgotten, the drone of a thousand crickets. Trying to ignore the throbbing in her finger, she strains to pick up an individual tune – something like the melodic call of the pet cricket her grandmother had kept in their courtyard, caged in pretty bamboo. Its insistent whirr, its lonely song. But the din is too loud, each cricket drowned out by the others. Ying thinks back to the pet cricket and purses her lips, whispers *wi-wer-wi-wer-wi-wer*, the sound contained to the close space of the tent, where she feels more alone than ever. Where is Lai Yue? What is her mother doing? Su? Lai Cheng?

Gingerly, so as not to knock her wound, Ying lifts open her trousers and peers down at the cloth pad. A smudge of dried blood, but hardly enough to soak into the sand, eking out stubbornly, as though her body is loath to give it up. Perhaps it is because she is no longer drinking her mother's herbal tea. She would never have believed it when she was younger, but Ying now misses its bitterness, wishes she could nibble on the barky flower shapes her mother used to grate into the boiling water. The steam's pungency as Ying added the safflower petals and thistle, watching the yellow, oily swirls follow the whisk of the chopstick.

Ying turns her head, stares at the jar of water. Her arm, thin as a reed, feels too heavy, her head too light. Finally, with a grunt, she pulls herself up onto her elbow, and with a shaking hand brings the jar to her lips. The water slides through her insides, a cool eel slipping downward through the coils of her stomach. Returning the jar to the ground, she flops onto her back.

Ying feels absolutely leached of life. Of blood. Maybe that is why her bleeding doesn't flow. She hasn't enough to spare. But when she presses her fingertip to the groove of gum against her front tooth, it comes away in a wet smear of red, just as it has for many weeks now.

5

The clouds crouch low, an iron dragon, exhaling waves of grey vapour. Lai Yue can almost feel its breath press against his skin, but there's no breeze, no whisper of air, as the heat – cloying, suffocating – envelops him. Trickles of sweat form gullies behind his ears, streak down his neck in tributaries that drench his shirt.

He whittles away at a piece of wood with rhythmic swipes. Its heft fills his left hand, its splintered edges jagged in his grip. Shavings curl and fall away with each stroke.

He's carving a figure of a bird, something like the rosefinch of home. When he'd picked up the fragment of branch, fallen from someone's fire, it was already in the sway-shape of a bird, and the timber's blushed hue matches that of the finch. When it's finished, he will give it to Ying. Back home, hidden in the pots of herbs with which his mother litters the courtyard, are all the figurines he's sculpted over the years. In the pot of parsley a snail traverses the moss, while a frog, a little wonky and sculpted from soft soapstone, guards her wolfberries. It's been many weeks since Lai Yue's fingers haven't been too sore, stiff, to wield his sharp knife thus. He hasn't carved anything since the sloping pipe he made for Ying to disguise her femaleness when she passes water. He's not quite sure what she does, but somehow, standing with her back turned, she guides the trickle to the ground like any other man.

The knife stops mid-scrape as he glances towards their tent. To where Ying lies, unconscious, for the third day now. Returning to his knife-work, he tries to concentrate on the wicking sound of blade against wood, each scrape steadying the competing thoughts that muddy his mind like writhing, splashing carp, searching out bits of dough.

He lifts his eyes, takes in the water, as dark as soybean paste; the patches of rocks he has slipped on countless times, rolling his ankle, straining his neck. The dull green of the leaves, how they crumple underfoot. The sandy earth that somehow finds its way into the very seams of his clothing, the cracks at the corners of his mouth, his eyelashes. Nothing like how he imagined it would be in the weeks they careened across the sea. Hadn't they been told that this southern land was a heavenly refuge? Heavenly. Conjuring up images of trees heavy with ripened peaches, pigs fattened and content. A land fertile with hope, yielding reefs of gold. Reefs. Layer upon layer of gleaming metal.

All they had to do was get themselves there, they were told, and the riches would come easily.

But this land is barren, hardened, unwilling to surrender its fruit. The heat's hostility like a bite to the hand. And the white people. Those ghost people. Just as unwelcoming. He thinks of the hiding they received that night when their pickaxes and metal pan were taken. The sharp taste of blood in his mouth where his teeth punctured lip. How the stinky curs had gasped with glee, doubled over, winded with the exertion of it, as they fired shots into the ground, spurts of dirt showering ankles.

Lai Yue's knife slips, slicing the bird's wingtip from its body.

'Is your brother any better?'

Lai Yue looks up at Ah Poy. The doctor is a small, plump man. The pores on his shiny nose are wide, craterous, and hairs creep from his earholes like ferns reaching through a crack in the wall. His stance is lopsided due to the weight of the wooden box he carries by its top handle.

'Yes, yes, I believe he is,' Lai Yue says, taking to his feet with a grunt. He didn't ask the doctor to return. Why is he here? Lai Yue feels the familiar tap-tap of irritation. 'He seems much cooler today. Less flushed.'

But was she? Maybe Ying's lack of colour was a bad thing; maybe her energy was slowing down, making ready to leave this world.

'He was in a dangerous state when I saw him two days ago. I would've returned sooner except I was called upriver to a man who was crushed by a wagon.' The doctor shakes his head, tsking tongue to teeth.

'You needn't have worried about us.' Even as he smiles, and bows respectfully, Lai Yue's shoulders stiffen, his stomach tightens. His thoughts alternate between a desire to retain each skerrick of gold he owns and a fear that his sister might be in dire trouble. He doesn't want to hand over any more of his meagre riches to this charlatan of a man, with his box of powders and leaves. The more gold he and Ying can collect, the sooner they can return home, repair all the damage. He stares at Ah Poy. He's sure there's an acquisitive gleam in the doctor's eye, that his free fingers itch for Lai Yue's gold. Lai Yue wants to kick the cotton seat of his pants, chase him from his camp site, but a rumble of unease for Ying gives him pause.

Ah Poy enters their tent. Inside, the air is close; it has a feral, sweet note. Ying lies on her back, eyes shut, her shadow a silhouette of sweat seeped into the bedding beneath her.

'The swelling in his feet has not come down. See here? And here?' Ah Poy says, pointing with his little finger, its untrimmed nail a good two inches long, as yellow as a piece of elephant ivory. 'Did you manage to buy any ginger water?'

Lai Yue is forced to look at his sister's feet. They're bloated – sallow and stippled in dark smudges like the skin of a bull frog. She isn't better after all. He doesn't have time for this. He doesn't have the money. The ants have returned, marching over his bones, nipping at his skin. 'There is none available. Only rice wine or whisky.'

'You must buy your brother as many green vegetables as you can afford. Catch some fish.'

Lai Yue does the calculations in his head. By the time he pays the doctor, buys extra food and herbs for his sister, their meagre stash will be greatly diminished. They will need to spend more months in this place. He imagines their ship home is far out to sea, too far to swim to, too far to call back.

'Have you been using the poultice I left with you?'

'Of course. Can you not smell it?' Lai Yue points at the lump of cloth tied to Ying's infected hand.

The doctor lifts his nose, sniffs. 'The onion is decaying. I will make a fresh one. I have managed to come by some herbal powder that will be perfect.'

He leaves the tent and squats, opening the lid of the box. First he lifts out a stone mortar and pestle, which is much bulkier than Ying's set. From a hessian sack he takes an onion. He whisks the peel away, starts pounding, so that specks of onion pulp splatter the fallen leaves and dirt. He rummages among the bottles and trays of herbs in the box. He mutters to himself as he reads the label on a blue jar, before replacing it to bring out a small cane basket of

41

cloves. After tossing a pinch of the spice into the mortar, he returns to his box to lift out a tiny glass vial. Carefully measuring out a portion of the yellow powder, he sprinkles it across the onion, where it settles like a layer of silt. Taking up the pestle, he grinds the mixture together.

'How did you want to pay me today?' he asks Lai Yue. 'I'm happy to take gold again, or your coin is good enough too.'

Lai Yue clenches his teeth. He feels a bit sick at the thought of parting with even a flake of gold but, glancing through the open flap of the tent at his sister, motionless, with cracked lips and sunken stomach, he knows he will have to. It's as though he's drowning in sand – as soon as his feet find purchase, he sinks backward again.

But where does the doctor think someone like Lai Yue would come by money? Is he being tricked? Does the doctor somehow know something? Lai Yue's eyes dart around his surrounds. A few men pan by the river despite the sun sinking behind the distant mountain range. The Wu brothers, who've taken over Chee Fatt's tent, pass a pipe between themselves, while the youngest one scrapes mud from his slippers. Have they been watching him? Do they know what he's done? Is this a trap?

The rabble of grey birds make a racket in the brush, their gravelling uproar piercing Lai Yue's unruly thoughts. He watches as the doctor continues to pulverise the poultice ingredients.

I told you there would be trouble when you stole Chee Fatt's things, Shan whispers in Lai Yue's left ear. *Didn't I tell you?* Her voice is sad.

But you were there, he thinks. You were there, Shan. You didn't try to stop me when I took Chee Fatt's purse.

He'd felt horrible, sick, when the white men had taken Chee Fatt. He would never have stolen his money, his paperwork, if he'd

42

known the warden and his mob of thugs were going to inspect their camp. Chee Fatt lives here now, in this land that smells of dried bay leaves. He's never going to return to their homeland. He can stay here, find more gold. He has time. Shan knows how important it is that they return home as soon as possible. Find the children. Save his mother.

Guilt tugs at Lai Yue's heart, though, as he remembers the jangle of chain, and Chee Fatt's bowed head as he was led away. Lai Yue closes his eyes for a moment. Chee Fatt still has time.

Lai Yue's gold remains nestled in the belt around his waist. Hard little nuggets he sometimes imagines might melt with the heat of his skin, liquefy, dissolve into his body until he and the element are melded together, a golden man.

He can't bear to give any more away. Each time he hands over a piece of gold, he feels as if he is parting with that exact shape of his younger brother's flesh. He decides to offer the doctor some of Chee Fatt's money.

'I swapped some gold for coins the other day.' He watches the doctor's back, alert to his reaction, but Ah Poy continues to stir, stone grating stone. 'A trader came through the camp. Said it would be easier for us if we carried some money instead of gold. Offered good rates.'

You talk too much. Shan's voice is sharp.

Lai Yue jerks his shoulder at her. 'I'll fetch it from the tent, Ah Poy.'

His fingers scrabble in the dirt beneath Ying's bedding until they touch the silk of his purse. He burned Chee Fatt's suede pouch in their camp fire the night he stole it, watched Chee Fatt sip tea at his own camp not four strides away while the leather charred and warped in the flames.

43

When Lai Yue exits the tent, the doctor stands up, his hands pressed to his back as he straightens. 'I've made you up a new poultice. Just bind it to your brother's hand again, like you did the last time. Throw away the stale one. And find him some greens to eat. Mush them up if you have to, add them to his porridge.'

Lai Yue nods. He shakes several muddy-coloured coins into the palm of his hand. They have the metallic whiff of blood. He holds them out to Ah Poy, who picks through them, choosing a tarnished silver coin and three pennies. The doctor's hand hovers a moment, his index finger twitching as though it's smelling the money, before he plucks up one more.

Lai Yue slumps to the ground next to his sister. He's disturbed her slumber by swapping over the poultices, but her eyes are still closed, her breathing a little ragged. He thinks of the doctor's last words, as he made his lopsided way to another part of the camp site: 'You'd better get your brother to Maytown before the wet season sets in. He'll never survive in his state, confined in that damp tent.' They'd both looked up at the foreboding sky, laden with dark clouds.

There will be more of those ghost men in town, Lai Yue knows it. Again, he thinks of the beating they received. The clump of dirt in his hair muddy with blood. 'They're not all like that,' Ah Kee tells him and Ying almost daily. 'I have met friendly Englishmen. Really, I have.' But Lai Yue isn't convinced. He stares at Ying. Without her, how would he even understand their jumble of strange words? His throat tightens at the thought of mixing with them. As always, the embers of dread fuel his simmering rage.

Clenching his fist, he imagines ploughing it into a white man's dog-stomach. He can't be scared of them. He pulls his shoulders back, breathes air into his lungs, ignoring the flutter of fear in his chest.

Lifting the purse, he feels the clink of coins, the rustle of paper. He slips out Chee Fatt's folded licence, opens it out flat onto his lap. When he'd found it in Chee Fatt's things, he couldn't return it without drawing attention to the stolen money as well. He tucks it back into the silk folds of the purse. His father's purse. One of the few things he managed to salvage after the old man's death.

Pulling the drawstring taut, he rubs the pond-green silk between his thumb and fingers. He tries to block memories of his father, can feel the ants scuttle around his ears, warm his throat, as he puts the purse aside and picks up his little knife and piece of carving. He tries to find his rhythm, slashes the blade away from himself, again and again, but it hitches on the uneven grain of the wood, matching his rutted thoughts. If only the old goat had stuck to tending the garden. Hadn't given up on the trees after one bad winter. Those mulberry bushes, bright leaves dancing and dipping in the sun, reduced to sad, misshapen beasts with brittle bones and gnarled twig-fingers. Blighting everything around them. First the sow, struck down with wheezing breath and lesions on her hooves, and then their five hens refused to lay: just sat at the back of the shed until their legs were too weak to carry them from their deathbeds. Not long after that, mice found their last store of grain. Lai Yue lifts his wrists to his ears, tries to blot out the memory of his mother's wailing.

And what did his father do? The ants well up in Lai Yue's throat; he thinks he might vomit them up onto the ground. A flash of blood-red anger blinds him. It's always the way when he thinks of his father: how he gambled their savings, their belongings, their smallholding. He gambled away the very lives of his children.

Lai Yue stares at the knife's blade, which glints in the dark. He experiences an urge to press the fleshy part of his forefinger into its tip to cloak the wrenching he feels inside. The night he found the old man in the filthy opium shack, cold – blue-cold – lying in a knot of blankets that reeked of stale urine and sweat, Lai Yue could've gladly kicked his useless, lifeless body, the rage in him rising in a torrent, but his uncle was there with him, muttering prayers, or perhaps curses, under his breath. Lai Yue had to swallow the bile, like he does every time he thinks of the wrongs that brought him to this place.

Shhh, warns Shan, her thin shadow leaning into him. Her head is neat, and small, the shape of an apricot kernel. He can smell the oil of her scalp. *You must not have such unfilial thoughts. He will hear you. The gods will hear you. And then what? Have we not had enough bad fortune? Think of something good about your father. Quickly, before it is too late.*

His mind sifts through the memories, like a mah-jong player flipping over tiles. The best ones are from when he was very young, when his father was the most absent. Lai Yue takes a deep breath and pulls his mind back to the early days, when his father left the breakfast table before the rooster crowed or the nightsoil man clanked his buckets. When he'd only leave the orchard when Chang'e, the moon goddess, gazed down upon him from the violet sky. Often their father would find him and Ying in their beds and tell them stories. The tale of the dragon that ate the wealthy man – Lai Yue can't remember why; the man was cruel or greedy or something. And the one about the princess and her magic paintbrush – Ying loved that one. But some of their father's stories didn't make any sense to Lai Yue. Little parables his young brain couldn't unravel.

These are good memories of his father.

'Well, I am no longer angry,' he mouths to Shan. But the heaviness on his heart is worse.

He lifts the flap of the tent. The sun has disappeared, and the moon is a mere sliver of coconut husk, shedding no light. The surrounding gum trees are illuminated by the camp fires that dot the riverbank. His neighbours, the brothers, lie by their fire, ankles crossed, hats hitched over their brows. He's envious of their relaxed limbs, how the youngest brother murmurs to himself, painting pictures in the sky with his finger. A breeze shivers through the camp, bringing the sweet scent of opium smoke on the air. Lai Yue eyes the pipe that lies by their fire. Suddenly he hungers for their lassitude. He, too, wants to think of nothing, to dream of colours only, to forget where he is, who he is. He reaches into his purse, caresses Chee Fatt's riches. Bringing out a coin, he considers the brothers, wonders if they have opium to spare.

6

Meriem drags the bucket from the water, almost falling backward onto the riverbank with the weight of it. A cooling breeze lifts the hairs that wisp from her braid. She can smell the smoke from the bakery's chimney on Leslie Street, and the wood fires that smoulder in the Chinks' camp further along the riverbank. Behind her, at the other end of High Street, a thick haze accompanies the acrid stench of the glass smelter next to the lemonade factory. Meriem turns back to the river and stares out past the stream and straggle of tea trees towards the mountain ranges that surround their township. A bushfire rises high into the sky, dark smoke mingling with the clouds. A rim of orange flame momentarily flickers.

'Them fires are lit by the blacks, I'm told,' a man says as he leads his horse past her and down to the river.

'So I've heard,' she replies, tilting her head the better to look at him. But there's not a lot to see behind the filth caked onto his face.

'Can smell the smoke day and night. Don't know whether to be more 'fraid of them attacking us or their fires wiping our camp out.'

She nods, gives him a half-smile as he walks his horse back up the bank, where he joins a woman. As they turn to go, a small child darts from behind the woman's skirts. In a matter of moments, the girl's over the rise and out of sight, leaving Meriem with an impression of a blue satin sash that's come undone, and tangled hair the colour of wheat. Reminding her of her baby. Pattie, she'd named her, in those few grim hours of dawn they'd had together.

Two parrots startle from the branches overhead, squawking, a flash of crimson and green.

Pattie, short for Patricia, after Meriem's best friend at school. She doesn't know what the Marneys ended up calling her.

The water purls by gently, whisking her back to when she was thirteen and her father took them all on a long journey to the bay. They were to see off her oldest brother, Tom, who was starting work on an oyster boat. Her toes, unfamiliar to the tingling chill of sea water, felt their way through shallow pools that reflected the sky as clearly as a mirror. The soles of her feet slipping on black stones that had the glisten of ice but were warm from the sun. The pebbly sand, the brittle starfish, the tabby-striped seashells. How the tender, wavering anemone flinched from her touch. She couldn't believe the unpleasantness of one minuscule grain of sand caught between her teeth, gritting like chalk against slate. And later, as the wind picked up and they sat on islands of grass overlooking the ocean, she and her little sister, Milly – only seven years old but as game and tumbling as their brothers – had shared bread and butter, laughing as seagulls plucked bits of crust from between their toes, and from the top of Milly's head. Milly squeezed her eyes shut so she missed seeing the white bird dip, wide wings hovering. A squeal bubbling up her throat, only released when the weight was deftly lifted from her head. Her flaxen hair caught in the gale, so that it spun itself into an untidy wren's nest.

Her father tried to take Ma's hand, but Ma slapped him away. Roused on Meriem for putting too much pepper on the ham.

Meriem hopes baby Pattie has found a home on the coast. Hopes her new mother is more forgiving than Meriem's own, her new father of a stronger will. Meriem presses her eyes together to see her little girl, from behind only, her wheat hair, blue sash trailing in the wet sand, pudgy feet leaving their footprints. It's all she can conjure of her daughter.

'What on earth are you doing, Merri?' Sophie comes to stand next to her, hands on hips, pale eyes surveying the murky river.

Two speckled finches flit away as Tinker snuffles around in the underbrush.

'I was thinking of the time my father took us to the seaside.' Meriem feels Sophie shudder against her shoulder.

'I hope I never see the ocean again.' The faint cadence of an Irish accent colours her speech.

'Get seasick, did you?' Meriem asks, a smile dispersing her heavy thoughts. The dog lopes his way to her, presses his wet snout into the palm of her hand. Licks.

'You could say that,' Sophie says, eventually. 'Can't escape the rough seas, even in a first-class cabin.'

Meriem peers sideways at Sophie, but she's turned her head away. Sophie often talks of a comfortable past. Of luxury, of respectability, of a husband named Jonathan. But Meriem wonders how much of it is true, and how much is made up to compensate for a dreary present. There are certainly no photographs of this Jonathan around, although it's true that she doesn't know what Sophie keeps in the papier-mâché box under her bed.

'Well, there's no chance of seeing the ocean from here,' Meriem says, funning. 'A long tramp you'd have ahead of you if you had a yammering for a bit of salt air.'

Sophie just nods, moves off. Meriem bends down and lifts the pail of water. She follows, the handle digging into her fingers as the pail bumps her leg with each step. She knows she's the servant, but she can't help but feel a tiny squeeze of irritation that Sophie doesn't offer to share the load, or that she didn't bring another pail with her to fill to save Meriem from having to do another trip.

Leaves crunch underfoot as they walk towards their house, and soon the heat of the afternoon suffuses Meriem's cheeks as she puffs along. They pass behind a Chinese gaming house and she is mystified anew at the curious clack-clacking that can be heard from within its walls. A grog shanty, on a lean like the inebriated diggers inside, has taken up residence next to the Petersens' lodging house. Another grog shanty is being cobbled together across the way. Four men load rocks from the riverbed into a cart. One of them tips his hat to Sophie, but his mate nudges him. The other two grin, pausing in their work to run their eyes over her.

'What are you doing?' Sophie asks the first man.

'We're laying cobblestones, miss. For outside the post office. Mrs Porter asked us.'

Sophie moves on, seemingly heedless of their tittering, of their crocodile stares. As Meriem strides past, she tries to catch their attention, wants to challenge their rudeness, their boldness. But not one of them looks her way. Their eyes follow Sophie's swinging gait, the bounce of her bonnetless fair curls. And although Meriem would scratch their eyes out if they were to stare at her like that, chagrin also clamps its jealous fingers around her throat. She might as well be invisible. A packhorse. A dreary old mop, cast into the corner of the outhouse. Nobody ever notices her. Not in the way they're aware of Sophie. Meriem's thoughts, as bitter as quinine, dwell upon her own shortcomings: her smudgy face, prone to spots, and far too pale for the climate; her thin hair, which drops ringlets as soon as they're set. Only Ned ever really noticed her. Really looked at her. At least, that is, until he got what he wanted.

Sophie stops abruptly and Meriem walks into her, water slopping over the rim of the bucket and onto her skirt.

'What is it?' Even as she asks, she looks to where Sophie gazes at a tall man leaning against the front door of their house. Another Charlie, she thinks, but then catches sight of Sophie's blanched face, how her body is stiff, alert.

'It can't be,' Sophie breathes.

Tinker pauses with them. Usually placid, a growl grumbles from his skinny frame. He doesn't dart forward, though, barking and corralling like Meriem's old Boney would have done. Instead, he lags behind, sniffing the ground.

By the time they reach the man, Sophie's regained her composure. She smiles up at him, says, 'Well, well, well. Clement Morrison. Come to search for gold?'

Her voice is light, but Meriem senses the tension in her, a taut viola string humming through her body.

'Ye dinna expect me to find you so far?' He has a thick Scots accent. When he smiles, Meriem notices his teeth are straight, although his upper right tooth is chipped, almost in half. Meriem finds it difficult not to stare at his pale blue eyes, at how the bunched laugh-lines leave a fan of dirt when his grin relaxes.

'It's been a long time, Sophie.' His voice is low. Beguiling. Sophie seems to sway closer, almost as though she can't resist the magnetic pull of him.

Meriem squeezes past Sophie, carrying the pail of water to

the tiny scullery at the back of the house. She glances over her shoulder, and sees they're still by the door, like a silent tableau in a parlour game.

She plunks the bucket onto the floor, fills a pan and sets water on to boil. Rinsing two teacups, she turns the second one in the dim light, admires the russet flower pattern, the faded gold rim, and thinks for the umpteenth time how nice a piece of porcelain it would be if not for the crack down its side. She splashes the hot water over fresh tea-leaves; she's quite certain Sophie won't want this particular gentleman caller to be served with the dregs from their breakfast. Pouring her own tea into a pannikin, she peeps out at Sophie and Clement, who are now seated at the table in the living room as though he were a morning guest, here to leave his card. How very strange. Usually if Sophie has a male guest he's whisked straight into the bedroom, a friendly arm around his shoulder, a soothing word on her tongue. Or, in some instances, a group of returned diggers might crowd the table and drink and horse around, sing songs, gamble their gold away. Sophie can almost make as much blunt from playing them at cards as sleeping with them. Chinese men too, sometimes, with their funny long hair and peculiar-smelling pipe smoke.

Meriem shakes her head, rubbing the condensation from her spectacles with the hem of her petticoat. She doesn't know how Sophie can bring herself to do it.

She senses that this guest is different. Their conversation is polite, restrained. She catches some of their talk of Sydney and someone named Ruby and a comment about an operetta they watched. His right hand rests, relaxed, on the table, and one finger taps a steady beat into the timber. Like he's waiting for something, expecting something, but patient with it too.

As Meriem sets out the tea things, she notices Clement looking about their home. He takes in the rough, grey floorboards, the walls that are fortified with bark, splintery and thin, and Meriem knows that to him their house must look no better than a shanty. A far cry from her family's neat timber cottage in Queanbeyan, painted a white as crisp as a peewee's breast. She can't understand how quickly she has become accustomed to such things. Counted herself lucky, even. Suddenly she feels as embarrassed as if he were her guest.

Meriem moves to the crate where they store the spirits, but Sophie catches her eye and shakes her head, almost imperceptibly. A bird scrapes its way across the tin roof. Tinker, who's refused to enter the house, scratches behind his ear in the doorway.

'Would you be wanting something to eat, Miss Sophie?'

Sophie pulls a face at her, half grin, half frown. Meriem knows it's because she called her *Miss*, something she's never done before. She's not even sure why she did so now.

'Yes, Merri, I'm famished. Can you rustle up something?'

In the scullery, Meriem lifts down the cake tin from the shelf. Inside is the batch of soda biscuits she threw together the day before. She breaks the corner off one, pops it into her mouth to check that they haven't become too stale. Setting aside the broken one, she places four biscuits onto a plate. She grapples open a tin of herrings and scrapes the fish into a bowl, leaving the last briny spoonful, scooping it onto her biscuit. Hands on hips, she scans the shelves through her skewed vision to see if there is anything else to offer. Two dirt-red potatoes wait on the bench, but they're as yet uncooked. Salted beef jerky wrapped in a kerchief, presented by one of Sophie's more regular diggers. Behind the sugar canister, Meriem knows, there is a prized can of peaches. She shakes her head. She won't be sharing them with this man. Herrings will have to do.

She places the plate of food on the table just as Clement is saying, 'I've seen the yellow bastards leave their own men to die on the field. Bunch of sneaky heathens, if ye ask me.'

Meriem's heard the like before. It troubles her how many Chinks troop through town. Most of the time there seem to be more of them here than there are white people. She's heard Cooktown is even worse. She's not sure it should be allowed. And she's not the only one who senses the menace of so many Chinese here; she heard one of the hoteliers' wives discussing the problem with the doctor just last Sunday after mass. But then, Jimmy seems all right, with his neat little shop. She likes him, even. And the Chinese man with the garden next door – fine cabbages he gave them two weeks ago.

'Ha' to escort a bunch of the slant-eyes the other day. They dinna have no horses, nor arms, so it's bloody slow work. Good money though – got another lot on the morrow. Poor buggers. Not allowed to carry arms, and too yellow to fend off the blacks themselves.'

Meriem glances at Sophie, wonders if Clement knows about her Chinese customers: the four regulars, the odd one passing through. She wonders if he knows about her custom at all, but then he says, 'It's a terrible thing to think of the stinky bastards rutting away at ye, Soph.' He laughs, a series of three humphs. His finger continues to tap away at the tabletop.

Meriem's ears burn red as she hurries back to the scullery. Snatching up her biscuit, she carries it outside. She takes a seat on a tree stump where Tinker joins her. She stares up into the sky, the light dappling through the gums, peeping around the edges of the gap in her eyesight. She pops the biscuit whole into her mouth. It's dry and crumbly and the herring leaves a soapy taste on her tongue. She wishes she'd brought out her pannikin of tea to wash down the crumbs but decides against returning for it. Perhaps if she lingers long enough, they'll retire to Sophie's room, leaving Meriem to clean up in peace.

A hand grasps her shoulder and she starts.

'Tie this around the tree,' Sophie whispers into her ear, shoving a green ribbon into Meriem's hand. The ribbon she uses to signal to prospective Charlies that she's unavailable. 'And stay out here. Steer the stubborn ones away. You know how they get with a belly full of rum.'

Meriem goes out to the dirt road, stopping at the ironwood. She draws the ribbon about its girth and ties a jaunty bow. As always, she inspects the scar tissue in its bark, an oval shape that has been cut from its flesh. Twice the size of a meat platter. She always marvels at how it looks as if the tree is birthing. Her fingers play along the edges of the scar, stroking the time-smoothed gradient between timber and bark. Evidence of the gentle healing it's achieved since the trauma of delivery. Meriem hopes that her wounds too will mend, that her jagged edges and disfigured depths will fade. Disappear. That one day she is restored enough to abide a loved one's touch upon her skin.

7

Sand flips into her slippers as Ying climbs the shallow rise. She turns and takes one last look at the camp that has been her home for so many weeks. The trees watch over the glossy water that mirrors the trembling foliage. Her eyes scan the sandy banks of the river and, further downstream, the darker soil of her plot. A bird, aqua with brown tips, lands on the bough of a tea tree that extends over the water. With her thumb, she presses the ridge of hardened skin that has knitted over the cut in her finger. The small wound that no longer aches but has taken such a toll on her body.

'Why did Ah Kee have to sleep in so late?' Lai Yue mutters behind her as they wait for the others to gather. 'Stupid goat. Now we will still be walking when it gets dark. Why do we have to wait for him?' He swears and hawks on the ground.

Ying flinches. She hates it when he uses coarse words – words their father would never have said. And Lai Yue wouldn't have spoken such things under their mother's roof either. But here they mix with all sorts of men, and Lai Yue is shedding his sense of delicacy like a skink shrugs off its skin.

Ying watches her brother's jaw bunch as he grinds his teeth. Stress vibrates from beneath his skin. She feels bad because she knows that they haven't amassed enough gold yet, due to her illness. By the time she crawled from their tent, the water in the river had lowered with the lengthening of the days. She remained too weak to work full days on the dig, so Lai Yue decided it was best they head to the nearest township and find other employment.

'They said Ah Kee's necessary because he can speak with the English guards.' She glances at the men on horseback. One has his wide-brimmed hat pulled low, a red scarf tied about his neck. She can only see his wide mouth, his neat nose, as he waits patiently for her party to gather. The other guard is shorter, fatter, has a rifle holstered on each side of his skittish horse.

'We should never have waited for Ah Kee. I don't know what the white devils are thinking. You know the white tongue now. You can talk with them for us.'

Ying shakes her head. She's not confident enough to communicate. And the short guard looks like an impatient type. He's as put out as Lai Yue is at the hold-up.

'If we were only allowed to have our own guns, we could take care of ourselves,' Lai Yue complains as he helps Ying hoist her bamboo pole across her shoulders, baskets swaying on either side. 'We wouldn't need to pay for these guards and we wouldn't have to wait for Ah Kee.'

When Ah Kee finally joins them, they line up in single file behind the horse of the taller guard. Ying and Lai Yue take up the last two places, and while Lai Yue positions his pole Ying counts the straw hats ahead of her. There are thirteen in all. She knows several of the men have found enough gold to repay the syndicate and return home, and that Wah Sing is merely going to town to buy extra provisions before returning to the dig. The others she is not sure of, but she thinks that she and Lai Yue couldn't be the only ones retiring from the gold field in order to seek out other work that might be more promising, less harrowing. She has no idea how much gold they have actually accumulated either. Lai Yue is a tightly folded fan when she asks him about their savings, so she shies from the subject.

They trudge up a hill, the short guard taking up the rear just behind Ying. A little while later, peering over her shoulder, she can no longer see the river. And she feels nothing. No plunge in her stomach like when she stepped onto the boat, leaving China.

She remembers, though, the fissure of wonder that hummed along her spine when they first spied this land's coastline from their steamship. The beauty of it. The aquamarine water; the mountains sloping towards the sea like slumbering beasts. Once landed, they had to wade through the shallows, clasping the brambly mangroves to steady themselves. Lai Yue discovered some nuts growing on a tree near the shoreline – something like almonds. She cracked one open to eat straight away, and slipped three more into her pocket for later.

She wonders if that tree is naked now, stripped by the hundreds of fingers that arrived after her.

Ying and Lai Yue reach the next rise, passing a cluster of men, who rake leaves, stack stones. The cemetery. Ying heard a poor fellow died the day before. Bitten by a snake. Perished so far from home. She hopes someone cares enough to disinter him one day soon, return his bones to his home soil.

The path, trodden clear by so many feet, winds upward through bush. Already Ying's legs feel like aspic, her knees wobbling against each other as she tries to maintain a steady gait. She's aware that her load is much lighter than her brother's, but it's not long before her arms ache. She repositions the pole into the gristly grooves of her shoulders, between bone and skin, bunching the fabric of her

59

shirt to cushion the hard bamboo. If they stop to rest soon, she will remove two of her monthly cloths from her belongings and use them to pad her shoulders beneath the pole.

Ying knows this walk is only for one whole day, perhaps two if Ah Kee has indeed held them up. She thinks of their initial hike from the coast to this field of gold, in a small band of men, much like this. The countless days upon days upon days, torturous, relentless. The tight embrace of the heat. Shuffling through scrubland, branches whipping her arms and cheeks, leaving a map of scars across her skin. Tramping over arid land, no surrender in the sun's brutal rays. Striding through waist-high water was bad enough – they lost a sack of rice that way, and a full crate of chickens – but Ying hated it when they had to make their way through gullies; how the softened, damp skin of the blisters on her feet tore open, became oozy.

Worst was the weight of the poles – laden on either side with rice, panning equipment, water, her grandmother's medicines and mortar and pestle, which she was sorely tempted to desert – against the soft skin of her shoulder blades. Ying reminds herself that she must place the cloths under the pole. She looks up at Lai Yue, walking ahead. There is still the shadow of blood across the fabric of his shirt from where the constant scrape of the pole broke skin. The bloodstains on Ying's shirt are no longer visible; hers has become a uniform rusty colour of dirt and sweat. But she remembers those evenings – gently peeling the material away from where it had melded with the wound, meshed with the dried blood. Unbearable. But not quite unbearable, because didn't she make it? Isn't the skin on her feet tough now? Gnarled like the trunk of a banyan tree? Didn't her shoulders heal, with barely a scar?

But the fever has taken its toll on her body. She can feel the whoosh of her weakened heart as she places one leg in front of the other.

'*What a beautiful jasmine flower ...*'

Ah Kee's singing voice, low and pleasing, rises above the buzz of the cicadas and the twittering of the birds.

'*What a beautiful jasmine flower ...*'

Ying is panting now, but she mouths the words, her steps moving in time with the tune. Her eyes are on the rubbly soil, which, in some places, is scorched black from bushfires, but in her mind's eye she sees her mother, winding silk onto spools, singing, '*Sweet-smelling, beautiful ...*' Her mother used to sing this song, again and again, as she took the cocoons from the twig frames and soaked them. Ying wanted to squeal with the frustration of hearing the sweet tune so often. Now, she has just enough energy to smile a little at the memory, but her chest burns because she misses her mother as much as she would miss her own shadow.

Two men ahead of her take up the song: '*Fragrant and white, everyone praises ...*' A pheasant darts from the underbrush, its plumage rich, earthy, though not as vibrant in colour as those painted on the scrolls that used to hang in her father's bedroom. Ah Kee switches to another song. The grass, straw dry, tipped in flame orange, sways against her knees. The heat is terrible. Ying feels as if she's being suffocated, that she's being poached by the sun, that her insides are congealing. She shifts her thoughts to one of her favourite daydreams – where she is a girl once more. She used to relish the times she could crouch in the garden with her father in a pair of torn trousers, or when Lai Yue allowed her to join him fishing in the stream, but now, after being trapped in this man's world for so many moons, she wants to feel the weight of an embroidered smock, perhaps a jade green with gold trim, or black silk with a butterfly pattern. And her hair will be long across her scalp, coiled behind her ears, and her hands, her hands won't be stained any longer. She grips the pole, slippery with sweat. They will be as pale as a lily, smooth ...

'We will rest here,' announces the guard. He leads them into the shade of some ironwood trees. One of their group hands out balls of sticky rice, and Lai Yue offers Ying a drink from the water pouch. She sinks to the ground against a tree. She nibbles the rice while running her free hand across the blackened tree trunk.

After too short a time, the tall guard says, 'Time to go. We can't tarry or else the blacks will find us.'

Lai Yue has to help Ying to her feet and, as they march forward, Ah Kee returns to the jasmine song. Ant hills dot the dirt road; little mounds that look like burial markers. She tries to kick one over, but it's tougher than she expects and she only manages to chip away some of the chalky outer layer. Lai Yue joins her, kicks it hard so the whole top half topples over, revealing a honeycombed nest of white ants, worm larvae. Lai Yue walks off, but Ying feels sorry for them, so she replaces the broken tip, hopes their broken home is repairable.

Perhaps a mile further, a commotion brings the trek to a halt.

'What is it now?' Lai Yue's eyes search the surrounding trees. Fear creeps up Ying's spine too. The shorter guard shouts something, his horse stamping the ground just behind her. He slides a gun from its holster.

Lai Yue tells Ying to stay where she is and shoves his way through the men. Not many minutes later, he returns. 'Someone's collapsed by the side of the path.'

She wonders who it could be, and then realises it could be any of them. No one is robust any longer.

'We don't know him. He's from another clan group. They must have left him behind.'

'How will we help him? Can someone carry him?'

The men in front of them hoist their poles and resume walking.

Lai Yue puts his own pole into position and frowns at her. 'Don't be stupid, Ying. We can't help him. We have our own things to carry. It's too unsafe to wait around.'

'Brother, we can't just leave a man here. He will die.' She looks for shapes in the distant mountain ranges. 'He might be killed.' Her voice hushes on the last words as she catches sight of the abandoned man. He's emaciated, and his eyes are as dull as a dead bullock's at market. His mouth hangs open. His front teeth are missing.

'Brother,' she says again, her hand clutching his sleeve.

Lai Yue snatches his arm away. 'Ying, there is nothing we can do for him. Before long I will have to carry you. Do you want me to have to carry him too?'

The others keep plodding ahead, ignoring them, but Ah Kee looks back.

Her brother nods towards the departing men. 'We don't even know him, Ying. We don't know where he's from. I owe him nothing. We owe him nothing.' Lai Yue's voice is harsh, his colour heightened, yet his eyes plead with her.

She looks down at the itinerant man. The hair on his pate has begun to grow back in soft tufts. There's a large sunspot on his right cheekbone. Where is his group? Where is he from?

Ah Kee says something to the guard at the front of the group, who calls out to his partner. She doesn't catch what he says, but she does hear the short guard swear, then shout, 'It's a waste of time, Clem.'

'Just do it, would you?'

The short guard shakes his head but swings down from his horse. He points at Lai Yue and another man, and between the three of them they sling the prone man over the rump of the horse. The short guard remounts and, twitching his crop, tells them to get a move on.

Ying squints into the bright sky and watches a wedge-tailed eagle catch the breeze. The worst of the heat has abated, but her limbs ache, and her arms are weak, rubbery, from holding the pole in place.

They are scrambling over boulders up a hill when her legs give way and she slides back down on her rump, her pole falling behind. With a click of his tongue, Lai Yue picks up her pole and its baskets, adds them to his. She feels sorry. She wants to remonstrate with him, but her mouth is dry. She stands up and her head spins as she walks, lurching as she did those first few days on the steamer.

Finally, she knows it is time. She takes the preserved plum from her pocket and, her arm heavy, she edges it past her lips. She has to roll it in her mouth three times before there's enough saliva to taste the sugar, the aniseed.

As they move ever on, her vision plays tricks on her, shimmers across the shape of things. A leafless branch becomes a snake poised to strike, a log a lazing lizard. But she continues to shuffle forward, too exhausted to sort the real from the deception. She concentrates hard on savouring the plum's flesh, which dissolves away until she's left with just the pip. Her tongue rubs its rough shell. Still sweet. She spits it into her palm and returns it to her pocket. She can suck on it later.

Her fingers find the sore patch on her shoulder. Taking her hand away, she peers at her fingers, damp with perspiration. No blood.

They tramp down the other side of the hill, passing three white men who are excavating a mine shaft. The miners watch them pass. They have no words of greeting for Ying's group, not even for the guards. Their eyes are watchful. Narrowed. One of them murmurs something to his companions, shaking his head.

Soon after, the guards allow them a rest, a very short one, for a drink only, for they still have a few hours to go. The short guard dances around them, waving both hands, urges them to hurry. Ah Kee confers with the taller of the guards and reports back to the men.

'They say it's best we keep going. We might be able to make it, but if it gets too dark, we will have to camp out.'

Even without her pole and belongings, Ying feels her weariness as though she's hauling a ship's anchor through the undergrowth behind her. What little energy she has wanes with the light of the day. The group picks up pace; the prospect of town spurs them on, but Ying starts to fall behind. Lai Yue doesn't notice, and the short guard, on horseback, edges away from her, keeps close to the rest of the group. Further ahead, smoke rises from between the treetops in the next valley. She can smell the smouldering brushwood. The leaves that stroke her arms are tawny from where the fire has already visited.

They wade through a shallow stream, and Ying is too exhausted to take off her shoes like some do. The water trickles through the fabric of her slippers, presses its cool fingers between her toes, squelches as she steps. Adds to the weight of walking. The stream follows the flow of the river around a bend by the side of a mountain, and as they climb yet another rise, weaving between tall gums, she hears a popping sound. Something like firecrackers, set alight to ward off evil spirits.

The men before her pause as they reach the top of the rise. By the time she reaches them thick, grey smoke billows into the sky from behind a straggly copse of quinine trees. The tall guard calls out, puts his hand up for them to halt, and she wonders if they've found another deserted digger. Her tired eyes are drawn to the man slung over the short man's horse. He hangs limp, like a fox pelt. She wonders if he is already dead.

Two gunshots pierce the silence and the guards duck their heads, shout at the group to run away. Two more shots, then a volley of four. She can hear more shouting but, worse, something louder, in the distance: a shrieking that rises into the still, humid air. A spray of birds scatters from the treetops. One more shot.

Her companions flee halfway down the hill, finding coverage behind some scrub. Ying's weak legs collapse beneath her, and the best she can do is crawl backward, until she's hidden by a large rock stuck deep into the earth. Three more shots crack forth, and she can't be sure if they're simultaneous, or if her hearing now matches the ripple in her vision. Dogs bark, a frenzied yapping. Who's attacking them? She didn't think the natives had guns. And surely white diggers wouldn't attack the guards.

She wants to stand, run to the others, take cover, but when she tries, her whole body shakes like a plate of jellyfish until she falls to the dirt again. Her breathing comes in sobs, alarm beats loudly in her ears, and yet she still hears the shouting, the screaming. Three more shots in quick succession.

She pulls herself back, so her head rests against the rock. Waits. The smoky air has a brassy trace to it. A grasshopper lands on her knee, hops onto her arm. She flicks it away with a trembling finger.

Seven heartbeats, and no gunshots. No more shrieking.

'We're friendly! We're just passing through!'

Ying is pretty sure it's the tall guard calling out.

Another voice, further away, responds in its own tongue. She can't make out what they're saying.

More voices drift closer. The tone is affable. She peeps over the ridge of the rock.

Two white men come out from among the quinines. One has on a wide-brimmed black hat, with a rifle slung over his shoulder. His companion carries his rifle cocked, ready. The tall guard walks down into the valley to meet them. She watches as her group rise warily to their feet, but they stay where they are behind the shrubbery. Lai Yue weaves back and forth, clearly trying to find her. She raises her hand and waves, enough to catch his attention. He gestures for her to stay where she is, then pushes towards the front of the men crowded together, craning to see what's going on.

The white men move towards the copse of trees, and she can just make out that perhaps three more men join them in the shadows. They gather under a sprawling paperbark and peer up into its branches. She can't see what they are looking at, pointing at.

Something is not right; Ying can feel it in the hairs that lift at the nape of her neck. A large crow lands on the boulder, shakes out its blue-black cloak, tweaks its inky plumage with its sharp beak. It lets out one loud caw, cocking its beady black eye towards the action further down the hill.

One of the white men looking up into the branches of the paperbark laughs loudly, and the man next to him follows his gaze. The tremor of a fly's wings buzzes close to Ying's ear, fades out. The man with the black hat steps forward, raises the barrel of his rifle and aims high. Even though Ying knows it's coming, the bullet's loud report makes her flinch like when she was young and fearful of the furious firecrackers at New Year, fingers plugged in her ears.

Something tumbles to the ground, lands with a soft thud, lost at the feet of the men and in the long grass. The others slap the man with the black hat on the back, laugh some more. The strangers disperse into the trees and their guard climbs up towards them.

Ying pulls herself to her feet. Her legs are still shaky, but she manages to buckle her way down to her group. She reaches Lai Yue, thinks he will be relieved to see her, but his skin is pasty as he stares towards the top of the hill.

Following his eye-line, she sees that the crow has flown off.

The guards indicate for them to lift their poles and ready themselves to continue walking.

'Sir, what happened?' Ah Kee asks the tall one named Clem.

The guard's mouth widens into a wolfish smile, revealing a chipped tooth. 'The niggers got a dressing, that's what happened.' He spurs on his horse as the group of men form an orderly line.

Ying takes her place behind Ah Kee and asks, 'What does *dressing* mean, Ah Kee?'

He turns to her and his lips pull down.

The light takes on an unfamiliar tone. The setting sun limns the world ochre: the pebbly sand, the coarse soil, the river rocks. Her shoes. Her skin.

They're close now. They plod along in a cloud of dust, and it's difficult to see much further ahead. They cross shallow creek beds and, as her feet slide across the slippery stones, she catches hold of the fibrous bark of the trees leaning over the water. The path curves around the side of the river and that's when she first glimpses the outskirts of Maytown – the flock of tents, the men who glance up then lower their heads to their tasks. A bullock stands in the shallows of the river. Stares at them, before slowly turning away.

8

Lai Yue peers into the wooden cage where the fight will take place. The cage is small, tube-like, and the two crickets have been segregated from each other by a thin partition. The larger one, caught in bushland close by, is a dull black colour, solid-looking, as though it's clad in battle armour. Its wings lift, vibrate, set forth a whirring sound for a few seconds before settling back into silence.

Lai Yue's eyes switch to the other cricket. It's sleeker, more delicate, dark in frame with glossy amber legs.

'This one's from good lineage,' the bet taker says, a fat man with oily skin. 'All the way from Shanghai.'

Lai Yue stares down at the cricket, wondering if it's aware that it is so far from home. If it also misses eating its usual fare or breathing in the lick of something familiar – perhaps the rain when it hits the vegetable patch's freshly tilled soil, or crispy duck roasting over a fire, or even the malodorous run-off wafting up from behind the village houses. At least the tiny creature has its own quarters to live in. Not like Lai Yue, who is reduced to cramming into a tent by the muddiest part of the river with five other men while waiting for a job shovelling or lifting, which will hopefully pay enough to tide him over to the next day.

He crosses his arms, hoping Ying sleeps well where she is, that she appreciates her good fortune to be working in Jimmy's store. When Ah Kee approached them, not a month beforehand, he made it clear that there was only sufficient work for one of them in the shop and, of course, it made sense that Ying take it. Everyone else might think her a boy but, being a girl of only seventeen, she couldn't possibly be left alone in that damned camp, surrounded by so many itinerant men – scrabbling, swindling men – desperate for anything to salve their appetites. Lai Yue knows this. Had insisted she take the work, in fact. But still – he hugs his arms even closer to his body, stifling the prickling that rises in his chest – surely he can be pleased for her and, at the same time, unhappy for himself.

Heat lies heavy in the tent and he wipes a slick of sweat into the skin of his neck. Others jostle him from the side, poke elbows into his ribs, as they, too, try to scrutinise the insects, try to evaluate which to risk their money on. Lai Yue observes the hard, black cricket that is native to this strange land. Surely it will win. It looks tougher. It's on home ground. Lai Yue clutches his pouch tight, feels the few coins still remaining.

But the fine one, with the pedigree all the way to China, perhaps it is in its blood to fight, to win. Anxiety clutches Lai Yue's stomach, rises to his throat. He can't afford to lose.

When he was a child, he pinched his grandmother's cricket to fight his friend's in the alley behind his home. Grandmother's cricket won, and Lai Yue went home with his opponent's cricket pot – lovely, it was, yellow, decorated with a lotus flower – and a mooncake. But this is serious. He hasn't been able to find good work apart from some trifling carrier jobs, and they won't get very far on the income Ying ekes out in that simple store. Lai Yue has to somehow win their way home to their village. In the thirty-two

71

days he's been stuck in this wretched town, he's watched Ah Kee win so much coin at fantan and mah-jong he could return to their homeland and come back again. But Lai Yue has not been so lucky. His silk pouch grows damp in his fist.

'Come on, man, choose which one or move to the side,' the oily man tells him.

'The black one. I'll place money on the black one,' Lai Yue says, pointing at the bigger cricket. He digs one coin out of his pouch and hands it to the man. Lai Yue moves a few steps away to allow others closer, folding his ticket over, then over, then over until it's a tight wad.

An old man comes up. His shoulders are bowed slightly so that his head rests at an uncomfortable angle. He withdraws a switch of dry grass from his pocket, dangles it through the thin bars of the cage. First, he flicks the straw at the black cricket, then once more until it pounces forward, opens its mouth. The crowd murmurs its approval. Lai Yue is relieved; it has a large mouthpart, good for a brawl. The old man then turns to the other cricket, tickles its antennae. It retreats a little, draws its hind legs up into a steep triangle.

The men cheer when the referee pulls away the partition separating the two opponents. Lai Yue presses ahead, into the fevered crowd. Between two men standing in front of him, he can only catch fleeting glimpses of the sparring crickets. The black cricket lumbers towards the other, which remains stock still in its corner. Another man moves in front of Lai Yue, cutting off all view, and Lai Yue curses him, tells him to take off his hat. The two crickets now seem to be grappling – they look like they're dancing, like they're embracing, except his black one seems to be widening its jaws. Someone shoves in beside Lai Yue and his view is cut again, until he finds another gap to look through. They're still head to head, but the black one can't seem to make purchase with its sharp mouth. The crickets fall apart, and the men let out frustrated groans, then cheers when the crickets re-engage. They wrestle some more but, after not too many seconds, the black one backs up. The crowd waits, quiet. The old man steps towards the cage, pokes the straw through the bars, tries to agitate the black cricket to return to the fight, but it just retreats further, turns into the corner.

The sleek Chinese cricket lifts its hind leg and lets out a loud, long chirrup. Sweet and high. Lai Yue's stomach drops. He gazes down at the grimy folded ticket in the palm of his hand.

Lai Yue watches others clamour around the bet taker, demanding their winnings, and he could almost weep. He has only two coins left. And the special pocket in his belt is empty of gold too. He can barely survive two more days on so little. He might have to resort to asking Ying for some of her coin, but then he'd have to explain himself. His face burns at the thought.

A tall man, his queue coiled around his head, opens up the side of the cage that holds the local cricket. He scoops it out and pops it into an earthenware pot.

His smile is friendly when he catches Lai Yue watching. 'Lost your money on my poor little friend here, did you?' he asks. 'He certainly looked the part when I caught him, but he doesn't have a fighting spirit.' He lifts the lid of the pot and Lai Yue looks down at the black cricket. It rears, its antennae angrily twitching, but it quivers all over too. 'You seem to be quite taken with him,' the man says. 'I'll sell him to you if you want.'

For the slightest moment, Lai Yue considers parting with one of his remaining coins for the poor creature – he might make fine company, they seem to be akin.

But you have me, Shan whispers.

Lai Yue shakes his head. 'No, I won't buy it.' He can think of something more worthwhile to spend his money on. Something that will make him forget lost gold, lost family, lost time.

9

Usually when Sophie has male guests – even if the tiny sitting room is full to bursting – Meriem is fine with plunking pannikins of brandy on the table, sweeping up the ash, shoving drunkards out the door. But when Clement visits, like today, the pressure builds, like water put to the boil.

Sophie always makes sure her other guests are absent whenever Clement returns from his trips away and comes a-courting. Meriem knows that's the wrong word for it, though. It's more like he comes a-prowling like an animal, reminding Meriem of the song her ma used to sing: *A frog went a-courtin' and he did ride, Ah ha*. She hums the tune as she lights a candle to deter flies. *Sword and pistol by his side, He rode up to Miss Mousie's door ...* But Clement is more like a tomcat to Sophie's mouse.

Clement is seated at the table, relaxing, and he brings a hip flask out of his pocket and swigs from it. He doesn't say much. Just stares at Sophie, who looks bored but the slight quiver of her voice, the pull of her spine, belies her calm.

Meriem refills Sophie's gin and, as she moves away, Clement clasps her wrist.

'Leave the bottle, lassie.'

He's finished his flask. Takes a swig of gin. His eyes are red;

they don't leave Sophie's face.

Clement leans over, runs his hand through Sophie's hair at the nape of her neck, strokes the side of her mouth with his thumb. Her short upper lip, lifting the bow of her lips in a seemingly perpetual humour. She closes her eyes, her lips parting a little.

Meriem freezes, caught short by the intimacy of the exchange. His hand moves lower, and she turns, walks quickly through to the rear of the house and out the back door. Bumping and humping she can abide, but *that* … She gives a short shake of her head as she sits down on the log.

She takes her glasses off and gives them a good rub with her apron. For some reason she feels tears tighten her chest. Stupid. Stupid girl. To be jealous of such a thing.

Tinker joins her. He always makes himself scarce when Sophie has custom – useless bloody watchdog he's turned out to be. He lies down on her foot, hoping for a pat. Meriem wonders what it would be like to have a man – Clement – gaze upon her like that, with such ardour, such ownership. Her heart quickens. She's always thought of Clement as a brute of a man, but now she allows herself to imagine what it might feel like to lie beneath his sinewy weight, to have his rough skin pressed to hers. To be taken.

Ned never looked at her the way Clement stares at Sophie. Ned was admiring – leering, truth be told – but like a boy with a new tin soldier, not a man with his woman.

A warm draught rustles through the bush like a rush of water, and a lonely bull bellows from down near the river. She watches the Chinaman on the next plot hoe the soil. He has a nice crop of radishes growing and many rows of cabbages. Today he's planting a small tree that has fresh bright leaves by the side of his hut. He's trickling some water over it when she hears Clement ride off, leaving a cloud of red dust in his wake.

When Meriem goes back inside, Sophie is again seated at the table, drinking gin straight from the bottle. She's naked, her skin flushed and dewy like a peach at morning market, but there are also red patches of friction, on her chin, her shoulder, the top of her hip. Meriem goes into Sophie's bedroom – holds her breath from the musk, the intimate odour of bodies – to fetch Sophie's robe. As she hands it over, she notices the fingermarks around Sophie's upper arms, the raised blood on her bottom lip.

'He seems very taken with you,' she says.

'Ha.' Sophie swallows down some more gin. Her eyes fix on a spot on the table. 'Not enough to hitch his horse to mine, though. But if he's in town, I have to make sure he gets all of me.'

'Or?'

Sophie doesn't reply, just stretches out her arm, presses the bruising. A blush of colour, white, blush of colour, white.

Meriem busies herself with heating up the chicken soup, sweeping leaves from the floor that have blown in on the breeze, washing up crockery. When she goes to strip Sophie's bed, Sophie stops her. Says she'll sleep with the sheets as they are.

Meriem shrugs. 'Fine by me. Less washing in the morning.'

Sunset casts its dreary gloom through the doorway, lingering over their meagre belongings, before slowly withdrawing, inch by dark inch until Meriem lights the two lamps. As she whacks the dust from the floor mat, she notices that the green ribbon is still tied about the tree. She looks over her shoulder to see Sophie is slumped forward, face pressed into one arm, bottle of gin embraced in the other. Meriem decides to leave the ribbon. Sophie is in no state for extra custom.

She places a bowl of hot soup in front of Sophie, who ignores it.

Still on her feet, Meriem dunks a stale piece of bread into her own soup. She thinks there is enough bread for another helping, and is eyeing off the cooling soup in front of Sophie when she stirs.

'Oh, Merri, I miss the champagne and oysters of Little Lon.'

'I wouldn't know about that. Never tasted either.' And why would Sophie have left such luxuries to work here, in dusty Maytown? It just didn't make sense. 'Long in Melbourne, were you?' Wondering if that's where she lived with her husband, Jonathan. Wondering if he actually existed.

'Wild nymph of Tipperary, they called me. Bastards. Not even from Tipperary.' Her words slur. 'When did your family come over, Merri?' Her voice is muffled against her arm.

'Father came here before my ma. He'd been here four years before he returned to England to fetch her.' The usual pang at thinking of them. She swallows some soup to douse the fire.

'So you weren't on the ship?'

'No. I was born here. In Queanbeyan.' Sophie knows all this. Has asked a number of times, over numerous rums, countless whiskies. 'When did you arrive, Sophie?'

Meriem expects her question to be ignored as usual, but Sophie rests her chin in the crook of her arm. Her eyes are bleary as she swirls the soup with her spoon. 'Three, four years ago. Can't remember. Don't care.' But a tear, crystalline by the light of the lamp, streaks down the side of her nose. She wipes it with the back of her hand.

'Came out on the *Arabella*. Two hundred and twenty-two passengers departed England on that ship, Merri. A hundred and ninety adults, thirty-two children. One adult lost to tuberculosis. Two infants born, three perished. Only two hundred and twenty landed safely.'

She reaches forward, rests her finger on the hot glass of the lantern until it must sting.

'Imagine,' Sophie whispers, 'listening to those babies who survived. Crying through the silence.' Her eyes swim towards Meriem's, who thinks of a blue sash, hair the colour of wheat. Meriem's free hand finds the folds of her soft stomach.

10

Ying stops to bend down and rake at the midge bites that circle her ankles, her nails scraping the crusty tips so that her fingers smear bright blood across her skin. After many weeks in Maytown, the constant itch from these insect bites has become the worst torment of living in the place, and the only reprieve to be found is when she can rub mint oil into the sores. Her shoulders have healed, she feels strength in her thighs again and, each night after the evening meal, her stomach is as hard as a pumpkin. Her first two nights in town, camping down by the river, she was so hungry she even contemplated creeping across to the temple to steal whatever fruit withered in the heat, but at Jimmy's, where she now lives and works as his shop boy, she eats well.

Shaking her head, she marvels at how lucky she is that Ah Kee recommended her to his friend. She rubs her hand over her stomach, satisfied, but then feels a dip of guilt, wondering if her mother is so well sated. How her mother would enjoy the pickles that Jimmy puts in the soup, and the spices that Yip Sow Kwai's cook adds to the bullock meat. And poor Lai Yue, still without work, one among many squatting by the river. Perhaps, later, Jimmy will let her take him some cabbage to add to his congee, or a handful of dried shrimp.

She straightens the pole on her shoulders and trots along Butchers Creek. The empty baskets swing, giving her steps a jaunty air. Across the narrow bight of water she can see the Chinese camp, a bustling colony of comings and goings. She keeps her head down as she brushes past white men building an extension onto the back of the Imperial. She pauses behind Miller's bakery, sniffing the air, wondering if she'll ever dare enter their shop to taste their bread. She hopes so.

Lo Pak's plot is towards the end of town, past Petersen's hotel, one of Yip's gaming houses, and numerous shanties. When Ying arrives at his garden, Lo Pak is kneeling over a small tree, rinsing each leaf between finger and thumb with a sprinkle of water. Each day she has worked for Jimmy, he has sent her here to collect the shop's supply of vegetables.

'What sort of tree is that?' she asks the gardener. Movement catches her attention, and she watches as a plump young woman with glasses on the adjacent allotment shakes out her apron and walks into the back of her house.

'Longan.' He wipes his hands on his trousers, lets out a short groan as he stands. 'You tasted longan?'

'Of course.' Sweet flesh, translucent as the moon. 'But how long until it fruits?'

Lo Pak gazes down on the tree fondly. 'Not long.'

'A year? Two years?' She's perplexed. Surely he won't be around long enough to see it bear fruit.

He chuckles. 'Sometimes they take five years. Seven, even. But worth the wait. Yes, worth the wait.'

She stares at him. Seven years.

'And when this tree is large enough, I will take a graft, plant its offspring elsewhere.' Lo Pak nods. 'Everywhere I settle, I will replant a piece of this tree.'

'You mean when you return to China?'

His laugh is like the wheezing honk of a goose. 'No. China doesn't need more longan trees. Here is where they are needed. I have heard of an area a little south. Mountains. Fertile soil. They are already growing bananas there, and a lot of sugar cane. I will go there when I have saved enough money.' He shrugs. 'Won't be long until all the gold runs out. Always happens. Lo Pak will be ready.'

As she helps Lo Pak pile beans into her baskets, she puzzles over his attitude. How could he think of staying? She peeps at his smooth skin darkened by the sun, at his relaxed mouth, at the sweat that grimes the creases of his throat. Perhaps he doesn't have loved ones across the ocean far from here, waiting for him. Perhaps they are lost. She has heard of her countrymen who have fled violence and homelessness to come to this place. But to not return! She's never considered the idea.

Lo Pak balances a large plantain on top of the beans, tells her it's especially for their supper.

'I almost forgot.' She roots around in her trouser pocket. Her fingers flick aside her latest stash of pocket food – a stick of cured sausage this time – and bring out a knob of garlic. 'A crate just arrived into town. Jimmy thought you might want some.'

The cleaver whumps down on the cutting board as Jimmy swiftly chops the frog meat into pieces. 'As my mother used to say, *The rice is already cooked*. Ah Kee, it's done. I don't understand why you become so angry.'

Ying peels the papery shell from the garlic and cuts the bulbs into fine slices, its oil sticky on her fingertips, stinging her eyes.

Ah Kee smacks his lips on the rice wine. His cheeks are flushed. 'It's unfair. We need to do something. Write up a petition of some sort about the obnoxious taxes we incur. I can't believe that we are taxed so much more heavily than people from other lands. I simply can't believe it. It's unfair. Many of the diggers here are as foreign as we are, speak other languages, cook different foods ...'

'But they are white.'

'Yes, they are white.'

Ying takes her board across to the fire. 'Should I put the garlic in now, Jimmy?' She calls him Jimmy, unlike Ah Kee, who sticks to his real name – Wui Hing. Jimmy tells her it is better that she becomes accustomed to using his English name in the shop.

'Yes, yes,' he answers, picking up the plantain to peel.

'And what about the message they painted on your front wall last week, Wui Hing?' Ah Kee says.

Ying scrapes the garlic into the bubbling oil in the wok, thinking of how her fingers looked almost bloodstained when she had to scrub away the words *Go bac chink* that were scrawled in red paint. She sniffs at the garlic on her hands. Places her fingertip to her tongue, where the raw garlic burns.

'I'm not convinced that was written by the white men, Ah Kee,' Jimmy says.

'But who then?' Ah Kee's voice rises in incredulity.

'I have wondered if it was another shop owner, trying to be rid of competition.'

'You mean Yeeh, next door, or Chan Poon?'

'Let's not think of it anymore. It is past. And you, Ah Kee, you have enough riches now.' His voice soothing. 'Why don't you return home? Find yourself a nice wife, have some children. I would say, have some beautiful children but you'd have to find a wife that is very beautiful indeed to make up for your shortcomings.' He smiles at Ah Kee.

But Ah Kee won't be diverted. 'I still think it was one of those red-haired devils.' He makes a sucking noise out the side of his mouth. 'There's a law, Wui Hing. There's a law that says they should treat us how we treat them when they come to our lands. They want to be treated well in our lands, but the curs won't reciprocate. Yip Sow Kwai and his men were talking about it last night.'

Jimmy adds the meat to the wok. Ying's belly stirs at the aroma that lifts with the steam. She sucks on her finger.

'Don't get too involved, friend. Perhaps you should go home for a little. Return here at another time.'

Ah Kee slumps against the tin wall. 'But I like it here.'

Jimmy laughs as he scrapes the food into three bowls. 'You like the gambling. You like the revelry with your new friends. You don't like the work.'

'That's not true, Wui Hing!' Ah Kee's voice rises, strident. 'I worked hard on the dig. I helped others. Anyway, I like the weather here. I like the busyness of this small town.'

'You like that you're not shackled to the traditions or expectations of your father,' Jimmy teases.

Ah Kee smiles reluctantly. 'You are right, my friend.'

'Then there is no use railing against the white man's laws. There is still plenty here for all of us, even with the extra taxes.'

'Wui Hing, that is not true. Have you seen how the poor beggars live down by the river? There is a sea of them – hungry, hopeless – thrown up on the shore like a thousand salted whitebait.' He shovels rice into his mouth with his chopsticks, glum.

Ying scrapes the flesh from a tiny bone with her teeth, wondering if Jimmy, too, has dreams of staying here. It is not her place to ask him, so she remains quiet, concentrates on her meal. She wonders how tall Su will be when she returns home. She wonders if she'll even recognise her siblings. Of course, she will always know Lai Cheng from his birthmark, mulberry red. But her sister?

Ah Kee picks through his pieces of frog with his fingers instead of his chopsticks and Ying is surprised that Jimmy doesn't remonstrate with him. In her time in his shop, Ying has learnt that Jimmy is quite refined in taste. He reminds her of the scholar who used to teach Lai Yue in their village. Jimmy has the grace of a crane, his soft face is long and his hair thins a little on top. Behind his spectacles his eyes are kind. He doesn't allow spitting, smoking or swearing in the shop, and always insists on a washed face, clean hands. On her first day he'd handed her a new set of clothing, told her to burn her own in the fire-heap at the bottom of his allotment. Gave her a pail of water and cloth to scrub the dirt from her body. It was the first time she'd realised how bad the stench was that clung to her skin, that drenched the fabric of her clothing. She still feels the heat of shame when she thinks of it.

But when European custom walks through the door, Ying notices a change come over Jimmy. He beams, he bows. Ying was a little embarrassed for him at first, at his clipped English, his scraping ways, but she now suspects his act is a shield, that he becomes everything they expect of him.

After dinner, Ying washes their dishes while the two men go out to join a mah-jong game. She unpacks small boxes of a brown powder favoured by their white customers – *cocoa*, Jimmy calls it – and pours more salty plums into the jar on the counter. After sweeping out the shop, she visits the privy, almost as smelly as the grove at the dig site, but at least more private, canopied in canvas. Finally, she lies down on her pallet by the back door and is lulled to sleep by dreams of her mother, and cicada song.

11

Wake, Lai Yue. Shan's lips are close to his ear. *Wake.*

Lai Yue rolls onto his side, folds close to her warm body.

She's shaking his arm now. He doesn't understand her urgency.

'Lai Yue! Wake up!'

Lai Yue opens his eyes, realises that he's lying against another man – that he's lying among many men, perhaps twelve in all. His vision is bleary as he gazes up at Ah Kee, who stands over him.

'What?'

'Lai Yue, I have some news for you. Clean yourself up and come outside.'

Lai Yue rolls onto his back. It's uncomfortably hot, lying with so many dreaming men in the tent behind Yip Sow Kwai's shop. There's the stink of flatulence, stale food. But it's not as bad as being alone, with a clear mind and nothing to occupy it. The rain beats a steady tap upon the roof. Yip's servant, Yook, lifts the flap of the tent and enters, ushering in three more customers. Dawn glimmers through the opening. So Lai Yue has been here the whole evening. He's surprised the small portion of opium he could afford lasted so well.

He watches as Yook weighs out a pea-sized portion. He's careful to take the newcomers' money before heating the opium over the spirit lamp. The opium becomes as golden, as treacly, as Lai Yue's memories of the night before – languorous dreams of Shan, of lying in the field beside the family's mulberry farm, of smoking a pipe with his father. His mind is blurry, but he drags himself up onto his elbow. With a soft groan he staggers to his feet, steps around prone figures until he's out in the ashen light of morning.

He gulps down water from the canteen that Ah Kee offers him, and asks, 'What is it?'

Raindrops splatter his face and the bald skin of his scalp. The low rush of the river reaches his ears, and he can smell breakfast fires being lit, the first of the bread being cooked. His stomach constricts with hunger, but he tightens it further, denying its appetite. The lovely, sleepy blanket lifts from his shoulders, and he feels the return of the sharp edges of the present.

'I heard talk last night of some Englishmen looking for a carrier and cook to accompany them on a surveying trip. The pay sounded good, so I told them of you.'

'What did you tell them?' That he was destitute? A thief? Is that why Ah Kee is trying to be rid of him?

Shan joins them, says to Lai Yue, *Calm down.*

'I told them I knew of a man – a hard-working man – who could do the job.'

Lai Yue frowns. 'Where is this trip to?'

Ah Kee holds his gaze. 'It will be for many miles. They're looking for land to set up a cattle station. You may be away for several months.'

Responses jostle in his mind like a cup full of fortune sticks. One stick falls forward.

'Well, that's ridiculous,' Lai Yue says. He leans against the rough bark of a tree. His mouth is dry, his tongue furred. 'I cannot leave Ying for that long. Or Shan. The great bird might appear again. If I am here, it will take me first.'

Lai Yue notices the odd look on Ah Kee's face. He's sure of his words, but muddled too. He shouldn't have said them. And did he just mention Shan? Another stick falls from the cup in his mind. 'Ying needs my protection.' Cold sweat swathes his skin with the effort of making sense to the other man. Ah Kee doesn't understand. He's not as aware as Lai Yue is; hasn't been enlightened with the secret, echoing laws that brighten Lai Yue's own world. How can Ah Kee know the risks?

'Ying is fine here, Lai Yue. Your brother has steady work. Wui Hing is good to him.'

'Jimmy.' Lai Yue sneers at the storekeeper's anglicised name. 'Kowtowing to the white ghosts.'

'It works well for him. He has more than one coin left in his pocket.'

Lai Yue glares at Ah Kee. 'What does it matter to you, anyway? I can find my own work.'

'It matters. You have to think of what's best for your family and your clan. You have to think of Ying.' Ah Kee turns to go. 'The man's name is Sullivan. You'll find him at the Imperial Hotel. Go take the job before one of the other hundred starving here does.'

Lai Yue wipes rainwater from his face as he watches Ah Kee walk away. He slides down the tree until his rump rests on the ground. The township slowly wakes around him: two men trudge past with kindling; others gather under the large red gum, awaiting their ration of rice. He should join them, but he won't. He deserves the nauseous hunger that rests in the pit of his stomach.

The sky is bleached with rain, and he stares up into it even though it hurts his weary eyes. A bird croaks from the branches above, and he startles forward, mouth loose, searching it out, hoping, hoping, sick with hope, that it isn't that huge black bird.

He knows why that bird was watching on the day they travelled to this place. Death. The black bird of death. He knows it. *Knows* it.

Four parrots quarrel in the branches, shredding leaves that flutter to the ground like confetti. Their shrieks remind him of that day.

Lai Yue was closer than Ying, who was hidden safely behind a boulder. He saw the native man stumble, look down incredulously at the cavernous bullet wound the white man's rifle had blasted into his chest. His blood a splatter of pomegranate seeds. Another white man stepped forward and fired into the back of his skull. Three mongrels circled the body, barking, nipping, skidding in the brushwood. Lai Yue saw the woman scramble up into the high branches of a tree. Keening with fright. The whole tree – the leaves, the boughs, the feathery buds – trembled with her. And that black bird, watching on. Seer or source, Lai Yue's tangled thoughts cannot decipher. But he's sure that the black bird was there for her. Knew it as the white man lifted his rifle and aimed it at her. Knew it as her limp body plummeted to the hard forest floor.

Lai Yue's as fearful of the natives as anybody; he's relieved the white men seem determined to finish the natives off before they attack more of his people. But the woman? A flash of sinewy arm, the wave of her hair. The cry wrung from her lips.

Acid waters his mouth. He gulps. He has to get home. He doesn't feel safe in this cursed place.

You are a good man, Lai Yue. You will do what's best, Shan says.

But I don't know what to do, Shan. Lai Yue feels for his pouch. One coin left.

You are noble, my beloved. You will do the right thing.

I have to return to China as soon as possible.

Yes! Yes!

But I need money, Shan. Or else I cannot find my way. Lai Yue thinks of Ah Kee's offer. If I go with these white ghosts, Shan, I can save the money.

He closes his eyes, and guilt settles as heavily on his skin as his rain-soaked shirt. If only he hadn't spent all his savings on opium, on gambling. He feels unwell thinking of how his selfishness hasn't honoured his siblings, his mother. He's unworthy of their forgiveness. He's unworthy of anything pleasant, anything kind. He should be whipped. He deserves to suffer. If only, if only there was another like him. Perhaps with the same small ears. Round head with the flat pate. But taller. Or shorter. Or the same. What did it matter his height? As long as he was older. The oldest son. The one to go home, the one to save the family, embrace them, feed them, grow old for them.

Go with the white men, Lai Yue.

Lai Yue's eyes blink open. The syndicate. If he goes on this trek, his clan's tong will take his money after he collects his pay; perhaps they will demand all of it. He probably owes them that much. For him. For Ying.

He can't let Ying know his plans. Or Jimmy. Especially Jimmy. He'd probably run straight to the Sip Yee tong, let them know he's taken work from the white men. And where would that leave Lai Yue? Poorer than he is now.

And Ah Kee – why did he offer him this work? If it's so good, why doesn't he go himself? He is trying to get rid of Lai Yue. He thinks of Ah Kee's last words – that he owes Ying. Has he been speaking with Ying? Perhaps they are both trying to get rid of him.

The ants march out from their cavity in his chest, sting and prickle his flesh. Has he become such a burden?

He'll take the white man's work. He will show Ah Kee, and Ying, that he can do something right.

You should go with them, my love. Better you don't tell anyone. Leave with the white men as soon as they are ready.

Yes. He will leave. He won't farewell Ying. If that's how she feels – that he's a burden – then he will go, and only return when he has proven otherwise.

He glances up into the branches to confirm the black bird isn't there. His jaw aches from being clenched for so long. Groping in his pocket for his pouch, he looks back towards the opium tent. He'll dream just once more, and then he will go find this Sullivan.

12

'Where did you hear of this bush dance?' Sophie scoffs a little on the last two words.

'There was talk of it after the prayer meeting the other day.' Meriem heard the McLean girls discussing it, and then Father Joyce – the retired priest who leads their prayers, recently come to Maytown to try his hand at gathering gold and flock – mentioned it in his community news. Meriem thrilled at the thought of whirling about a dance floor, at swinging her skirts to the lilt of the music.

The last ringlet falls from the curling iron. Sophie's hair is done.

Meriem returns the iron to the top of the wood stove. 'I should have put my hair in rags last night,' she says. 'It's almost too hot to bother with curling my hair now.' But she's determined to this once. Wants to look her very best for the dance.

She takes a seat next to the stove and takes up the ironing tongs. She rolls some of her hair around one long tip. Holds for a few moments, until she smells it burning. As she releases the iron, her hair slips free, more a loose tangle than a ringlet.

'Oh, let me do it,' Sophie says, slapping Meriem's hand away from the iron. 'I can't stand watching you scorch your pretty hair.'

Sophie combs out a small handful of her hair. Meriem draws herself inward, almost crouched. 'Don't be so scared, you silly girl.' Sophie laughs. 'I'll not burn you.'

But Meriem is not afraid of the iron; she's just not used to someone else tending to her, touching her. Nobody has fixed her hair since she was much younger. Her mother, in fact. And that not done in a gentle or very willing manner. Her mother had snapped at her to hold still as she wrenched the brush through her knotted locks or twined it into a tight plait. Meriem will always feel the weight of imposition, will always think of others' ministrations as a terrible embarrassing chore for everyone concerned.

'I have made soup for your supper,' she tells Sophie.

'Mmm.' Sophie picks a hairpin from between her lips, presses it into Meriem's hair.

She worries that as soon as Sophie is finished the humidity will undo her fine work. She reaches for the piece of scone she's left on the bench, brings it to her mouth.

'Stop fidgeting, Merri!'

Meriem can feel the heat of the curling iron as it beds against her scalp. Sweat trickles between her breasts. 'I hope I remember the dance steps tonight. It's been so long.' Since Penny Doolan's wedding. The stroke of Ned's thumb down the side of her hand. His thigh bumping hers.

'Some things are never forgotten,' Sophie says, grinning. She nudges Meriem's shoulder. 'Isn't that right?'

Meriem is glad of the heat that already flushes her face.

'There, that shall do.' Sophie steps back. 'Lovely, indeed. Go peep in my mirror.'

Sophie exaggerates. While the waves in Meriem's hair have taken on a hopeful gleam, and Sophie has pinned one of her own silk flowers behind her ear, Meriem's face is blotchy from sitting by the fire. She takes off her glasses. That's better. She refuses to dwell on whether that's because she's removed her glasses or because her eyesight blurs.

In the alcove where she beds down of a night, opposite the scullery, Meriem removes her apron and day dress. She lies down on her mattress for several minutes, hoping to cool her ruddy skin, but when she finally does pull her good clothes on – the dress she keeps for Sunday service, the lace collar she hasn't had reason to wear in many a month – the linen sticks to the perspiration on her legs, hitches on her damp shoulders. The sweaty ringlets cling to her neck, and she has to hold them aloft, savouring the kiss of cool air.

She wonders if her appearance is neat, but she doesn't want to ask Sophie for the use of her mirror – which, in any case, is too small to reflect her whole length. She's glad of the lilac flower Sophie has lent her, but she wishes for the pretty basket of trumpery that used to sit upon her mahogany dressing table. Left at home at her mother's insistence. Meriem wonders if Milly misses her when she magpies her ribbons and combs; whether it's with reverence that her sister wears her brooch with the tiny seed pearls, or if she grasps it with greedy fingers. Meriem tightens the sash around her waist. Tightens until she can barely breathe, can barely feel the pain in her heart. Her hand finds her stomach, presses the fabric and petticoat beneath, until her fingers sense the shape of belly fat, low slung; a memory or a cover-up, she's not sure. She walks across to the benchtop and shoves another piece of the scone in her mouth. Smears the last of the jam onto the rest and swallows that too, until she hiccups with indigestion.

'Don't go just yet,' calls Sophie from the other room. 'Wait until it is a little darker. You want to make a grand entrance. Also, if you are too early, the old cats will make you help arrange the bloody flowers or set out all the refreshments.'

Which is exactly what Meriem had planned to do. She thought that if she turned up early to help out, the women might look upon her more favourably, might share a word or two with her. Perhaps she might even engage a dance or two with some lad or other before the finer young ladies traipsed in. Apart from Maggie Gilhooley's girls and the three women Meriem's heard of who are shacked up by the Chinese camp – and Sophie, of course – there are only a small number of young, single women in Maytown. The rest of the women are either married to their tradesmen husbands, or old widows, like that Mrs Porter who runs the new post office.

Meriem can see, though, that Sophie wants company before her evening visitors arrive, so she takes a seat at the round table. Sophie pours a generous tot of rum, pushes the tumbler towards Meriem.

'Warm yerself up,' she says. 'Loosen your limbs for dancing and all sorts.' She winks at Meriem. Taking a large swig of rum herself, Sophie shuffles the notes and coins in front of her into a semblance of order, counting under her breath as she goes. She puts apart a note and five coins. 'Here's your pay. Don't blow it all on punch and sermon books, now.' Smiles to take the bite from the words. She packs the rest of the money into a red coffee tin. 'Hide it away, will you, Merri?'

Meriem picks up the coffee tin and drags a chair towards the scullery. She stands in the shadows and climbs up onto the chair. On tiptoes she lifts a sheet of roofing, slides the tin under.

Before she leaves she helps Sophie don a frilled petticoat and a muslin dress so fine, so translucent, Meriem thinks she might as well remain naked.

'The johnnies love a bit of peek-a-boo,' Sophie says.

The dance is a rowdy affair by the time Meriem arrives at the newly built hall behind the Empire Hotel. She pays the coin entrance fee, which will go towards re-stumping the post office. An assortment of lanterns – brass and glass – are strung up around the hall, casting their mellow, uneven light across the wooden floor and the capering revellers. The sharp fragrance of fresh sawdust, kerosene, oily candles and sweaty cologne combine in a heady scent. The din is incredible, almost enough for Meriem to want to cover her ears. Clapping, yelling, the stamping of feet. The butcher, Mr Doughty, slaps the bow up and down the strings of his fiddle, while Mr Cowper's accordion wheezes the notes forth from between his flapping arms. Three men tend to a barrel of beer.

From the corner of her good eye, Meriem notices Mrs Cowper glare her way, before turning sharply to mutter something to her clowder of cronies behind the laden cake stands. Meriem pushes her way to the right, past a group of men who smoke their pipes, tap their feet, watch the few women bounce by.

The room is crowded with men – diggers, tradesmen, bankers, newsmen, builders – but there are perhaps only eleven women in total in the hall: five women on the dance floor – tall Kitty O'Halloran; the Foster girls; and Mrs Joyce, Father Joyce's sister-in-law, visiting from Gladstone – four women tending the food and drink; and Mrs Porter chatting with two men in the corner. A brawny fellow, who smells of cologne slapped over sheep grease, grabs Meriem about the waist and whisks her onto the dance floor.

He hops and thrashes about with more enthusiasm than skill, and she's relieved when the dance calls for her to be flung into the arms of her next partner.

Between dances, Meriem washes up next to the Foster girls against the back wall. She's puffed out and thankful for the breeze that comes through the window. She turns towards the youngest Foster girl and grins. The girl returns the smile, but lowers her eyes quickly.

Kitty sails up to them – Meriem is quite envious of the burgundy frills on her pink gown – and asks, 'What can I fetch for you ladies to drink? Frances?' Frances murmurs that she'd enjoy a lemonade. 'Josephine?' She, too, would like a lemonade. 'Evie?' A cup of tea would be lovely.

Meriem's parched, is hopeful that this is her opportunity to obtain a lemonade without having to approach Mrs Cowper or the other forbidding women guarding the jugs and teapots. But Kitty's gaze does not transfer to her, cuts short as though Meriem isn't there. Kitty smiles graciously at the other young women and walks away.

Meriem glances over her shoulder, out the window, as if she hasn't heard the exchange, as though she accepts she has no place in their party.

Perhaps she should take a turn around the room, but she would hate for anyone to think she was peacocking. She wishes the music would start up again, cranes to see what the musicians are about. People are yelling to make themselves heard, the lantern-light flickers against the dark spot in her vision, a man steps back, his heel landing on the tip of Meriem's toe.

'Here, love, take this. It's a sherry cobbler.' Mrs Porter hands her a punch glass.

'Thank you.' Meriem's fingers wrap about the glass. She has a sip of the sweet brew, and then another, and the spirit and the postmistress's kindness warm her.

Accordion music bounds into the room, and Mrs Porter taps her foot to the rhythm. She's shorter than Meriem, perhaps forty years old, and fair, with lovely rosy cheeks. When she drinks, her tongue finds the edge of the cup first, before she takes a sip.

'How long have you been here now, Mrs Porter?' Meriem asks, leaning in close to be heard. She wonders if the postmistress knows who she works for, if she's heard Mrs Cowper's gossip yet.

'Six weeks.' Mrs Porter smiles at her, eyebrows raised. 'Long enough to know what's going on.'

Meriem doesn't know what to make of this, so she simply nods. 'Did you have far to come?'

'From Sydney, I am. My brother-in-law arranged this post for me when my Walter passed away.'

A lanky man joins the two musicians, brandishing a button concertina. Meriem's stomach stirs at the distant fragrance of roasting corn and butter.

An older fellow, whiskery, a patchwork of ruddy veins spreading across his nose and cheeks, claims Mrs Porter's hand for the next dance. Meriem's heart lifts as a skinny digger, hair oiled, cuffs clean, walks towards her, but he is pipped by Father Joyce, who slides in front of Meriem.

'Meriem, how nice of you to find the time to join our little dance.'

She's pleased Father has approached her, singled her out. She's sorry the young women are no longer close by to notice this small gesture of respectability. Of course, she has shaken Father Joyce's hand on exiting his Sunday service, bobbed a curtsy, but she's never had a word with him. Each week Meriem looks forward to the prayer meetings in the back room of the Mayweather. She relishes the ritual of pulling on her gloves – worn, and much too warm for the climate – and tying the ribbon of her good straw hat under her chin. She tiptoes past Sophie's room, and walks to the Mayweather on roads that are not yet billowing with dust and drays. For close on an hour, once a week, while Father Joyce delivers his sermon, she imagines she's cloistered by people she knows, people she loves and who love her in return. She closes her eyes and imagines Father Joyce's sonorous voice is that of Father McHugh's, back in Queanbeyan. It's only on the hot walk home that she allows resentment to creep into her heart as she pictures her family gathered for Sunday lunch – Milly demanding the last drumstick, her mother slapping her father's newspaper away, him teasing Tom about his newest waistcoat. She scourges herself with these cruel thoughts.

Back in the hall Father Joyce's voice is kind, conciliatory, as he says, 'But perhaps you are too busy to stay that much longer. Perhaps you are needed at your … home.'

'No. It's perfectly fine for me to stay longer,' Meriem says. Baffled, but deeper down, a glimmer of his meaning squirms its way in, and the breach in her vision widens, blackens, until her right eye can barely make him out.

Mr Cowper's barrelling baritone fills the room.

The wind is fair and free, my boys, the wind is fair and free

Perhaps Meriem didn't hear the father properly.

The Palmer we will see, my boys, and Cooktown's muddy shore

Father Joyce looks across the room to Mrs Cowper, who pours a cup of tea, lips pursed. He continues, 'There is some concern that your line of work … That the younger ladies …' He pulls a handkerchief from his sleeve, rubs it across his mouth.

Suddenly, Meriem is terribly conscious of the crush of people. A group of diggers share loud stories to her left, their backs to her, but two men – a lad who helps out at the Imperial Hotel and a grey-haired man sucking on a cigar – stand so close they are virtually a part of her circle with Father Joyce.

'Don't be like that, Father,' the older one mutters, smoke wafting from his nostrils.

'I hear there's a shindig over at Gilhooley's tonight. You and that Irish harpy might want to go there,' the other one says to her.

Father Joyce tuts, frowns over his spectacles at the young man, but doesn't say more.

I'll stay no more down south, my boys

Whatever distress Meriem feels from Father Joyce's sentiments is choked off by the lad's teasing words. Meriem is thankful for the lace collar that covers the blush creeping across her chest. But there's nothing she can do about the heat in her ears. She's sure they must be as red as Kitty's blasted frills.

I'll stay no more down south, my boy

So let the music play

She forces a smile, says, 'I am sure you are right, Father. I am very tired from such a long day. I will listen to one more song and then I will make my way home. I have a busy day tomorrow.' She curtsies and lifts her chin to watch the band.

To lend a helping hand, my boys, where the soil is rich and new

Meriem concentrates on the dark smudge in her right eye. Concentrates so hard she can't see the father, Mrs Cowper, her attendant cows, Kitty, the crowd. Waits for the interminable song to finish.

They say the blacks are troublesome,
and spear both horse and man

She taps her foot to the music, just as Mrs Porter had, and grits her teeth, her cheeks straining into the semblance of a smile.

No sooner does the last note squeal from the accordion than Meriem pats her skirts neat and focuses on walking in a leisurely manner towards the door. She looks to the darkness beyond the doorway, a haven from the guttering lights, the roar, the stench of sweaty bodies and tobacco smoke. The cooling night air smites her face, breathes life into the ache in her heart, but small clusters of men, smoking and drinking, stand about in the courtyard, and she must keep herself together for a little longer.

'Do you need a hand, miss?' asks one kind digger, which almost undoes the wound's stitches, but she manages to gasp, 'No, thank you' before hurrying on her way.

The moonlight is so dim there is no chance that anyone will see the tears that slip down her cheeks. She walks past the lemonade factory; Maggie Gilhooley's, where, indeed, there does seem to be a party going on; and numerous shanties. The blacksmith is still at work, his fire gleaming and orange, hammer ringing out against anvil. In her haste, her shoe slips on the edge of a newly laid stone slab. Her ankle rolls, and she crumples to the ground on all fours. Her left knee cracks on stone, the pain giving her pause. She's quiet though. Doesn't want to call any more attention to herself. But her glasses have fallen from her nose. Her hand searches the ground, brushing gravel and leaves. She rests back onto her haunches and covers her bad eye with her hand, searching, searching, with her good eye. What more? What more could possibly be in store for her?

She flinches with fright when something is slipped between her fingers. Her glasses. Someone has placed her glasses into her hand. Meriem slides them onto her face and struggles to her feet, wondering if the nice digger had followed her after all. The sharp, dry scent of peppermint oil reaches her nose and, by the light cast by the blacksmith's fire, she peers at a small man clad in black pants and a black smock. A Chinaman, no less.

13

The weight of only a few hours' sleep presses behind Ying's eyes. The dogs in town begin barking to each other almost before the roosters crow. She yawns wide, her eyes watering, as she places three tomatoes into a paper bag for a digger, says, 'Hand under bag. Watch bottom. Hold care, please' just as she does every time she passes over a parcel to one of Jimmy's customers. She's intimate with the flimsiness of those bags, having made them herself out of newspaper squares glued together with a paste of flour and water. She often hears the rustle, deep in the night, of cockroaches nibbling on their seams.

She yawns again as she unpacks tins of the pungent orange spice the white inhabitants of Maytown favour.

Jimmy lights a joss stick, placing it next to the altar. 'Where were you last night?' He sits on a stool and considers her. Leaning his elbow on the counter, he drapes two fingers over the bridge of his nose, as he is wont to do, his thumb stroking the nub between his nostrils.

Ying turns away to avoid his scrutiny, sliding the tins onto a shelf next to the baking powder. She's taken to stealing out at night-time. Slipping along the streets in the dark, peering into shops or establishments to see how others bide their time. She's familiar with the rumble of talk, the scuffle of cards and tiles, the bilious smoke that emanates from the Chinese gaming houses, and the low murmur of her more devout kinsmen who pray in the temples. It's looking in on how the Europeans spend their time that she finds fascinating. How, in Carr's eating house, the men clatter metal forks against enamel plates, shovelling stew into their mouths; and in the Empire Hotel, several times a week, a group of men gathers to play a game where they toss a sharp shaft at a round target, cheering each other on, clenched fists waving in the air. How, in the Mayweather, a tall man in a striped waistcoat crashes out a tune on a dusty piano most evenings until he drinks too much whisky and topples from the stool. Ying knows to stay clear of the beer shanties, to avoid the inebriated men who roll through their doors. And usually she doesn't go far at all, is aware of her own vulnerability, but last night, while she watched the blacksmith at work, she saw a young woman fall to her knees, losing her spectacles in the dirt.

Ying rubs mint oil into a mosquito bite on the back of her hand. She didn't realise Jimmy knew of her absence; she is never gone long and is always careful to return before he does.

'I was helping a lady. The one who comes here sometimes. She bought those hard sweets you ordered in from Brisbane.' There's something about the woman that Ying finds pleasing. Ying admires her narrow nose, as slender as an owl's beak – not fat and wide, like Ying's own. And the skin on her arms is thick, creamy, has the pale lustre of roast pork belly.

'Miss Merri? Why did she need your help so late in the evening?' Jimmy asks, frowning.

'She fell over in the dark, very hard, on her knees. I made sure she arrived home all right.' Ying doesn't mention how Merri waved her hand at Ying, told her to shoo, as though she were a pesky mongrel sniffing around for a scrap of meat. But by the light from the blacksmith's, Ying saw the tear that coursed down her cheek, the glisten of snot on her upper lip. Ying felt a tug of sympathy despite the girl's rudeness. She kept a fair distance between them, watching Merri as she limped her way back to the little house next to Lo Pak's.

'Listen, Ying, you should be careful of that lady. Yes, she is a good customer, but ...'

Three men stamp the dirt from their boots in the doorway. Ying feels their noisy presence vibrate up through the soles of her shoes and their bulk blocks the light as they crowd into Jimmy's shop.

The first man – pale face clean-shaven, wearing a shirt greyed with sweat and soil – picks up an earthenware jar of fermented bean paste and lifts out the cork stopper. His nose screws up and he swings the jar in front of the taller of his companions. 'Here. Smell this.' Laughs when his friend reels away. 'Bad, innit?' The jar clinks against others as he shoves it onto the bench.

There's a looseness to his gait as he walks towards them. Beer fumes are strong on his breath. He taps a coin on the counter and grins down on Jimmy, who smiles back.

'Got any rum, John?'

'No. No rum here, mister. You try Mr Ming Long down there.' Jimmy points to the left, further along Leslie Street.

'What about whisky? Gin?'

Still smiling, Jimmy shakes his head.

The tallest one pushes up beside grey-shirt. A crusty trail of gravy travels down the breast of his brown waistcoat. 'Your coin's no good to him. He only wants gold.'

'You only want gold, John?' grey-shirt asks. 'Want to add it to your stash, mate? Look after it for your Chinkie friends, I'll wager.'

The tall one pulls a green and blue woollen cap from his greasy curls. 'Sure, them chows always have gold around, the greedy buggers.'

'Of course he done, Dermot,' pipes up the youngest one, who has stayed back, lingering among the food stores.

Grey-shirt leans on the counter, bobbing his head closer to Jimmy. 'You lot want to take it all back to China with you, or what? What?' He's still grinning, but there's a reptilian set to his fat features.

'Yeah. Greedy fucking buggers,' jeers the younger fellow, swiping a bag of cornflour onto the ground, where it lands with a powdery *oof.*

'No gold, mister,' Jimmy repeats. He arches his head as though to greet new customers over grey-shirt's head.

Ying drops her gaze as she carefully winds the lid onto the bottle of mint oil, turning her head away from the man's terrible breath. With so many Chinese people in town, she wonders why these men have chosen Jimmy to taunt. Perhaps it's common knowledge with the white people of Maytown that Yip Sow Kwai's henchmen are skilled with knives, or that the Sip Yee men carry rifles wherever they go. She wants to melt away from their menace but doesn't want to leave Jimmy alone. She glances sideways at him. He's still smiling, but a shaft of red colours his throat, creeps across his jawline.

'No gold,' Jimmy says again, straightening up the row of spinach that lies atop the counter.

'Well, if you have no gold, mate,' grey-shirt says, 'why don't you go back to China, you yellow heathen? Open a shop there.'

It's not the first time Ying has heard this sentiment flung at them through the shop's doorway, or when she walks around town.

And it's not the first time she's felt an answering barb of annoyance, either, glad of its ability to dissolve some of the fear. She backs away, her eyes finding the wooden stake Jimmy keeps under the counter for when he might need to chase thieves.

Grey-shirt sighs dramatically, bringing a flask out of his coat pocket. He takes a swig, offering some to the tall man, Dermot, who also drinks. 'Have a cooler, mate,' he says, offering the flask to Jimmy. 'Or is it against your Chinkie religion?'

A digger, swarthy with mud, enters the store. Ignoring the others, Jimmy asks the man what he can fetch for him.

'Fill this pouch with tobacco, would you,' the digger says.

'That it?' grey-shirt says to Jimmy from the end of the counter, brandishing the flask. 'You don't want to have a cooler with us?' Dermot swats his friend's hand away, and grey-shirt guffaws. 'I wasn't really going to share my whisky with him, Dermot. Do you think me mad?'

Jimmy continues to fill the digger's pouch with tobacco.

'Where's your gold, mate?' grey-shirt resumes his chorus. 'Our gold. I know you have it hidden here somewhere.'

The digger turns towards grey-shirt for the first time, a confused frown on his face.

'Thank you, mister,' Jimmy says, ushering the digger from the store. 'Please come again.' The digger pauses, glancing back towards the counter before finally leaving.

Jimmy no longer smiles. 'Please, mister, you go,' he says to grey-shirt and his friends. 'I do not speak to you—'

'You know what's funny, mate?' grey-shirt says. 'People from here don't hide their gold. They don't take it back to some godforsaken land full of long-haired monkey-people.'

Dermot's laugh is surprisingly high-pitched; it ends on a snort.

'Come on, that's enough of that.' Maytown's solicitor, Mr Grange, stands in the doorway, the digger at his shoulder. 'There's plenty of room in Maytown—'

Grey-shirt waves his arm, some whisky slopping from his flask. 'But look at this Chink, would you, mate.' He turns to bellow at Jimmy, 'Why don't you go back to China, mate? You don't belong here. I belong here. I was born here, mate.' His spittle lands on a tin of oysters.

Mr Grange shakes his head and moves on, encouraging the digger to follow suit. Grey-shirt slurps up more whisky while Dermot continues to snigger. But it's the sound of tins tumbling to the ground that turns Ying's annoyance into something more brittle.

'What if I born here?' she says.

Grey-shirt's eyes swivel around to her. He takes up a bullish stance. 'What's he saying?'

Ying's heart races. 'What if I born here? Will I belong Maytown?' Looking at their confused faces, she tries again. 'If child born here, will child belong Maytown?'

Grey-shirt's mouth falls open, flummoxed.

'Does he mean have a babe with one of our lasses?' Dermot asks, outraged.

'No, no,' Jimmy says, shouldering Ying out of the way. He shakes his head at their misunderstanding. Sweat trickles from his hairline.

'Break it up, would you,' says a deep voice from the front of the shop. Sub-Inspector Campbell stomps into the small space, looks about. 'Heard there was some barney brewing here, which is very unwelcome, lads,' he says to grey-shirt and his companions. 'Come on. Let's go over to the Mayweather. You buy me a pint, and you won't hear anything more from me.'

The policeman rounds up the men, who shuffle from the shop, glaring at Jimmy and Ying as they go. The youngest one kicks a sack of oats on his way out. 'Bloody Ching Chongs.'

The fish head rises to the top of the soup, nestled among the cabbage and mushrooms. Wide, milky eye; gleaming skin as speckled as an old man's. Ying's mouth waters as she dips the spoon into the earthenware pot, serving herself a small bowl. She takes only a couple of flakes of flesh, leaving the rest of the silky fish head and the soft scallop of its cheeks for Jimmy and Ah Kee.

They haven't had the opportunity to tell Ah Kee of grey-shirt and his friends because, since his arrival, Ah Kee has been complaining of his losses in one of the Sip Yee gaming houses.

'Those men are cheats, Wui Hing. How else could I lose so much money in one sitting?'

'How many cups were you in, friend?' teases Jimmy.

'That's not the point. And now they demand a huge amount in interest on top of what I owe. I won't pay it. I won't. I'll give them what I owe from last night, and that is it.'

Jimmy eyes his friend. 'You lost that heavily? You haven't lost your passage home, have you?'

Ah Kee tsks. 'Nothing I can't fix.' He folds his arms, slumps further into his chair.

Jimmy ladles soup into a bowl, hands it to his friend. 'Be careful, Ah Kee. The Sip Yee tong is far-reaching, after all.'

He brings out a newspaper from home – three months old, only a little tattered at the edges – and places it between himself and Ah Kee, pointing out an article about a famine. 'Look. They say people are eating roots and clay.' He shakes his head in dismay.

'While here we are enjoying fish head soup,' Ah Kee responds.

Ying wonders why Jimmy doesn't tell his friend of grey-shirt. It is probably for the best; Ah Kee is made of more volatile stuff than Jimmy. Why excite the man? Or perhaps Jimmy isn't troubled. Perhaps he is more accustomed to such behaviour than Ying is, or thinks it is best not dwelt upon. But for Ying – as she helped restack the shelves that long afternoon, lugged pails of water from the well, swept leaves from the shallow stoop with the straw broom – the sight of that man's lips set in a snarl, and the sound of the youngster chanting 'bloody Ching Chong' springs to mind unbidden, as irritating as a hidden burr, scratching her skin at unexpected moments.

She stirs her soup, closing her eyes to banish thoughts of grey-shirt. She doesn't want her enjoyment of the meal to be tarnished. She carries her stool outside and settles down to watch the last of the sun sink beyond a rise of grass as dry as wheat, punctuated by clumps of bright green foliage. Before eating, though, she sifts the soup for flies that might have fallen into its depths, stunned by its heady steam; searches for tell-tale wings or the crooked leg of a roach. Thinking of how her mother would scold her for being so fussy. She gulps down five burning mouthfuls before looking up again.

On one side iron sheeting has been cobbled together to divide Jimmy's land from that of Chan Poon's. The other side is bare of fencing, and Ying watches as Yeeh's servant beats the dirt from a rug, the swirl of brown dust settling on his shoes. Behind his shop, at the end of the allotment, Yeeh has planted a tree from his village, its first creamy buds a bold contrast to the dull palette of its surrounds. A tiny white finch balances on one of the branches, at one with its sway. Ying admires how its beak slopes straight down from its forehead; the fawn pattern upon its wings like the links in armour; how a black ring outlines its head in the shape of a helmet, reminding her of the warrior painting that used to hang next to Lai Yue's bed at home.

Thinking of her brother ruptures Ying's calm. Ah Kee told her of the work Lai Yue found with the white men that would take him far away for a time, but she doesn't understand why Lai Yue left without saying goodbye. She turns her head to glance into the shop where her bedding lies, knows that among her things packed neatly in the burlap sack is the bird carving her brother left for her. Sometimes she takes it out and gently rubs the curve of its head across her lips, inhales its spicy scent, which always takes her back to their tent by the river, so hot and so wearisome, but also where she last shared the damp air with her brother. She feels the creak of something inside herself at the thought of how far she has been cloven from those she loves.

'Ying, wash the plates,' Jimmy calls, from inside the shop. 'I am going out with Ah Kee.'

A mosquito hovers near her ankle. A stripy cat leaps over the makeshift fence, catches sight of Ying and darts across the yard into Yeeh's.

After rinsing the bowls and earthenware pot in the pail, Ying throws the dirty water across the grass. She gives Yeeh's servant a spoonful of tobacco to watch over the shop and follows the road around to the left, making her way along the side of the river to Lo Pak's. In the dark, she sees the outline of the tea trees weeping over the restless water, reminding her of the willows back home, and of her mother bent over the tub, her black hair dripping into its depths. Ying brushes past groups of men preparing for their long walk to the gold sites on the morrow. A pedlar offers to sell her a bag of salted fish; another, a shovel and pickaxe. Ying continues on her way until she is near Lo Pak's. His hut is in darkness, but there's a cheerful glow through the open doorway of the house next to his. A green ribbon is tied in a saggy bow around the tall tree out front.

Ying wonders why Miss Merri was crying the night before. Could she be feeling lonely, like Ying does? Or had she heard sad news? Ying wonders if Miss Merri has friends here, a companion to talk to. Someone with whom she can share a meal, the long hours of the day, her thoughts, her memories. Ying stares hungrily at the square of light but doesn't dare move closer.

14

The days pleat into one another. Their boots crunch over rubbly earth, tack across dry granite. The terrain alternates between belts of slate and beds of desert sandstone. Bloodwood, red gums, ironbark, more bloodwood. The land scathing during the day but alluring – sly – by night, its cool shadows and soft burring a fragrant veil cast across venomous creatures and watchful natives. The mountain ranges aren't broccoli-neat like those at home, but are languid, unkempt, have the undulations of a recumbent woman.

Lai Yue feels like a live carp being nibbled away. He wishes he didn't have to hold his laden pole in place – he wants to stride at the forefront like Sullivan, who slashes the dense scrub with a tomahawk as he leads his horse forth. Lai Yue wants to tame this hostile shrew of a place. Each insect bite that pockmarks his skin, each welt that scores his flesh, reinforces how unwelcome he is, how his banishment is almost complete.

They splash through a stream, and he looks up into the sky, feels dizzy for a moment as the dry leaves of the stringybarks whirl above his head. Two crows gaze down at him. But not the great black bird with its blue-black shine, its knowing eyes.

Sullivan chooses a camp site for the night by a fast-flowing creek where the trees sway along its craggy shoreline in supplication to the sun. Sullivan's face is smudgy from too much drink and his stomach folds complacently over his belt. When Lai Yue approached him for work, he asked Lai Yue something in English, and when Lai Yue couldn't immediately catch his meaning, he talked slower, louder.

'What … is … your … name?'

'Lai Yue. Lee Lai Yue.'

'Lie what? Sounds like you're hacking up something. We'll call him Larry?' Sullivan looked around at the other men in the room, who nodded in confirmation. There are six of them in all. Fritz, a big sandy fellow who forsakes a shirt in the terrific heat, so that his sunburnt back takes on the hue of Chinese sausage; and Hagerty, a bovine-looking man who drank so much whisky on the first night he pissed his pants. Two brothers: Bengt and Lucas. And Lai Yue and Sullivan. The kindest to Lai Yue is the younger of the brothers, Lucas. He has the colouring of a white mouse, the same sniffy snout. But he smiles at Lai Yue encouragingly when the day draws out into a stifling abyss and sometimes he even shares a pinch of his tobacco. He offers English words to Lai Yue, asking for Chinese words in return.

Lai Yue stokes the fire while the brothers search for extra kindling and the others try their luck in the stream – Sullivan for gold, Fritz and Hagerty for fish. For a moment he considers joining them, would like to feel the cool water reach the sweet spot at the nape of his neck. Fritz calls out something to Hagerty, splashes water into the other man's face, and Lai Yue decides against it. His presence would just accentuate his separateness. He will cook some duff to go with the kangaroo the red dog dragged into camp at dawn. It's their fourth time eating the fragrant meat. It's the men's favourite, after fish and frog. Kneeling at the bright yellow timber board he'd chopped from a tough Leichhardt tree, Lai Yue pours some of their precious flour into a dented pot, adding a trickle of water. The preserved fruit is long gone, as is the sugar. He kneads the stiff dough and then halves the mixture – he's learnt the hard way that if he breaks them into smaller rolls they become almost as tough as those biscuits the whites like to break their teeth on – and places both pieces on the board. When he's filled the pot with water, he sets it over the flames.

A jolt of nausea hits Lai Yue's stomach with the scrap of meat he swallows. He deserves the hunger that corrodes his insides. He will only eat enough to sustain himself, and no more. The joys of eating will not be his until he returns home, among his mother, brother and sisters.

He tears off another charred chunk of kangaroo meat and offers it to the kitten. Part of his job is to keep the small creature fed and watered, this offering the white men are taking to their friends at some distant sheep farm. The kitten lives in a wicker cage that has an unpleasant, sour reek, but Lai Yue likes sitting by it. He calls the kitten Jie, after a favoured cousin. Its fur has the mottled colouring of a snail's shell, and long wisps grow from the tips of its ears.

The others mostly ignore Lai Yue in the evenings, so he pets the cat through the bars of its enclosure, chats with Shan. He's found a nice piece of wood, slender, golden. He brings out his sturdy little knife and scrapes it down the smooth grain. No breaks, no knurl. He starts roughly, with long sweeping cuts so that several thin slices of the wood peel away. He's going to make a sculpture of Shan, but he'll keep it secret for now.

How long will we be on this terrible trek, Lai Yue?

I'm not sure, Shan. Tension tightens his breathing, rattles the ants that rest in the crawl space of his chest. His fingers tremble and he longs for opium's obliging pall. He lays the knife in his lap for a moment, leans in to tickle the kitten's soft forehead.

I think perhaps you made a mistake coming on this trip, Lai Yue.

Lai Yue tries to concentrate on the cat's soft purr.

What else was I to do, Shan?

I don't know. Her voice is sad. *It's a pity …*

Lai Yue frowns, picks up his knife, continues whittling excess chips of wood away.

It's a pity what, Shan?

Her voice becomes plaintive. *It's a pity … It's a pity …*

She can't say it, he thinks, his knife gouging the wood. She can't say that it's a pity I lost all our savings. That we are in this cursed position because of my actions. But didn't I do it all in order to get us home?

Sullivan shouts in his ear and the blade skips off the timber, glancing against the side of Lai Yue's thumb. Sullivan waves his pannikin about three inches from Lai Yue's face. More tea. The others are still seated around the fire and Fritz and Hagerty smirk, shake their heads, but Lucas smiles at him, nods, lifts his pannikin too. Lai Yue glances down at his hand. His blood, dark and syrupy in the firelight, seeps into the grain of the wood.

Sullivan and his men bed down for the night while Lai Yue rinses the cups and pots in the stream. He sleeps several feet from the other men. He's not too afraid because he lies near the dogs. Their stiff ears and quivering noses seem to be on constant alert for trouble. When he's finally finished packing away the cooking utensils, he rests on his swag and breathes deeply, staring up at the slender moon that reclines in the sky. His body is so weary, yet these slow, empty moments – hours – are the very worst for his hectic mind. If he closes his eyes, perhaps Shan will think he sleeps. The fire crackles and spits; crickets' calls drawl in and out. Tiny insects splutter against his swag.

Something prods his arm, and he grunts in fright. But it's only Lucas, squatted next to him, smiling. He holds up a dark bottle in one hand, grasps two cups in the other. Gestures for Lai Yue to join him. Lai Yue is slow from his bedding, puzzled. He follows Lucas to a fallen tree, a little way from the fire, and sits next to him. The moon emits an amniotic glow from where it's hidden behind thin cloud, but Lai Yue's eyes can make out Lucas pouring a generous measure of the amber spirit into a cup for him. He sniffs it: rice wine but sweeter. He takes a sip, and it bites his throat. The spirit lingers on his lips, tingles, not unlike the feeling of sunburn on the shoulders.

'Rum,' Lucas says.

Lai Yue nods. He's shy of repeating the English words. Both stubborn and unwilling to appear foolish.

Lucas points up into the sky. He talks, explains something to Lai Yue. He leans in, his shoulder nudging Lai Yue's, and his finger circles a bright star in the sky, and then traces a rectangular pattern, says a word three times. Lai Yue gulps more rum. He appreciates the man's friendliness, but he feels awkward too. What does he have to say to this pallid mouse? He's no longer practised in niceties, can't find his way into showing his gratitude. They sit quietly for a while, watching the black sparkle of the water's surface. Lai Yue swallows the last of his rum, makes ready to stand, and Lucas pulls at his shoulder so that he remains seated. Lucas shuffles closer to

Lai Yue to pour more rum into his cup, doesn't shift away when he's done.

The rum warms Lai Yue's flesh, slinking down his throat, settling in the skin of his chest. He wonders if he's actually swaying, or if it's all in his swirling mind. He takes another sip of rum. Feels the heat of Lucas's leg.

What are you doing?

There she goes again. Nagging at him. But he doesn't care. 'Don't care, Shan.' Lai Yue dribbles the words, tilts forward, and his laugh is loud, huffing. Lucas shakes his arm, says, 'Shhhh' and Lai Yue topples into the scrubby dirt. He lies on his back and although his laughter is now softer, wheezy, he continues for so long his stomach muscles start to hurt. A tear trickles from his right eye into his ear cavity.

He is a nice man, and you are making yourself look stupid.

Lai Yue's mouth claps shut. She's right. What is he doing? A drop of rain hits his cheek. Another his left eyelid. He will lie here, watch the stars, the tree shadows, the moon whirl above him. He reaches for the thoughts that usually trouble him, but they're nowhere to be found. Another raindrop splashes his forehead.

Lucas says something, rising to his feet. Lai Yue's head hangs backward, heavy in the sandy earth, as he tries to haul his upper body up by his elbows. He rolls onto his side and then has to rest on all fours for several swaying moments before he can grasp the log and pull himself into a standing position.

Staggering after Lucas's retreating figure, he finds his way to his swag, pauses. He can hear mewling. Squatting by Jie's cage, he peers in at the small creature. Its fur is matted with rainwater. Its eyes gleam at Lai Yue, its little pink mouth mawed open upon a cry. Lai Yue unlatches the door of the cage and reaches in to gather up the kitten. Clasping it to his breast, he wriggles his way into his swag so that he's fully encased like a worm in silk. He listens to how the patter of raindrops against the fabric matches the staccato tap of the kitten's quick heartbeat. His palm cups its bulbous tummy, and he can feel the kitten's thin ribs beneath his fingertips.

That liquor Lucas shared with him is almost as good as opium for banishing bandit thoughts. He feels muffled, as though he's sinking from the world. Sometimes – times like this – he allows himself to dream he's under water. That he drifts, leaden, weightless, in midnight waters. With her. With Shan.

Join me. Join me. Be with me, my love.

15

The bullock meat Clem has brought sticks to the bottom of the pot, and Meriem can tell that no matter how long she cooks it for, it will remain tough. Its aroma, though, rises through the steam, filling her with hunger. How she misses roast lamb sandwiches, the slices of meat cool from the ice box, the soft bread lathered with butter and mustard. As soon as she has saved enough money to return to a proper town – in New South Wales, hopefully – she will buy herself a roast lamb sandwich in some reputable eating house. Follow it up with a large piece of sponge cake with fresh cream. Trying to ignore the ache that comes with the realisation that no sandwich or cake would ever taste as good as her mother's, she jabs at the lumps of meat.

'My friend here is right. Sure he is,' says a rough voice in the next room.

Meriem shudders, hidden as she is in the scullery. She's lucky nobody looked her way when Clem arrived with that man in tow. The very same man Meriem witnessed kicking the dog's rump that day by his butcher tent. As soon as he pulled the wool cap from his head, the oily stink of his scalp filled the small room.

'Thank 'e, Dermot,' Clem says. 'I cannae persuade Soph that there's nothing good about them.'

They're arguing about the Chinese again. The more that Dermot drinks, the more strident his voice becomes, the more his words slur. Meriem chops up two carrots, adds them to the meat with a little water and cornflour. Stirs the muck about, watching the swirl of oil rise to the top of the stock. She often wonders what Sophie would do if she were to fall pregnant to one of her Chinese customers. Doesn't it fill her with fear? Meriem's own eyes widen at the thought. She's not sure how Sophie safeguards herself from pregnancy. Perhaps the next time she's really drunk, Meriem will ask her. There's a wry twist to her mouth as she thinks of how such information would have been useful to her a while back. A wisp of wheat hair comes to her mind. A plump, waxen cheek. She dries a damp dish on her apron and looks in on Sophie and her guests.

Dermot fills his pipe, tamping down the tobacco, and says, 'I don't know how anyone can tell the smelly buggers apart.'

Meriem recalls the Chinese boy who helped her after the dance. He was familiar somehow. Reminded her of a wood duck, with his tuft of dark hair at the back of his bald pate.

'Dinna I read in *The Week*, Dermot, about the Chinese mob that robbed two hundred pounds from the warden?' Clem says. 'Tied his poor sod of an orderly up. Said they'd shoot 'im if 'e followed.'

'Thievin' rascals.'

Meriem places a plate of damper on the table.

'The Chinese are probably trying to recoup some of the very money that the warden has stolen from them in the first place,' Sophie says in a teasing voice. She tosses down the rest of her gin.

An ugly frown descends upon Clem's face. 'You always take their side. I ha' just about enough of it.'

'Oh, don't be silly, Clem,' Sophie soothes. 'I'm just saying.'

'Well, dinna say it,' he shouts, and thumps his hand down on the tabletop.

Tension cloys the air. Sophie simply bites her lips inward, ignoring Clem. 'How much longer 'til the stew is ready, Merri?'

'Half an hour, I'd say.'

Dermot's eyes are bloodshot, loose in their sockets, as he stares at Meriem. 'Didn't notice this fine filly afore,' he says, his gaze wandering over her bosom, her hips, down her skirt, resting on her bosom again.

'She's my maid, Dermot. Nothin' more,' Sophie says, filling his glass.

'Dinna fuss, Soph,' Clem says. His voice is light, as though trying to ease the strain, but there is a warning note as well. 'He's only bein' a wee lickerish for the lass.'

Meriem moves heavily as she returns to the scullery. Feels the pressure of the men's eyes as sure as if they were to have their hands on her.

She steps outside and stands against the wall. Takes a deep breath in. Next door the Chinaman's hoe thwacks the soil in a steady rhythm. His hens cluck in their laying box. A breeze has arrived with dusk and she's sorry to have to turn back into the stuffy house. She tends to the stew, rearranging and cleaning the scullery shelves rather than return to the main room.

The others have begun a game of round robin, which Dermot starts up with surprisingly tuneful vocals about a 'fair young girl', Lady Margaret. Meriem can't quite make out the words of the song that drunkenly overlap. Somebody kisses someone, twice, three times, but then Dermot sings something about a 'corpse asleep'. Meriem frowns. Sophie joins him in singing the last bit in the round:

Fair Margaret died today, today,
Sweet William died the morrow,
Fair Margaret died for pure true love,
Sweet William died for sorrow.

They repeat it three times until Clem grumbles for a new song.

Sophie sings 'The Wild Rover' in a low, pretty voice, straining only slightly on the highest note. Dermot claps along with her, and even Clem sings, *And it's no, nay, never. No, nay, never no more.*

Meriem places the only flat plates they own in front of Clem and Dermot. Sophie will have to make do with an enamel bowl. Serving the stew straight from the pot, Meriem gives Sophie only a small helping because she can tell Sophie's already too far gone on gin to do more than pick at her dinner. The men, however, fall on the food, dragging pieces of damper through the gravy.

Her own bowl of stew she carries outside with her. It's become so dark it takes her a few moments to discern what is night and what is the breach in her vision. She offers some damper to Tinker, who grasps it between his front teeth and trots a few feet away to roll it in the dirt before chewing on it. Inching further into the darkness she sits down on her tree stump, lifting her nose to sniff the smoke from the Chink gardener's fire. Whatever he's cooking smells delicious, much more appetising than the mess she's thrown together. She places her bowl on the ground, leans her elbows on her knees. She stares at Sophie's sheet, which still hangs on the line, a patch of white in the gloom. One of the men's horses snuffles where it's tethered at the side of the house. Perhaps it is as restless and bored as she is. She allows her mind to forage its way through useless things – the softness of her bed in Queanbeyan, how long Milly's hair must now be, Pattie, Pattie, Pattie – almost enjoying the scalding that accompanies the thoughts, for it reinforces the righteous pity she feels for herself. She likes to be consumed by the hurt until she finds strength in its resultant anger. Its heat reminds her of who she is, hardens her to it; if she were to soften, after all, she might disappear like a drop of rain in the sea.

A gust of wind flaps Sophie's sheet. 'Better get it down,' she mutters as she rises to her feet. She's slipping it from the line when strong arms circle her waist from behind, heave her backward against a hard body.

'Let go of me, Dermot.' For she can smell it's him. She tries to peel his fingers from her body. In an effort to sound cajoling, wondering just how drunk he might be, she adds, 'Come on, Dermot, let me go. That's enough funning for now.' Prays that if she's reasonable, he will be too. He nuzzles her neck, and she grimaces at the rub of his stubble and his stagnant breath.

'Ye'll be good-natured for me, won't you, lass?'

She senses the more she struggles against him, the more excited he's becoming. She tries to remain still, slack even, repeats, 'That's enough, Dermot. I have to get on with my chores for Miss Sophie.'

'Sure, it won't take long to do a little chore for me.' His voice has become raspy and he releases his right hand to bend over and yank up her skirts.

'No, Dermot,' she says, breathless from the tight hold about her middle. She strains her face towards the doorway and calls for Sophie. 'Sophie, you need to help me,' she calls, ending on a short squeal. 'Sophie!'

There's no movement inside the house, and Meriem realises that Sophie and Clem have most probably retired to the bedroom, their own noises masking Meriem's calls.

Dermot clamps his hand across her mouth and forces her towards the closest tree, shoves her face to its coarse bark.

'Be good-natured, now, lass,' he gasps, ramming her to the trunk. 'Be good-natured.'

The bark grazes her fingers, lacerating her chin where it is squashed against the tree. She yelps when he squeezes her breast hard. Pressing her into the tree with his groin, he lifts her skirts. She feels the night air on her exposed thighs, then higher, on her rump.

A dull, metallic thud rings out. Dermot grunts, slumping onto her, before his body slithers to the ground.

Meriem swings around, shoving her skirts down. She closes her bad eye, the better to see the black silhouette before her, a hoe grasped in its hand.

'Come,' the Chinese boy says to her. 'Come. To there.' He points towards the bushland that leads out of town.

There's a rustle by their feet and they both look down. Dermot rolls over on the dry leaves and dirt, groaning. They run.

16

Weak sunlight twinkles through the canopy of leaves, and Ying wipes the sleep from her eyes. The fabric of her shirt and pants are damp with morning dew, as is the grass that surrounds her. Ying looks across at the young woman, Merri, but she's still asleep. Her mouth hangs ajar, and her left eyelid twitches. Her hair is the colour of red earth, as fine as a silkworm's thread. When Ying led her here the night before, she thought they would hide for a short period only. But Merri sank to the grass, resting her hands in the nest of her skirt. She gazed up past the paperbarks to the stars, and that's when Ying saw she was crying again. She said many things, in a hard little voice, too swiftly for Ying to quite catch their full meaning.

Sunbirds whirr among the drooping leaves; a honey sucker, as sombre as a monk, lands on a branch, watches her for several seconds and then swoops off. Ying blinks up at the circle of sky and thinks of how she's like a bird – a migratory bird, perhaps a swallow – having fled her home's winter, with hopes to return in its spring. She recalls that first night at sea, when she lurched against Lai Yue's shoulder in the creaking dark, the choppy seas hurtling them far from home. How sure she was that they'd made the wrong decision, how determined she was to board the very first boat home, whatever the cost. But try as she may, Ying cannot remember what she felt in those panicked hours; she can't re-create the sensation of loss, heavy in her stomach, or the disquiet that must have scrabbled its talons behind her ribcage.

Because now she feels content. Revels in her life in Maytown, working for Jimmy and exploring the township at night. She feels bad whenever her thoughts are drawn back to her mother, Lai Yue or her younger siblings, but mostly they lie beneath diverting layers of routine and small pleasures. Indeed, Ying has lain in this very spot many times before, staring up at the clear sky in snatched moments between the errands she runs for Jimmy, and wondered if she could even return to her old life. She's not sure she would want to live without the freedoms she experiences here; freedoms, she realises, that are associated with both a lack of family to watch over her, and with disguising herself as a boy. How else would she have discovered her knack for adding numbers and returning change; or tasted the marvellous, tart sweetness of marmalade; or known about how men visit women like the one Miss Merri works for?

It's her new-found sense of exploration that led Ying to this private place. While waiting for Lo Pak to finish wrenching spinach from the soil, she had wandered down to the river, to gaze at the brackish water as it cut across jagged, black rocks. She'd continued until she came across a fisherman, lounged on a low-bearing branch, his feet swinging above the water. He frowned at Ying, so she retreated, dodging her way through a copse of tea trees. And that's how she came across this grassy mound, hidden within a ring of paperbarks and shrubbery.

Ying notices dark clouds massing above. Time to return to the shop. Face Jimmy's ire.

'Lady, we go.'

Merri blinks awake. Sitting up, she looks at Ying, and says, 'I cannot believe I fell asleep here.'

Her teeth are extraordinarily straight. Ying runs her tongue over her own front teeth, where one snaggles across its neighbour.

'Last night …' Merri begins, pushing her glasses up the bridge of her nose. She peers at Ying, slightly narrowing her right eye.

'Yes.' Last night, when Ying hit that man over the head. She'd seen the shadow of his face as he'd rolled over and was quite sure he was one of the men who'd taunted Jimmy in the shop that day.

'Last night. Why were you there?'

'Yes. Last night. There.'

'But why?'

Ying bobs her head. She thinks of how she often lingers outside the house at night, but decides it is easier to lie. 'I buy cabbage from Lo Pak.'

'Ah.' Merri nods. 'The gardener next door.'

Ying hears the word 'gardener' and bobs again.

'What is your name?'

Ying has an urge to tell Merri her whole name, her real name. Wants to share it for once. But also, she's awkward with it. Perhaps she will feel exposed; perhaps her real name won't rest comfortably on her shoulders anymore. 'Ying,' she says.

'Ying. Well, that's nice and easy. Ying.' Merri pulls a face as though surprised.

A raindrop plops on Ying's scalp. Merri wipes one from her cheek.

'We'd better head back,' Merri says. Her mouth draws down as she shakes out her skirt.

~

Ying can't tear her eyes away from the photograph grasped between her fingers. The Chinese woman is seated on a cane chair and at her elbow, which rests on the tabletop, are a slim crystal vase filled with ferns and a small brass clock. Ying can't tell what clasps the woman's sable hair, but pendant earrings hang from her earlobes. Although concealed by the sepia tones of the photograph, Ying's sure her smock is made of very fine heavy silk – of perhaps a golden colour – and her feet are shod in handsome shoes that curl slightly at the toe. The woman gazes off to the side. Her face is narrow, her lips full. She's as fine as a finch, and Ying feels an unlovely twinge of envy.

'She will be your wife?' Ying looks across at Jimmy, where he sits and smokes behind the counter.

Ah Kee laughs. 'If his mother has anything to do with it.'

Jimmy's eyebrows lift, but he continues to stare at the ground, his crossed leg swinging.

Ah Kee takes an English-speaking newspaper from his pocket. He waves his fingers at Jimmy, gesturing for the other man to give him his spectacles, and then peers through them at the strange script. Slowly, he translates the words as he reads: '*A Chinese lady* – they mean your bride, Wui Hing.' He chuckles before returning to the article. '*A Chinese lady … arrived by the Brisbane boat … a beautiful daughter of* – ah – *a beautiful daughter of the flowery land … with her servant … stared at by a crowd of Europeans* – the devil dogs – *at her painted lips, her eyebrows, her beautiful dress, her tiny feet.*'

Ying glances down at her own feet, so flat, so long. Her grandmother had bound feet, neatly nobbled like a pair of walnuts. But Ying's mother came to the family with large slippers, and Ying and her sister had to help out about the farm far too much to be hampered by such femininity. Ying curls her toes in as far as they will go.

'Your parents must be very determined to send her all this way,' Ah Kee says, folding the scrap of newspaper.

'Yoke Yee is simply visiting her uncle in Cooktown, Ah Kee.'

Ah Kee snorts. 'We will see.'

Jimmy brushes past Ying to place a fresh tomato in front of the altar. He's ignored her since she crept into the shop earlier that morning. She brought a basket of beans from Lo Pak with her – thinking she could pretend she was only gone since dawn – but knew from the stiff expression on Jimmy's face that he was aware she had abandoned the store the whole night.

She returns the photograph to where she found it next to the altar and lugs a crate towards the shelves at the front of the shop, its sharp edges digging into her shins. As she unpacks tins of turtle soup, the men argue over whether Jimmy's betrothed can be brought to Maytown or not. Ah Kee is amused at the thought of a retinue of carriers carting her, reclined in a sedan chair, through the bush, but Jimmy is still not convinced he will marry so soon.

'She would be the first Chinese woman here, Wui Hing.'

Jimmy nods, puffs on his pipe.

'You can make all the others red-eyed,' Ah Kee says. 'Imagine how incensed that stupid dog Yeeh will be that he doesn't have a beautiful young wife here with him while you do. I have seen his wife, too, the old buffalo. I caught a glimpse of her fat face when we were boarding the boat. She would never travel so far, away from the luxuries of home.'

Ying takes a raisin from her pocket and slips it into her mouth. The raisins here are smaller, meaner than those they get at the market back home. The skin is tougher, more wrinkled, but she enjoys worrying at it with her tongue, taking in its grooves, rubbing it against the roof of her mouth until, finally, a tiny tear allows some of its sweetness to peep through. This she can keep up for minutes at a time. Rolling the raisin in her mouth, she has an idea. She crouches down and searches for a jar she knows is on one of the lower shelves. Pushing aside two ginger pots, she pulls forward a glass jar filled with red berries even drier and smaller than the raisins. She remembers her grandmother used to chew these berries every morning, said they helped clear her vision. Ying peeps over at Jimmy. Ah Kee has left, and Jimmy is serving two Chinese diggers wanting to buy flour. Ying pours a large handful of the red berries into her left-hand pocket. After twisting the tin lid onto the glass, she shoves the jar to the rear of the shelf and hurries through to the back of the shop to fetch another crate of food to unpack.

'Ying,' Jimmy says, when she returns. His voice is heavy. 'Where were you last night?'

'I fell asleep.'

'You fell asleep where?' Sharp this time.

'Beneath the trees. By the river.'

Jimmy frowns at her. 'I will not tolerate a worker of mine wasting his time, and mine, on opium every night, Ying.'

'No, Jimmy. I have never smoked opium. I go for walks, that's all. Down by the river.'

Jimmy looks doubtful. 'I did wonder where you found the funds to visit one of the Yip opium tents.' His frown deepens though. 'But you're supposed to be here, minding the store while I am out. How are you to repay me if my shop is robbed when you are on one of these walks of yours?'

'I always ask Yeeh's servant to watch the shop, Jimmy.' She doesn't mention the spoonfuls of special red tea, tobacco or pickles she pilfers from the shop to pay him.

'You can't rely on that silly goat, Ying! This is not good. If you leave the shop unattended again, I will have to find somebody else to work here.'

Ying wants to cry out – how can she give up her evening excursions now? But she only nods, lowering her eyes. Specks of raisin dissolve on her tongue.

17

Drowning. Drowning. Lai Yue struggles to breathe. He opens his eyes but all is still dark. The canvas of his swag smothers his nostrils, his mouth. He flips the swag wide, takes a deep breath, squints up at the lavender sky. An aching throb jags at the lower right side of his skull, makes him cringe. His tongue is dry and spongy. He can smell the sour spirits on his own breath. Each morning he regrets his drinking spells with Lucas, yet every afternoon tension twists his muscles taut and he feels a giddy need for the release the rum provides.

He sits up, cradles his head in his hands. Someone clanks a pannikin against a pot, and Lai Yue almost groans. He has to get himself up, prepare tea. Breakfast. He dry retches.

Sullivan's voice is close, grates loudly in Lai Yue's ear. 'What the fuck is that?'

Lai Yue follows the man's line of sight to a mound of damp fur at his side. Lai Yue scrambles to make room for the poor creature. 'Jie, Jie,' he cries.

He turns the kitten over. Its forelegs cover its little face. Lai Yue shakes the kitten gently, but it doesn't stir, hangs limp from his fist. What has he done? He stares and stares at the matted body. What has he done?

He staggers to his feet, still holding Jie's body.

Fritz and Lucas come up behind Sullivan. Fritz says something and spits to the side.

'I took him to bed because he was crying,' Lai Yue tries to explain to the other men. It has become his custom to find sleep with Jie's warm body pressed to his heart. 'The lightning. He was frightened by the lightning.' He gabbles, but in his own tongue, and he sees they can't understand him.

'You bloody gowk,' Sullivan says, shaking his head.

Lai Yue looks from the disgusted expression on Sullivan's face to Lucas, who doesn't meet his eye.

Sullivan says something to Lucas, who then steps forward. 'Larry, did you want to eat it?' He makes the motions for eating – morsel in fingers, placed to mouth.

'No, no,' Lai Yue shouts. 'Jie. I named him Jie. He was my friend.'

'Eat? Does *Jie* mean eat?'

'No, no.'

Sullivan's mouth twists in disdain and he says, 'As bad as the bloody natives.'

This Lai Yue understands.

He shakes his head from side to side, but he can see that they've made up their minds. Fritz calls out to Hagerty, who's pissing against a stringybark. Hagerty gives a shout of laughter, says something about not being surprised. The men walk back to sit around the embers of the fire.

Lai Yue gazes down at Jie's body. The kitten's fine fur is a wet lick across Lai Yue's sweaty palm. His lip jerks, and he clamps it between his teeth. He must not cry in front of the others. That would be the worst. But really, he wants to weep – weep as he

135

did when he was a child and he nursed infant silkworms from the beginning of the season only to find them annihilated by an army of ants. A rampage of stinging and stabbing; soft, writhing bodies; a bundle of victims to cart away. Those ants. He executed each one under the savage print of his thumb. Perhaps that was when they took up residence in his cloudy soul. Marched forth when his anger stirred, bided impatiently when he was distracted.

18

Meriem stares up at the bruised sky, glad of the lull in the downpour. If the rain keeps up she'll never manage to dry Sophie's sheets. She thinks of the poor sods down by the river, barely protected from the deluge in their overcrowded tents. Better than a few years ago though, long before she arrived. Those earliest diggers who didn't reckon on how dire the wet season could be. Some had even found themselves cut off for weeks at a time without sufficient food, their animals and camps washed away with the rising river.

The shower picks up again as she returns to their house across the planks of wood the Chinese gardener helped her lay over the mud. From a distance, the gardener looks young, nimble, but up close she's noticed the white strands of hair that pepper his pigtail, that grow stubby from his cavernous nostrils. She thinks of the Chinese boy who helped her escape that disgusting pig, Dermot. Of how she spent the whole night by his side. Something about the idea makes her grasp her lips in her teeth to stamp out a smile. How very *audacious* it was of her. Meriem had almost told Sophie of it, but the annoyance she felt towards her had stilled her tongue.

By the time she returned to their house the morning after the attack, Meriem had whipped herself into quite a temper. She was going to tell Sophie exactly what she thought of her, leaving her vulnerable to the advances of a brute like Dermot. Meriem had a good mind to leave, find paid housework somewhere else – there must be countless whores who could use the services of a fallen girl, a disgraced girl. Her thoughts were savage. But when Sophie crept from her bedroom later that morning and Meriem saw her swollen cheek, she swallowed all the scalding words, and instead stoked the wood in the stove with vicious jabs.

Now, as Meriem steps into the scullery, rainwater trickles from between layers of tin roofing into a pot she's placed on the floor. A cup and a skillet catch the rain that drips onto her bedding. She tosses water from the brimming skillet out the back door, returning it to its position beneath the leak. Despite the cooling shower, the air within the house is steamy.

'Merri, can we have a cup of tea?' Sophie calls from the next room.

Meriem looks into the living area. Sophie is seated opposite Clem at the round table, fanning herself with a pretty paper fan, her robe hanging loose from her shoulders. Pieces of Clem's dismantled Colt are strewn across the table. He's wearing one of those new Yankee felt hats. Meriem's seen the sign outside Cowper's general store advertising them for seven shillings. Meriem had been afraid Clem might be angry with her, perhaps even strike her for what happened to his mate. But days passed and he didn't say anything, and Dermot hasn't returned, making Meriem wonder if Dermot had been so far gone with grog and the whack on the head he simply didn't remember anything of that evening.

As the kettle warms up, Meriem takes a seat at the back door, as far from the heat of the stove as she can get, and peels potatoes over a tub.

'It's disgustin', Soph. What if you have a bairn to one of them?'

Clem says, shoving a tiny wire brush back and forth through the holes in the gun's barrel. 'What sort of muddy-skinned little devil will you bring into the world? It's just no' right.'

'Clem, darlin', we've discussed this,' Sophie says, her voice sweet yet steady. 'If I don't take their custom, I'd not make any money.'

The boiling water stirs in the kettle.

'You should move home to Melbourne, then.' Clem drops the gun barrel to the table and picks up the wood grip. He dabs a spot of oil onto a rag and rubs the handle until it shines.

The kettle rattles on the stovetop. Meriem lifts it off, splashing hot water across the tea-leaves in the pot. She's glad Clem isn't drinking rum today. Well, not yet. When he's drunk, his Chinese rant usually ends with slammed furniture and marks on poor Sophie's body.

Meriem edges the teacups onto the table, next to the Colt's workings. Clem has the revolver's greased skeleton in his left hand, waggling screws and pieces back into its body. He drives the handle into its metal hoist.

Meriem returns from the scullery with the canister of sugar, but pauses on the threshold as Clem says, 'I'm fond of you, Soph. I'd hate to see you come to trouble.' He leans over and kisses her neck. He cups her breast with his free hand, runs his thumb across her pale skin, leaving a black smudge, then, jaw clenched, pinches her nipple until the skin around the tips of his fingers turns white. The fan crumples in her hand. 'You should stop invitin' them heathens,' he says. 'I mean it. No more.'

When Clem returns to his Colt, Meriem shoves the canister and teaspoon on the table.

'*Ching Chong Chinaman, velly velly sad*,' Clem chants, slowly, as he slides the barrel onto the gun's shaft. '*All his cabbage*,' he continues, levering the Colt's long, black nozzle into place, *'ha' gone bad.'* His voice is sarcastic when he asks, 'Does that make you sad, Soph?' As he stares at Sophie, his pupils rise like the sun in a white, stony sky.

Meriem drapes Sophie's coat over her head as she hurries towards Jimmy's shop. The rain patters the oiled cloth. She's glad of the coat's cover, not only for keeping her hair relatively dry, but also, she hopes, so Dermot doesn't recognise her. For the first three days after that night, she flinched each time a shadow fell across their doorway. Was it him, come to exact revenge? To try to claim what she'd denied him? She recalls his words to her that night: *Be good-natured.* What a bastard. Meriem thinks of the dainty pistol Sophie showed her when they first moved into the house, wondering where it's hidden. Not that Meriem would know how to use it.

Stamping the mud from her boots, she steps into Jimmy's shop, whisking the coat from her head. The tiny space is full of men – as stinky as drenched mongrels – ostensibly there to buy stores, but most probably avoiding the rain. She drops two cans of peaches into her basket and beats a Chinese man to the last pot of anchovies. Spying something green on Jimmy's counter, she joins the line, hoping it's spinach. She can cook a nice spinach pie with whatever meat she can get from the butcher – if she could only remember how her mother made pastry. Meriem's always comes out too short, so that her pie is more like some sort of meat crumble.

As usual, her eyes are drawn to Jimmy's gold and crimson altar. Incense smoke coils through the air, its sickening fragrance mingling with the stench of horse manure and dirt and all the odd foreign foods Jimmy sells. When a digger, his greatcoat splashed with mud but with a neat bowler hat perched upon his large head, moves to the side, Meriem catches sight of a photograph propped up against the altar. She tilts her head and moves closer, the better to see it. The photograph is of a young Chinese woman dressed in a sumptuous smock. She's a far cry from the skinny, half-dressed Chinese men who overrun the place. Meriem positions herself a little to the left, so her better eye can study it. Refined. That's the word she's searching for. The woman looks refined. Meriem's mother used to say the word when describing their schoolteacher in Queanbeyan. A thin British woman, she was. Took a squeeze of lemon in her tea, pressed a lace handkerchief to the cream on her lips when eating a scone. Meriem decides the Chinese woman looks far more refined than that Mrs Cowper and the other old cats here in Maytown.

'Miss Merri,' says a soft voice at her elbow. 'You want lolly?'

The Chinese boy – her Chinese boy – stands before her with a large jar of humbugs. What was his name again? Young? Will? Perhaps Sing, like the Chinese man who has a little barber's tent on High Street?

'Oh, I thought you looked familiar,' she says. 'I must have noticed you working here. Have you been with Jimmy long?'

The Chinese boy smiles. 'Yes. I work here.'

Meriem isn't quite sure whether to ask him for his name. She's pleased to see him; didn't he save her from Dermot? And when he kept her company that long night – she has admitted to herself upon reviewing their time together – she felt nothing but safe beside him. Comfort, almost. His presence benign, yet very welcome in the darkness, not unlike when Boney, her family's spaniel, used to lie beside her in bed.

However, glancing about the shop at the other white folk, and noticing Jimmy watching them as he packs potatoes into a paper bag, Meriem doesn't want to appear too friendly with a Chinaman.

'Yes, thank you. I will take two humbugs and a bunch of that spinach over there,' she says to the boy.

As she pays him, she nods towards the photograph. 'Who's that?'

'That Jimmy wife.'

Meriem's surprised, wonders why she isn't here with her husband. But when she glances at the photograph again, she can't imagine such a lovely creature enduring the dangers and discomfort of a move to this godforsaken place. 'Did she stay at home?'

'She in Cooktown. She Jimmy wife soon.'

'Soon?'

'Yes,' says the Chinese boy. 'Maybe later.'

Meriem shakes her head, confused, and turns to go. Squeezing past a group of new diggers entering the shop, she pauses on the front step while she rearranges the coat over her head.

'Please, Miss Merri.' The boy catches up to her, handing her a paper bag.

She sees that it's half-filled with a dried red berry of some kind. 'Oh, no. No, thank you.' She tries to shove the bag back into his hands.

'For Miss Merri eyes. Eat. Eat.' The boy points at his own eyes.

'I eat these?'

'Yes. Yes.' He holds up five fingers.

'I eat five berries a day?'

He nods vigorously, smiling.

'But how much are they?' she asks, still a little suspicious. 'How much money do you need?'

'No. No. From me. Please eat.'

Meriem stares down at the berries. She would rather not. They might be poisonous. Or taste terrible. She smiles at him, though, and says, 'Thank you. That's very kind ...'

The boy puts the flat of his hand to his chest and says, 'Ying.'

Ah, yes. She remembers now. 'Ying,' she repeats.

Still smiling, she turns onto the street, pulling the coat over her head. Delight coddles her heart as her boots splash through the mire. Touched that someone has thought of her – her especially. She banters with the butcher when she buys the bacon and compliments the baker on his vanilla slices. She thinks of how much Ying reminds her of a wood duck, and that perhaps Jimmy, with his long face and kindly lashes, is rather like a 'roo.

As she approaches their house, Meriem's quick trot slows despite the rain. Her spirits drop at the thought of the hot, confined rooms: the fusty, mushroomy smell, the wood stove that will be a bugger to light in the wet. And she really, really hopes that Clem will be gone, departed on the month-long trek he was telling Sophie about – heading west with a team of carriers that includes that bastard Dermot. Meriem looks forward to the peace, for each time Clem visits Sophie, it's as though he tightens his hold on her. Treats her as his chattel, refusing to pay his way. Stomping through a puddle, Meriem mutters, 'I don't know why she puts up with it.' But also, she thinks of the caution that slows Sophie's actions when she watches Clem, how it's mixed with some kind of longing. Meriem feels a curl of embarrassment for her. Sophie. Usually so merry and matter-of-fact with her other custom. Reduced to a pretty washcloth around that man.

19

Standing at the rear of Jimmy's shop, Ying can hear the rain slap against the rising water of the river. A caul of mist slips across the moon, swathing the township in darkness. She wriggles her toes, still damp in her shoes. She supposes they won't dry until the showers ease and it's almost impossible to believe that they ever will.

The canvas walls of the extension Jimmy erected behind his shop are covered in clouds of mould and have taken on a fetid odour, something like sweaty feet. Damp creeps across the ground despite being undercover, so that at night they have to pull their bedding up onto the shop floor to sleep.

It's too wet for Ying to go for her usual wander. Too wet, too miserable. It's been three days now since she walked along the diminishing riverbank and she can't help but feel heavy with the absence of something; she doesn't know what. Even when she lies down to sleep, she has a restless ache in her limbs, as though her legs might lift in the air, float away. She stares out at the black outline of eucalypts bowed under the weight of the rain, and wonders if Miss Merri is eating the berries.

Having lugged her blanket and mat up into the shop, she drops them onto the timber floor in the front corner, diagonally opposite where Jimmy positions his own bedding, near the counter, when he returns from his mah-jong nights. She lies down, and stares into the glare of the lamp on the counter until there is a glowing blind-spot in her vision when she glances away. Closing her eyes, she tries to settle into sleep by relaxing each part of her body, starting with her toes, just as her mother taught her. But she hasn't even reached her thighs before there's the familiar tingle of restlessness in her legs. She opens her eyes. Watches a cockroach's crooked journey across the ceiling.

Sitting up with a frustrated groan, she decides to continue unpacking the crates brought that morning by the teamsters from Cooktown – probably the last through for several weeks, Jimmy said. She goes behind the counter, stopping to peruse the photograph of Jimmy's betrothed again. How beautiful she is. Ying saw the way Miss Merri admired the photograph too and in that moment she wished so much that Miss Merri could see her, Ying, in her special yellow tunic, with its lovely sheen and the lotus flowers her mother had sewn at its breast. But, of course, that can never happen, for Ying is a boy now and the tunic is long gone. Ying studies the photograph, and she takes in the beads that adorn the woman's wrist, and how a butterfly has been embroidered onto the hem of her smock. When Ying is a girl once more, and owns such things, she will embroider a phoenix on her own smock, in orange and blue thread.

Ying wonders if Jimmy's betrothed is enjoying her sojourn in Cooktown. Does her uncle allow her to see much of the town, or is she confined to the back spaces of his store? She might have fine clothing and pretty ornaments in her hair, but Ying doubts very much if she has ever seen how the English people dance, grasping each other's waists as they twirl around the room. Or if she's tasted

145

lemonade or rabbit pie. With a welcome sense of superiority, Ying tuts with the pity of it.

She picks up a burlap parcel and unwraps a clutch of knives, sharp, with bone handles. Unsure of where to put them, she leaves them on the counter and continues with a box of heavy boots, which she lines up against the wall. She pries the lid from the largest crate and peers inside at the pile of moleskins Jimmy orders in for the white diggers. She stacks them on the shelf where they belong, hesitating at the last two pieces of a heavier material in a dark blue shade.

She shakes one loose, and it takes her a moment to work out that the length of fabric is a woman's skirt, the kind the Cowper lady might wear, or the woman who looks after the post office. She holds it to her body, but its hem hangs across her feet onto the floor, the waistband so wide she could wind it twice about herself. Ying lifts up the other skirt, which, although smaller, is still too large. Hugging it to her chest, she checks that the front door is locked. Calculates that Jimmy will be at least another hour from home. Without removing her trousers, Ying pulls the skirt up over her hips. She knows that the bunched fabric belongs at the back – for reasons beyond Ying's understanding, white women insist upon this hump of ruched padding over their bottoms. Perhaps it is to cushion a fall, but Ying thinks it is more likely in order to avoid a pinch from a man's wandering fingers.

Ying presses the skirt at her waist with her left hand, running her other down the skirt's smooth nap. She walks across the shop, enjoying how the fabric drapes her legs, swishes the floor behind. If only. If only it fit her a bit better, if only she were a little plumper; she is reminded of Miss Merri's creamy flesh. If only she could be a girl again, and stroll down the street in a girl's attire.

She catches sight of the photograph. Thinks that perhaps it is better to be a sparrow, after all, than a canary in a cage.

'Ying!'

She freezes.

'Ying, what are you doing?' Jimmy hisses.

She turns slowly. Jimmy's entered through the back and stands staring at her, eyes wide. Looks more confounded than outraged.

'Take that thing off and come help me.'

Ying allows the skirt to sink to the floor, kicks it away. She follows Jimmy, joining him where he crouches down next to a figure who rests on all fours in the rain.

'Help me get him inside,' he says.

Together they heave the man to his feet, walk him through the door of the shop. The man moans, tossing his head and, by the lamplight, Ying sees that it's Ah Kee. His nose is dark with blood, spirits strong on his breath.

'Sit him over there.' Jimmy nods towards his chair behind the counter.

It's not until they right him in the chair that Ying notices the nape of Ah Kee's neck. Brown and bare. She moves to his other side, confused, looking for his queue. She takes in the jagged hair at the base of his skull. Backing away, she knocks over a basket and potatoes bounce across the floor.

'Where is his queue?' Dizzy with the shock of it.

'He cut it off,' Jimmy says, leaning on the counter, contemplating Ah Kee, finger hooked over his nose. 'He cut it off himself, in front of everyone.'

'But why?'

'Tea,' Ah Kee mumbles, his eyes rolling towards Ying. 'Tea.'

The lip of the teapot clinks against the cup, her hands tremble so much. If Ah Kee has no queue, he cannot return to China. Not for a long time. Not until his hair has regrown.

She gives him the cup, and he spills some tea down his tunic before managing to get it to his mouth. 'I showed those dogs.' His hand flops to his lap, and Ying catches the cup just in time.

'I wonder if you will feel so proud in the morning, friend,' Jimmy says.

Ah Kee's mouth sets into a grumpy line. 'I'm sick of pandering to all those Sip Yee dogs. I won't do it anymore. And now they know I mean it.'

Ying looks to Jimmy for clarification.

'Ah Kee is late paying his debt to the tong, so some Sip Yee men beat him. Told him he had to return to China to work in one of their gaming houses until the debt is paid.'

Ying considers the blood congealing in Ah Kee's nostrils. Notices a tiny cut that brims his left eyebrow. How his cheekbone is swollen.

Jimmy continues, 'That's where we've been. Paying out his debt.'

'Thank you, Wui Hing. Great friend. I will repay you very soon.' Ah Kee's eyes close. Ying wonders if he's fallen asleep or passed out.

'Ah Kee handed over the money, and then sliced off his hair,' Jimmy adds.

One eyelid peels open. 'Did you see their faces when I brought out my knife, Wui Hing?' Ah Kee's grin is wet with spittle. 'Thought I was going to stab them.'

'I shouldn't have let you go to them after so much wine.'

'I will not be forced out by those dog-thugs,' grunts Ah Kee. 'More tea.'

'But,' Ying whispers to Jimmy, 'but he won't be able to return home. He will be executed.' They will hang him or perhaps shoot him or chop off his head for treason.

'Maybe you can say that a group of *gweilo* cut it off,' Jimmy says to Ah Kee. 'I've heard of it happening. We all have, haven't we?'

'Yes, yes,' Ying says. 'The authorities will give you special dispensation.' But her guts twist as she thinks of the taxman, his dead eyes as he gouged more and more levy from her mother.

'Not going back. I'm staying here. More tea, Ying.'

Ying pours him another cup and hands it to him.

'You should have seen me, Ying. I threw my queue at their feet, didn't I, Wui Hing?' he says, his cackle jubilant as he claps his free hand against his thigh.

Ying stands before him, almost crying. 'But, Ah Kee. You might regret this in the morning. You really might.'

Ah Kee pouts his lips, making an effort to think. 'Perhaps … Perhaps I will wish I'd kept my queue as a keepsake,' he says, a rueful smile lifting the side of his mouth. 'But that is all.'

As she lies in the darkness, Ying is careful to rest her hands by her sides on the timber flooring. Knows that if she rubs her face, the lavender oil that stains her fingertips will burn her skin. Just the smell of it always makes her eyes smart, and her breaths become shallow. But she didn't hesitate to wash the bloody crust from around Ah Kee's nostrils or dab the lavender oil across his wounds – hoping it would ease the pain, cleanse the abrasions – before Jimmy and she settled him for the night on Ying's mat.

It's not the hard floor that keeps her awake. Her fingers worry at the frayed wood, her skin hitching on thick splinters. Sickened by the dread she feels for Ah Kee. It's as though Ah Kee doesn't know, doesn't care, what trouble he's made for himself. She turns her head, tries to make out his shape in the dark. Amazed at his bravery.

But then, Ah Kee seems pleased with himself rather than distressed. Ying can't believe it. Rolling back, she stares above, blinking three times, testing the darkness. Everyone will go home sooner or later, won't they? Jimmy, Yeeh, the myriad kinsmen who have come here searching out gold. Even Lo Pak, after his sojourn south to plant his longan tree. She tries to imagine never returning – never seeing her mother again, the mulberry trees, the muddy lane – but each time she tries, it's as though a paper fan unfurls across her mind, blocking the trajectory of her thoughts. Instead she thinks of Maytown, its noise and filth and constant spectacle of triumph and hardship; of how she still has to try one of the pale buns at the bakery, with a spoonful of jam on top; how she's hoping Jimmy will allow her to have some of her pay to buy a pelt of soft possum fur. The longer she lies there, listening to Ah Kee's drunken snoring and Jimmy shift in his sleep, she feels an exquisite shiver of wonder, a loosening of her shoulders. No longer positive that Ah Kee has made such an impossible choice.

20

Lai Yue trudges some distance behind the others. He hangs back just enough to not lose sight of the men and their horses when they slash a path through dense bush or zag through tall forest. Since the incident with the kitten, the men have resumed ignoring him, although Lucas still offers him a sympathetic smile when the others are not looking. But the late nights of drinking rum are finished.

Lai Yue is stupefied by the humidity. He wades through the undergrowth, light-headed, drowning in damp air that laps at his chin, the bottoms of his earlobes.

How much longer? How much longer? Shan shifts on his back, wraps her legs more comfortably about his hips.

'I don't know, Shan. How could I know? I don't even know how long we have been away already. I don't know where we are going.'

Hagerty looks over his shoulder at Lai Yue, irritated. But he doesn't say anything. They all mostly disregard Lai Yue when he mumbles to Shan. They have no idea what he is saying, and Lai Yue no longer cares what they think.

After Jie died, he buried the kitten's wisp of a body in a shallow grave.

You might as well eat it. Eat it! You are starving and they think you killed it to eat anyway. You have nothing left to lose, Lai Yue.

But Lai Yue refused. He deserved to starve. He certainly didn't deserve to find succour from the tiny creature's body. Something inside Lai Yue has given way, though – perhaps because the others expect so little of him, or perhaps he has succumbed to their idea of him as an indiscriminate predator – for he has become as adept as the dogs at scavenging for meat. Wallabies, bush rats, possums. He scrambles over wormed gullies, yanking sand goannas into his sack by the tail; borrows Fritz's gun to shoot down large parrots, turkeys, owls. The easiest to catch are the poor pigeons that squat in the dirt when approached. A pretty pity. How are there any left? And he keeps a keen lookout for turtles in the creeks they pass, because their soft flesh is very popular with the others. It seems that as long as it's not a kitten, the white men will eat anything Lai Yue cooks up for them.

He adjusts the heavy pole on his shoulders, carefully balancing the baskets. He feels dizzy, as though he might topple or float on the air like a tuft of goose down. Sometimes he concentrates on the carving of Shan he keeps in his pocket. He floats in her world, withdraws from the rubbed skin of his feet, the smoke in the air, the rustling surfaces. But at other times he tethers himself to what's before him. Bengt lying in the dust, feverish, spent. The long grass, its sharp spurs piercing the fabric of his trousers, drawing long, nasty scratches across his skin. The horses, pushing through the same spear grass, a mingle of sweat and blood spiralling their spindly legs.

They reach a deep clough, and Fritz loses his footing and tumbles down the steep slope. The men laugh, even Bengt, weakly, from where he's slumped forward on his horse, but some slick of colour – umber, glossy – catches Lai Yue's attention, fades away into the scrub.

He drops his pole and baskets to the ground and draws his machete from its sheath. He skids down the slope, keeping his eye on the spot where he noticed the movement. Reaching the thicket, he nudges two loose rocks with his toe, prods the leaves with the tip of the machete. Gently he parts the scraggy twigs. The snake, as thick as his arm, takes off up into the branches, much faster than expected. Lai Yue focuses on its head as it rounds the tree, and his machete slices through the air. The blade lodges into bark, decapitating the snake. The two pieces fall into the lower branches with a heavy thud. Reminds him of another thud. His thoughts recoil. He forces himself to listen to his own panting, to read the scalloped pattern on the snake's varnished hide. Wrenching the blade of the machete from the tree, Lai Yue uses its tip to roll the snake's head closer. Metallic with a yellow band. Camouflaged eyes. With the tip of his knife he gouges out the snake's left eye, then the right. Deposits them in the well of his palm. He flicks the rest of the snake's head away.

Sullivan comes up behind him, grunts his satisfaction. 'Dinner.'

Lai Yue nods. He climbs back up the hill to retrieve his belongings and unpacks a hessian sack – worn, stained, rank – into which he hefts the snake's corpse. The eyes he pops into his silk pouch.

Two hours later, as they make camp, Lai Yue's ears pick up the winding call of crickets. One day he will catch a feast of crickets. He will spend the whole day searching them out. He'll need to roast many to fill up these men.

It's been six days since they passed through a township and the flour is running low. He makes up a tough damper, puts it onto the fire to cook. He lifts the snake's carcass from the sack and makes a neat slit down its belly. He shucks the skin from the flesh inch by inch until the snake is laid pink and bare. He guts it and slices the meat into four-inch lengths. After rinsing the slick from the bits of snake and his hands, he rolls the pieces in flour, bakes them over the fire.

The brothers eat with their fingers, noisily, but the others maintain some semblance of refinement, scrape spoons against bowls, wipe their snake-greased lips on their sleeves.

Lai Yue pours himself some hot tea and breaks off a corner of damper. He retreats from the circle of men, sits down on his swag. Once his hunger would have watered his mouth, but now the smell of the roasting meat just makes him feel a slight sickness in the pit of his stomach. He won't eat.

Yes, love, best you don't eat.

Lai Yue's irritated at Shan's words, but she is correct, after all. He will suck on some damper crumbs later, that's it. He's been such a failure – a thief, a killer – he doesn't deserve even a scrap of snake flesh. He opens the pouch, though, and drops the snake's eyes into his tea. Gulps it down, the hot water searing the skin of his mouth. The snake is no more. It has no way of watching him. No way of reporting to the black bird.

While the others eat, Lai Yue brings out his carving of Shan. He's trying to get her hair right – it's grown longer since he met her. It reaches the middle of her back now, between her shoulder blades. It's a lucky coincidence that the stain of his blood darkens the wood just where her hair slopes down her spine, and with his blade he nicks the spot where her hair ends. The timber is so soft it's like paring an apple.

How much longer, Lai Yue? I do not like it here.

'I know, Shan. I don't know how much longer. But the longer I'm here, the more money I accrue,' he mutters, thinking of home, of the spicy fragrance of his father's rosewood desk. Of his mother's corn soup. He wonders what Ying is up to in Jimmy's shop. Her feet won't be covered in blisters anymore. She probably even has a protective layer of fat over her ribs. He tells himself he's pleased for her, relieved, but the ants stir.

Lai Yue leaves his carving and knife on his swag and returns to the fire to gather up the empty bowls to wash. He leans over Hagerty to retrieve his cup, and Hagerty reels back, waves his hand in front of his screwed-up nose at Lai Yue's bad breath.

Most of the time Lai Yue can't smell it himself, but once in a while he catches a waft and is surprised, almost satisfied, by the hot stench that rises from the black depths of his stomach, which feeds upon itself.

'Like the stink of carrion, splayed, a slash of red, stinking in the heat,' he says to Shan. *A dead mouse squished behind the drawer.* Yes, Shan, something rotting. Dusty, sickly. *Like pig waste, the mud, runny diarrhoea. And bugs.* Beetles, picking their way through shit, *grubs twitching,* gorging, in the dark, crackle chomp chomp chew, *rancid meat gone grey,* maggots squirming, *feeding heaving,* burrowing in a snot-green wound. *And a deserted raw corpse, bloated.* Shrimp shells, their brittle pong, *bzzz bzzz,* a dog fart.

Lai Yue chuckles at their game. Hagerty stares at him. He can't understand Lai Yue's words but he looks outraged. Perhaps a little scared. Lai Yue scoops up a thin twig and uses it to pick at his teeth. He sniffs the tip for the intimate reek of decay.

21

Meriem crams her straw hat onto her head, ready for the prayer meeting. She sits on the log outside Sophie's, though, loath to be too early. She's sick of the good people of their small parish turning from her; much better to arrive just as the sermon begins, to take her seat behind the crowd.

She draws the folded piece of paper from where it's tucked into her bodice and stares down at the letter from her father, arrived not three days before. Meriem was confused as to how he came to know where to write to her, eventually surmising that he'd had her direction from her brother, Tom, who she's written to four times now. Her eyes rake through the lines once again, reading of her mother's illness, pausing on the words *great pain* and *weak with it*. But no matter how often she peruses the letter, she cannot decide whether he invites her home or not. Is it simply kindness that prompted Pa to write, or is he secretly imploring her to return to them? What would she do, though, if she were back in Queanbeyan? She once thought of becoming a teacher, but that is behind her now, what with her poor eyesight and indiscretions. The familiar hum of her loss courses through her body.

Perhaps when she has saved enough money, she'll move closer to her family, take up some cleaning work nearby. She glances over her shoulder into the house. And what of Sophie? Who will work for her then? She might have to join Maggie Gilhooley's girls and give up having her own place.

Someone is walking along the road and she jumps up, glad to shed her heavy thoughts. It's the boy. Ying. Striding towards her past the beer shanties and lodging houses, pails swinging from his bamboo pole.

When he enters the gardener's hut, she loses sight of him for several minutes. Lingering on the edge of the garden, she waits until he comes out. Making sure she has caught his eye, she gestures for him to follow her and sets out towards the copse. Twice she looks back to make sure Ying understands her. That he follows.

Meriem thinks she remembers the way to where they hid that night – that thicket of peace Ying led her to. She steps across the overflow channel – only a trickle today – and her shoe slips on fallen wattle seeds. Righting herself, she clambers through a clump of tea trees, the melancholy leaves brushing her face, until she finds herself at the grassy mound.

When Ying appears through the trees, he seems almost surprised to find her there.

'I wanted to say thank you for helping me that night,' she says. 'And for the berries.' She's thought about this quite a bit since realising Ying works in Jimmy's shop. She's noticed him a number of times at the Chinese gardener's recently, gathering vegetables and eggs, and she's almost sure that one night, when taking in the ribbon from the ironwood, she saw his wood-duck silhouette in the shadows.

She wasn't fearful, though. How could she be after that evening, when she slept at the boy's side, unmolested? Again, Meriem feels the ticklish curl at the audacity of it. A whole night spent with a Chinaman. And that's when she found herself wanting to thank him, perhaps talk with him, although that doesn't stop her from shying away from being seen in his company. Imagine if Father Joyce were to see her with Ying? Or that sour old prune, Mrs Cowper? It's only when she noticed him approaching the Chinaman's garden that this little mound of grass occurred to her as the perfect place to meet. Hidden. Private.

Ying unpacks a hessian sack from where it's tucked across a number of chokos in his pail and, opening it out to its full length, he drapes it across the grass. 'Sit, please.'

'Oh, aren't you clever,' Meriem says. With a huff, she lowers herself to the ground. Despite the rain having cleared overnight, the damp rises through the hessian to her buttocks. She pats the other side of the sacking. 'You can sit too.'

The boy squats at the edge, smiling at her.

22

When Merri cocks her head a little, to peer from the side, Ying is reminded of the dove that used to nest in the eaves of their house back home. Plump and tawny; a glint of wary intelligence in its eye.

Ying frowns with concentration as Merri speaks to her. Some of the words perch in her mind, fully formed, comprehensible, but others take wing, gone before she can catch them. Merri tells her that she's from a place called *Queanbeyan*. And she speaks of her *brother*. She says the words *boat* and *oysters*, and Ying nods that she understands.

Ying tells Merri that her *brother* is on his way to a *sheep farm. For Englishmen.* She tries to pronounce *carrier*, laughing with Merri, who says, 'Next time, *next time*, you' – points at Ying – 'you *teach* me' – points at her own chest – 'some *Chinese words*.' When Merri smiles, her top lip draws high, revealing as much ridged pink gum as teeth.

A bird whistles above them, a pretty tune. Ying looks up into the branches, but no matter how much she angles her head, she can't catch sight of it. Leaves tremble, and the bird's mate returns the melody. Suddenly Meriem climbs to her feet, saying something about dinner. She gestures for Ying to stay seated, and waves goodbye, disappearing through the thicket of trees. In the distance Ying can hear the ragged rhythm of a saw cutting through timber. Further yet, the steady clank of a miner's digging machine. One of Lo Pak's hens clucks loudly, boastfully, at the arrival of a fresh egg.

The next afternoon, Jimmy sends Ying out to sell rice balls and dried fish to the men camped by the river. Before she's even sold half her fare, though, she detours to the edge of town. Hurrying past Lo Pak's garden, she slows, delighted to see Merri hanging washing on the line behind her house. Merri spies her too and points towards their grove. Ying continues along the dirt road and darts in among the shrubbery by the river. Wondering if Merri is really going to meet her again. She can't remember the last time she felt such giddy anticipation spill through her body.

She roosts on a low-bearing branch that stretches towards the river, forming the perfect bench. She glances over her shoulder at a rustle, but it's only a lizard, nudging its way through the fallen leaves.

When Merri arrives, Ying gestures for her to sit, and the branch dips just a little as Merri carefully lowers herself onto it. Insects, too small to see, skim their way across the river, creating perfect, vibrating rings.

Ying digs her hand into her pocket and brings out some raisins. Feels so pleased when Merri takes two and pops them into her mouth.

'It is very peaceful,' Merri says, tilting her face to the sky. 'It's just as peaceful as church.'

Papery bark crumbles away from Ying's fidgeting fingers. She is familiar with what Merri means by *church*; she has seen the simple white building behind the Mayweather the white people use as a joss house. But *peaceful* she does not know. When she frowns, questioning, Merri closes her eyes with a soft smile. She slumps her shoulders, pretending to be relaxed. Puts her finger to her lips, *shhhhh*. Her eyes spring open. '*Peaceful*.'

Ying nods and looks across the river, at the slabs of stone surrounded by fields of uneven rockery. At the trees that encroach on the waterline, protective. Leaves whisper, a murmur of prayer, and smoke from countless wood fires mingle with the peppermint fragrance of the trees to form its own incense; its smell, for Ying, almost like the taste of honey.

It's too wet to meet again for four more days, but on the fifth, Ying asks Jimmy if she may visit the nearest temple to pray for her family. Instead she tarries at the edge of Lo Pak's garden for almost half an hour, waiting for Merri to appear. The heat peaks midafternoon, and the men loitering outside the beer shanties and lodging house retreat into whatever shadowy relief the tin and bark walls provide. She shuffles past Merri's house, scraping the soles of her shoes against the rubble. She's never been proficient at whistling like Lai Yue, and the best she can do is catch the air between her teeth, so that a high-pitched hiss rings out. She's only exhaled three times when Merri pokes her head out through the front door and nods at her.

As soon as Ying arrives at their grove, she pulls a log from the undergrowth that edges the copse. Positions it in the middle of their grassy knoll for Merri, who is following not far behind, to sit upon.

This time Ying has brought along something very special indeed for Merri to try. Her heart skips as she takes the tiny bundle from her pocket, hoping that Jimmy never works out that she's filched something so precious. She pulls the string free from around the folded newspaper, revealing three thin slices of pickled sea cucumber.

How Ying had stared at the wiry, dark man who lugged the vat of dried sea cucumber into the store. He'd come into town with the bush mailman and, as he measured out two pounds of the delicacy at the counter, Jimmy murmured to her in their own language, 'Native. From somewhere further north, though.'

Over the next few days, Jimmy had soaked and boiled some of the crusty creatures until they returned to their watery, knobbly state. He'd then preserved them in vinegar and sugar, their gherkin-shapes bobbing in the brine. Slicing the rubbery flesh into slivers, Jimmy doles it out to his more prosperous customers at such a monstrous price it might as well be gold.

'Ooh, it's quite slippery, isn't it?' Merri says, prodding a jelly-like piece with her finger.

Ying holds it close to Merri's face. 'You eat.'

'But what is it?'

'It like cucumber. From the water. Make you happy.' Ying grins for Merri. 'Make you ...' She doesn't know the word for *healthy*, so she puffs out her chest, pats it with the flat of her hand.

Merri looks dubious. She lifts her glasses and, bending down, peers more closely at the slimy flesh. 'Pooh. Smells a bit fishy.'

'You eat?'

'No, Ying.' Merri laughs, pushing Ying's hand away. 'I don't think so.'

Ying's disappointed, but smiles and nods all the same. She feels too shy, somehow, to pop the sea cucumber into her own mouth, faced with Merri's revulsion. She wraps the slices up in the newspaper and pushes them deep into her pocket.

162

She follows as Merri picks her way through brushwood, seeking a stick to clean the muck from her shoes. They catch sight of a small blue claw lying in the mud.

'Yabbies,' says Merri. Merri points at Ying's pocket. 'Let me have that string, Ying.'

When Ying brings out the package, Merri also takes a pinch of the pickled sea cucumber. For a joyful moment, Ying thinks that Merri might taste it after all, but – horrified – she can only watch as Merri gently attaches the meat to the end of the string. She dips the improvised line into the silty shallows.

'My grandfather taught us how to trap yabbies in the creek behind his house,' she says to Ying. 'Icy cold, that creek was.'

It isn't long before Merri draws the string from the water, and a small creature, slick and bristling, clings to the meat. Ying is swift to scoop it into her hat.

A spume of cloud, white and silver, froths the morning sky. A brisk shower catches them by surprise and they dart through the trees, stifling their laughter. Ying lets Merri rush home first, so nobody sees them together.

The next day Ying tells Jimmy she needs to visit the temple more often, that she is worried about her mother and siblings. Instead she hurries through the township towards the river. She wades through brush to reach their grove. A branch flops onto the top of her head, reminding her of Lai Yue, of how he used to tease her, but she doesn't feel the usual clutch in the pit of her stomach. It's difficult to imagine misfortune when each day offers so much.

23

Lai Yue can feel it. It creeps up behind.

The smoky clouds chase them from the east. Press down upon them. Hot gusts that breathe against the back of his neck.

Eyes. Eyes. Eyes. Dark. Watching. From behind the scaly trees. From up high on the rocky ridges. Spears with poisoned tips raised. Lai Yue twitches. Imagines being pierced in the soft flesh of his side, or perhaps under the shoulder blade so that the spear lodges between his ribs. He licks his lips with a dry tongue. Looks over his shoulder.

But perhaps it is only Ah Kee who follows? Or Sip Yee men? Keeping an eye on him. Making sure he doesn't run off with their money when he is paid. What would they do if he did? Lai Yue thinks of the threatened beheadings. The whippings. Maybe a stealthy garrotting in the alone hours of the night.

Is that the black bird, Lai Yue? In the tree there?

His neck muscles jerk. He stares through the branches, concentrates on a dark shape between the wide leaves and a sprinkling of sunlight. He can't be sure. Perspiration stings his eyes.

Sullivan calls out something and the men pick up pace.

Their shoes dig deep clefts in eroding red soil. A splatter of raindrops, then nothing more. They leave the cover of forest and trudge along the side of a river that peters out to blanched rock, wafered by sunlight and bygone water-flow. Fritz halts, points out something in the dry riverbed. They crowd around to gaze down on some sort of dusty stone. Lai Yue peers closer. A sun-bleached half-skull. Hidden among the rocks, forgotten.

Again Lai Yue turns his head to look behind. He bends over and rubs his hands in the chalky soil that surrounds the skull and rubs it across his face. Up and down his arms.

The landscape breathes open before them, broad and cleared of trees. A few animals – sheep? cows? – dapple the grass in the distance. The men stride forward, their steps long, more sure. The dark clouds finally catch up with them, driving rain against their backs. There's talk of whether it's safer to set up camp in the open or to find shelter in the clumps of forest that edge the fields. They decide to deviate through bushland, and Lai Yue is sorry. In the open space he can check behind to make sure he's not being followed. He can gauge the distance between himself and whatever is after him.

This is all your fault, Lai Yue.

He clenches his teeth tight.

We are all alone because of you. We have lost everything, everyone. Ying, Mother, Lai Cheng, Su. Nobody loves you anymore.

Sadness moors Lai Yue's steps, but he shakes his head, trying to dislodge Shan's whisperings.

'We are not alone.'

If not for me, you would be alone. Alone! These men, they only put up with you because you feed them, carry their smelly things.

Lai Yue's breathing catches in dry gasps. He stares ahead at the group of five men plodding through the downpour. Sullivan leads the pack, dogs at his horse's heels. Lucas rides alongside Bengt, pats his weary shoulder, while Hagerty and Fritz bring up the rear, discussing something, heads bent forward to keep raindrops from their faces. The ten feet between him and them might as well be walled up, across a deep ravine, or beyond the southern seas.

This is all your fault. I should have stayed in that stinking river back home.

'I wish you had,' he shouts. Only Lucas glances over at him.

Shan begins to weep, resting her face in the crook of Lai Yue's neck. He can feel her hot tears mingle with the chill rain.

The showers have eased by the time they come across the natives' huts. Sullivan dismounts, rifle at the ready. Lai Yue brings out his machete, turning out from the group, his eyes searching for movement in the surrounding bushland. Shadows shift and trick in the half-light. In their travels they have passed several natives' camps, mostly along the banks of fishing gullies. Deserted by the time they'd thrashed their way to them. This camp seems to be the same.

Fritz glances into the three bark huts, calls out that they're empty. Lucas and Bengt find what seems to be the storehouse. It's filled with fish, two spears, a woven bag that clacks with seashells, flints and a block of something that leaves red dust on Lai Yue's fingertips.

Sullivan points out a European-made axe, says, 'Bloody thieves.'

Lai Yue is following the others out into the open when there's a dull clunk at his feet. A stone rolls to a rest on the wet ground. Bengt howls as a stone pelts his shoulder, and Fritz ducks as a spray

166

of pebbles shower the broad brim of his hat. Sullivan takes cover behind his horse, readies his rifle over the saddle. The red dog yelps, scampers into the undergrowth, tail between its legs, but the mottled grey dog bares its yellow teeth, holds its ground.

A number of natives dash up the mountain slope, pausing only to brandish their spears at the group, their cooees a discordant clash in the air. Their cries root Lai Yue to the ground, an answering cry rising in his throat. A spear whooshes past his cheek, lodges in the dirt. He clasps the machete tighter. Bites down on the scream.

Run, Lai Yue. Run, you stupid man.

'Get out of here,' Sullivan shouts.

Lai Yue, hunched low, runs towards a thicket of trees. Looking back he sees Hagerty leading two horses, limping from where a rock connected with his ankle, but Lucas, cupping one hand over his wounded brow and holding his brother upright with the other, hollers at the black men. Lai Yue can't understand his words, but he seems to be gesticulating for the natives to come down, to confront him, his pale mouse skin pink with fury. Taking his hand from the welt that oozes blood into his eye, he gropes for his gun. Fritz joins him, rifle cocked, and they back up towards where Lai Yue and Sullivan wait, out of reach of the spears.

Aarrkkk.

Lai Yue spots the black bird perched high in the branches above their assailants. A sickly feeling of satisfaction settles heavy in his gut. He knew he'd see the black bird again. He knew it. Had seen it in his waking dreams.

The natives lower their weapons but continue to shout at them.

The bird is here for you, Lai Yue.

'No. No, it's not, Shan.'

Aarrk. Uck-Uck-Uck. Aaarrrkkk.

167

Bile rises to his throat.

The natives advance down the hill, perhaps eight men, but Lai Yue can't be sure as they meld in and out of dusk's gloom.

Lucas pulls the trigger, fires into the trees. Lai Yue sees two figures run up the hill, but one native, taller than even Sullivan, swoops through the grimy light. He hurls an axe at them. Hagerty's horse rears up, squeals. The native keeps coming, a short spear – club-like, razor-sharp tip – grasped in his hand.

He will kill you, Lai Yue. That spear is for you.

Not far now.

He'll want to finish the Chinaman first. You know this, Lai Yue. He hates you. Hates you. Knows you're weak.

Lai Yue can see it now. Can see the native's eyes are set on him. His eyes. Eyes. Always on him.

The native is closing in on the huddled group when Sullivan's bullet rips the flesh from the black's shoulder. He staggers, drops the spear.

Lucas runs forward and punches the man in the stomach and, as he doubles over, Lucas heaves his knee up, smashing the dark man's nose. The crack of bone, the splatter of cartilage, rings louder than the distant hollering, the cicada buzz, the black bird's caw. The native slumps to the ground, his face a glistening mash, and Hagerty turns and retches into the grass. Fritz giggles and swings his leg back, whumps his boot into the man's side. With a humph and a sharp elbow he throws himself down onto the native's midriff.

They all circle the prone man. A pack. Hagerty stinks of vomit, and Bengt steadies his fever-weakened legs by leaning on Lai Yue's arm. Sullivan lets off another volley of warning shots into the woods. The black mumbles something through swollen lips. His teeth are stained red. A tooth hangs loose from a string of gristle.

Lucas kicks him on the temple so his head squelches back towards Lai Yue. 'Fucking darkie vermin.'

The native's eyes – black pupil, an expanse of ivory – stare up at Lai Yue. See him.

Aarrk.

Aarrk.

Lai Yue bounds forward, kicks and kicks. Kicks until he feels the bone in his third toe snap.

Kicks until all is dark.

Nothing can be seen. Nothing can see him.

'Yes, Larry!' Sullivan shouts. 'Finish 'im.'

The white men close in around him.

Lucas pats his shoulder. Tells him that's enough.

24

Meriem pours the peanuts the Chinese men brought with them into a bowl. Drops a small handful into a jar to share later with Ying. Four of the men are seated at the table, shuffling coins back and forth. The fifth is in the bedroom with Sophie. This lot is fresh from Cooktown; Meriem has never seen them before. Not like Sophie's regular Chinese custom, the same men turning up on the doorstep every Tuesday, Thursday and Sunday nights, no matter how torrential the rain; the other days taken up with various diggers: old Cecil Powers from the Imperial, Dr Hamer and the baker's nephew, gormless yet nice.

When Clem is away, that is. When that ribbon isn't tied about the ironwood.

A lisping whistle reaches her ears. Hurrying to the front door, she peeps out, sees Ying amble past, wheezing air through his teeth. The secret code that's developed between them over the past few weeks.

Meriem sweeps up the basket she has at the ready and knocks on the timber screen that Sophie uses in place of a bedroom door, calling out, 'I just have to run over to the store' and trots out before Sophie has a chance to reply.

When she arrives at their thicket, Ying sits up from where he reclines on a canvas square, holds a finger to his lips, his other hand pointing towards the water. It's not the first time they've needed to be quiet due to the presence of someone fishing on the river close by.

Meriem places her basket on the grass and lies down quietly next to Ying, listening to the twit-twit of the emerald-breasted parrots in the branches above. The fisherman's line zithers through the air, the bait landing with a plop.

Meriem's hand rests on her lower belly, and she wonders if the comfort she finds in the gentle curve of fat above her pelvis lies in the memory it holds of her baby.

The fisherman hauls in his line. He breaks wind, a trebling sound that draws forth longer than Meriem would have believed possible, ending on a short, squeaky note. He sighs loudly.

Ying turns to face her, his face creased into silent laughter, and Meriem wants to giggle so hard she has to clamp her hand over her mouth so she doesn't give away their hiding spot. She huddles onto her side, her nose resting against Ying's heaving shoulder. The fabric of his shirt smells vinegary and of a spice she can't quite pinpoint.

They don't have to wait much longer before the fisherman gives up his spot with a dissatisfied grunt. Once the splash of his footsteps recedes, Meriem kneels at her basket, unpacking a tall, black bottle and a battered cake tin containing three scones. She pours a measure of sherry into a cup for Ying, and hands it to him.

'I am reminded of your name often, Ying,' she says, sipping the sweet liquor straight from the bottle. 'When I hear the words pray-ying, sway-ying, play-ying ...' She pauses, grinning at Ying, and adds, 'Annoy-ying ...' And even though she's not sure if he quite understands, she says, 'No, I am only teasing.' She rests her fingers on Ying's forearm for a moment and continues, 'I only think of you when I hear pleasant words, such as stay-ying, beautify-ying, dally-ying.'

Ying gives her a strange look, as though he understands, but also as though he doesn't. He continues to taste the wine, licking his lips with each sip, and soon Meriem is distracted by the flush that muddies his throat.

'You've got grog blossoms, like my gran used to get,' she says. 'Except her nose used to go red too.' Meriem takes his cup and pours him a little more from the bottle of sherry. A small treat she's bought for herself.

'It's my birthday today, Ying.' She looks away, studying the veins in a leaf that dangles by her cheek; although she still smiles, a tiny nerve tugs at the corner of her lip. 'My sister – Milly, her name is – and I have birthdays only one day apart.' The pain constricts her words, and she struggles to sound normal. 'Different years, of course. I'm a good six years older than Milly. Anyway, my mother used to make us a large fruit cake in Gran's square tin – dark, it were, rich with raisins – and after I'd blown out the candles, she'd cut us each a piece – for me and my brothers, for Pa, and Milly – until the cake was a smaller square, and that's what Milly would have the next day for her birthday. She cut it neatly, though, did Ma. It still looked good, especially when the candles were alight again. It was nice.'

Meriem knows Ying can't understand everything she says, but she's glad of the warm hand that pats the middle of her back.

25

Ying always thinks of Merri as pretty, girlish almost, but when she cries the skin of her face droops, like the folds of melting wax at the base of a candle.

Ying knows she should head back to the shop – Jimmy will wonder why it takes her so long to sell the leaf-wrapped rice balls to the flock camped by the river – but instead she pats Merri's back a while longer, then closes her eyes, flushed and relaxed with the wine.

Wanting to cheer Merri up, she searches her sluggish mind for the jasmine song her mother used to sing to her. She hums a few notes, finally hitting upon the right tune and murmurs, *What a beautiful jasmine flower; What a beautiful jasmine flower* ... She opens her eyes and smiles at Merri. Taking her hand, she swings it up and down. *Sweet-smelling ... Sweet-smelling ...* Ying repeats herself for she can't remember the rest of the refrain, until *Let me pluck you ...* and for the first time she wonders if the song is really about a woman and not simply a flower.

By the time Merri is smiling again, Ying is relatively sober, a slight throb at the base of her skull the only reminder of Merri's wine. As usual, she allows Merri to dash home first, before Ying leaves for Jimmy's.

'That took a long time,' Jimmy says, peering over his spectacles.

'I think Chan Poon's man went through the crowd before me, selling roast pumpkin,' she lies. 'So it took a while to get rid of all the rice balls.' She drops the empty pails to the floor. 'But I managed to sell them all in the end, you see.'

When Jimmy turns to serve a customer, Ying slips across the room to neaten the shelves. They are running out of sardines and corned beef, and the pile of trousers has diminished. Ying searches the bench for the two skirts she unpacked, but there's no sign of either of them. Glancing over at Jimmy, she wonders if he's sold them or perhaps passed them along to the Cowpers or another store. But she won't ask. She doesn't want to remind him of that evening, when he caught her in that skirt. He's never asked her about it, and she hasn't volunteered an explanation. But she does wonder if there has been a shift in his behaviour towards her. He's taken to stringing a sheet up between them when they settle to sleep, and he spends less time in the evenings playing mah-jong with Ah Kee, content to sit by his little stove, reading the newspaper, while Ying's legs jiggle with restlessness.

She decides to sweep the floor and, once finished, takes her rice porridge outside, sipping the soup as she meanders towards the bottom of the yard. Freezes as the dusty reek of Yeeh's chicken coop reaches her nostrils, shifting her memory back to the village marketplace, to that crate of geese she hid behind with Lai Yue when they watched the broker sell their siblings. She pauses, the bowl almost to her lips, back in their house near Broken Bowls Point, in the room painted serpent green. Back even further, lamplight as golden as a silkworm's cocoon, eating Mother's lettuce soup, elbow to elbow. But the picture has become less clear, as though she peers through cloudy glass. She lowers her head to take another sip of her porridge.

~

It's already late in the afternoon of the next day by the time Jimmy sends her to Ming Long's shop to ask when he expects the next lot of teamsters to come through with provisions. She'll pretend she couldn't immediately find him and, hurrying past Merri's, she whistles through her teeth.

They each burrow into the crook of a sturdy branch, hugging the tree's hard girth. Ying likes how the fine hairs on Merri's arm glisten gold in the pale sunlight; how her fingernails are curved, pearly, unlike Ying's own, which are as splayed as scallop shells.

She reaches across and places a salty plum into Merri's palm, licking the red, sour-sweet stain it leaves upon her own finger and thumb. She gestures for Merri to put the plum in her mouth. Pretends to chew. 'Quickly. Is best.'

When Merri spits the plum to the ground, eyes welling, squealing, 'Ooh, it's sour, you beast', Ying's mouth waters in sympathy. She folds over with glee. 'I trick you. I trick you', and Merri slaps her arm, tells her she's mean, but she's laughing too.

Ying watches as Merri squints through the foliage at the patchy sunset. For two nights now Ying's agonised over whether she can tell Merri her secret – not her whole secret, but a small part of it. She wants to hear Merri say her true name, not just the diminutive 'Ying' that she and Lai Yue came up with to fool others into believing she's a boy. She hesitates, though, for if it were to come to the ears of her own people, her secret would most probably be out. Her heart races at the thought of the shame, the outrage, that would ensue. But she also yearns to share something of her real self with Merri, this new, precious friend of hers. And nobody else will know. It can't hurt anyone.

Ying places her hand to her chest and says, 'My name *Mei Ying*.'

It doesn't feel as special as she thought it would. In fact, her name is awkward on her tongue after so long, and she's even a little embarrassed, worried that Merri might think she's been deceiving her up to this point.

Merri looks puzzled.

Ying says it again, slowly. 'Mei Ying. My name Mei Ying.'

'But I call you Ying?'

Ying points her thumb down to the ground. 'Here, my name Mei Ying. In Jimmy shop, my name Ying.' She nods at Merri, willing her to understand.

Merri smiles, revealing pink gums. 'Mei Ying. Mei Ying.'

Ying smiles back at her, her frame softening into the tree.

The air is muggy with the threat of rain and smoke. Bullocks clop through the shallows. They listen to the comfortable dollop of a fish breaching the water's surface, and, along the river's shingle banks, the branches of the paperbarks reach for each other and entwine.

26

Lai Yue and the red dog watch as Sullivan and his men are swallowed up by the driving rain.

'You'll be fine, Larry,' Sullivan said, as they watered their horses earlier in the day, ready to move on to a cattle station further west. They'd spent two nights at the Pennington sheep station. Sullivan and Hagerty slept in the main house, with its latticed verandahs, iron roofing and weatherboard cladding, while Lai Yue and the others dossed down in the bachelors' huts near the fowl-house. Lai Yue slept closest to the hens, could hear their brooding, their scolding, through the thin wall. Their lice burrowed into the fabric of his shirt, nipping and fretting at the skin around his hairline, under his arms, and their feathers dusted the floor.

'Pennington will give you eight pounds, four shillings to look after his sheep. You wait here for us and I'll give you the rest of your carrier money when we return to the coast. You'll be fine, Larry,' he repeated, and laughed. 'We've seen how savage you can be with the darkies.'

Lai Yue understood most of what Sullivan said. His purse lay heavy for once in his special belt. If he waited, it would lie heavier. Almost heavy enough to return to his own fragrant land, away from the dirt, the lice, the white brutes, the natives.

But will Sullivan really come back? Lai Yue stands in the doorway of the hut. The red dog's paws sink in the mud, and it yaps but doesn't follow the riders. Initially it tried to stay with the other dog, but Fritz drove it away with three well-placed cracks of his whip.

It took great fortitude for Lai Yue to resist running after the group, but he suspected they would've turned the whip on him too. He loathed them. Yes, he did. He did! But he was used to them, was familiar with their ways. He knew that Sullivan couldn't drink his tea without sugar; that Bengt and Lucas weren't really brothers, but something closer; that Fritz wept some nights, deep in the night; and that Hagerty had five children – the eldest a son, Pat – far away in a town called Galway. They weren't foreign to him like this new lot of white men who were already cleaved into groups, chary of the Chink. He clasps the purse in his belt, glancing around.

I wouldn't be surprised if you are robbed by these white curs, Lai Yue. Everything goes wrong for you.

The dog yaps again, without conviction. It glances over its shoulder at nothing in particular. They've been cut loose. Useless.

A burden.

Everyone thinks you are a burden.

Lai Yue bites his lips together, feels a force behind his eyes. He steps out into the downpour. If a tear rises to the corner of his eye, no one – least of all himself – will know.

Pennington hurries past, motions for Lai Yue to follow him to the stable.

Pennington is a lean man, his trousers hanging loose over twig legs. Beneath his wide-brimmed hat, his eyes are tired, his thin face prematurely lined. The farm hands are already at work around the station, but his shearers – three sturdy men – wait by the stable, chewing on their breakfast of damper and eggs.

'Can't hire any bloody shepherds to watch the bloody sheep because of the bloody gold rush,' Pennington says, leading out a grey mare. 'Get up,' he says to Lai Yue.

Lai Yue backs away. He hasn't ridden a horse since he was a boy, when his uncle lifted him onto his satin-black stallion. His uncle stayed close, led the steed only four careful steps before Lai Yue insisted on climbing down, back into his mother's arms.

'Get up.' Pennington says something else but Lai Yue doesn't understand. Pennington points to the horizon, waves his arm in and out. 'Far. Very Far.'

The shearers look amused. One – squat, with the physique and blunt nose of a fighter – approaches, signals that he will help Lai Yue climb up.

Shan titters. *He's going to lift you up like a baby.*

Lai Yue waves his hands at the shearer. No.

What a fool you'll look.

The shearer loops his fingers together, nods his head from the step he's made with his hands to the seat of the saddle.

Oh, get up, you big fool.

'I won't, Shan.'

You're just a big, frightened baby, Lai Yue.

'I won't climb up onto that beast, Shan. I'll fall off. Then I'll look like a fool.'

Lai Yue lifts his pole and baskets, rests them over his shoulders to show them that he'll walk.

Pennington sighs, shakes his head. Rubs his hand up and down his tired face as he goes back inside the stable. The squat shearer sits with his mates and they mutter among themselves, their pipe smoke mingling with the rain mist.

Lai Yue's not sure if they are discussing him. He wants to appear as though he doesn't care if they are – tries to divert his mind – by gazing out onto the grey morning. Through the waves of rain, past a vast paddock, he thinks he can see a waterhole. His mind acknowledges the aroma of baking bread, sizzling bacon, but only as a muted distraction, not as something he needs. His body has learnt to deny its craving, has learnt that it does not deserve this pleasure. He rubs his thumb along the protruding bone of his hip, satisfied.

Pennington returns with a short mule. He leads the docile animal over to Lai Yue, says, 'We have to go far. Get up.'

Lai Yue looks into the mule's grave eyes surrounded by long eyelashes. He thinks that perhaps he can trust this beast. The shearer and Pennington help him attach his baskets to its saddle. It's easy for Lai Yue to climb into the groove of the mule's back. The animal is so short Lai Yue's feet almost reach the ground. Pennington mounts the grey horse and they move out from the stable yard, the dog trotting at the mule's heels.

Rainwater splashes across the mare's rump from neat rills in Pennington's oilskin coat. Raindrops fall from the brim of Lai Yue's hat to form a steady tap on the tip of his nose. They pause for several minutes while Pennington has a word with four of his workmen who are hammering in rails and unravelling wire around sturdy posts. The fence circles a dam – still mid-dig, discarded shovels sunk halfway into the mire – and extends towards the horizon, past the expanse of cleared land.

The rain eases and, as the mule and mare plod past two more dams, Lai Yue's uneasiness builds. He glances behind, trying to gauge how far they have come from the homestead. He wonders how far away Sullivan and his men are now. He knows he'll never be able to retrace his steps to Maytown alone. To Ying. To home.

They reach a vast paddock where clumps of sheep graze on the rough meadow grass. As the men approach, the sheep surge away and then near, like waves on a beach.

Pennington pulls up in front of a hut that's constructed of bark stripped from local paperbark. Two men come out through the doorway, clamping hats onto their heads as they peer up at Pennington.

'You look like you've been asleep,' Pennington says. 'Fine shepherds you make. Go back to digging the dam in the western field. Try to get as much done before the blasted rain returns.'

The two men trudge off, without a word.

Lai Yue slides to the ground and, as he follows Pennington into the hut, the boggy earth and grass almost suck the slippers from his feet. On the right wall is a blackened fireplace lined with stones and clay beneath a rickety chimney. Propped up on the opposite wall is a chaff mattress. Pennington places Lai Yue's rations of dried meat, flour, sugar and tea into a wooden box in the corner.

Outside, Pennington observes his sheep. 'You watch the sheep, Larry. You are my shepherd. Shepherd.' His voice rises on the words he repeats for emphasis. His arm makes a sweeping motion. 'There, and there, you can see the fencing.' He looks at Lai Yue, to see if he comprehends. 'But there' – pointing at a stretch of lightly wooded land – 'we are still fencing. There is no fencing. You watch the sheep. Watch.' His eyes widen towards the sheep. 'And then at night-time, at night, you bring them back in here. Count 'em. There are one hundred and twenty-three. Too many for one shepherd, but ...' He mutters something about the gold rush again and stalks across to a large pen, sturdily fenced with logs and wire.

The ground in the pen is a mush of mud, and two drink troughs brim with water.

'I will send a couple of men to help you round 'em up when it's getting dark.'

Lai Yue looks around, at the expanse of damp green and the outlying forest, domed beneath a grey sky. Anxiety peaks, beats silent wings in his ears.

'Natives?'

Pennington shakes his head. 'No problem.' He strides over to his horse and withdraws two rifles from their holsters. He hands one over to Lai Yue. He holds up his gun, then points at the one he's given Lai Yue. 'You'll have no trouble from the blacks.'

The heft of the rifle rests reassuringly in Lai Yue's hands and briefly the wings stop fluttering. His thumb rests on the cool hammer, and he imagines the deadly heat of the steel block when fired. His senses quicken: he sees the dark leaves of distant trees, the gnarled wool of the nearest sheep, the swoop of two swallows cruising the field. He smells the fresh soap scent of Pennington, the unwashed, stable-yard stench of himself. The bleat of a sheep. A single raindrop on his right forearm.

'No. You'll have no trouble from the blacks. And watch out for wild dogs. If the sheep get injured or ill' – he clutches his stomach, mimicking sickness – 'come tell us.'

27

Meriem swerves, almost twisting her ankle. Changing direction, she heads straight for the bakery, hoping he didn't see her.

Dermot. Stepping out of Maggie Gilhooley's front door.

So they're back from wherever the hell they've been. Presumably that means Clem has returned too. She stares blindly at a basket of loaves, and tension constricts her breathing.

By the time she arrives at Jimmy's store, she's feeling clammy all over. Usually, she and Ying steal sly little smiles at each other, but today Meriem can do no more than grimace when he glances her way, and then shake her head when he looks enquiringly at her. How to explain the dread that congeals her blood, slowing her movements? Knowing that Dermot lurks around town again while Clem will haunt Sophie's. Perhaps he is there right now, just as before, the air so suffused with his malevolence Meriem can almost smell its yeasty presence.

But when she arrives home, Sophie is seated in the cramped living room, alone. The table is strewn with Chinese coins, and she's placing a teardrop nugget of gold into the coffee tin.

'I saw Dermot in town before,' Meriem says. 'He was away with Clem, weren't he? Means Clem will be back too.'

Sophie's face remains blank but her eyes darken. She sits very still while Meriem unpacks her groceries onto the scullery bench. She's bought two carrots and two potatoes but has forgotten to buy eggs.

The chair legs scrape as Sophie stands. 'Here, help me get rid of all this,' she says, sweeping the brass coins into the tin. She hides the coffee tin in its place beneath the roofing. Meriem collects the cards that litter the table and hides them in a shoebox with the funny little rake the Chinese men use in their game. While she sweeps away the pumpkin seed shells and peanut skins from the floor, Sophie lifts an earthenware jar of rice brandy from the table and, throwing her head back, swallows what remains. Licking her lips, she passes the jar to Meriem. 'Here, find somewhere in the scullery for this.'

They look about themselves to make sure all sign of Sophie's Chinese custom is gone.

'You want me to tie the ribbon about the tree?'

Sophie bites her cheek. 'What day is it?'

'Wednesday.'

'It would be best, don't you think?'

Meriem frowns at Sophie's uncertainty. 'Well, if you're expecting Clem ...'

Sophie nods. 'Perhaps it would be best. Tie the ribbon, would you, Merri.'

At the turn of night, a crisp shower brings a fleeting gust of wind. A steady ache has set up in Meriem's womb, just as it does each month, for several hours. She adds carrots to the stew from the day before, stirs in a little flour and water to thicken it. She almost adds sugar instead of salt, so distracted is she with listening out for

Clem. Each time a horse trots past, she holds her breath, stares at the doorway.

Sophie remains seated at the table. She's pretending to read a book by the feeble light of the lamp, but Meriem is sure she hasn't turned the page in over an hour. She's managed to down three cups of gin in that time, though.

Tinker sits at the door, watching. Meriem bids him enter, thinking she might feel braver with him in the house, but he refuses, his tail swishing in the dirt. Useless dog.

The stew bubbles as Meriem breaks apart some damper, pushing the pieces between her lips. She chews mechanically, rolling the dry dough in her mouth, wishing she could get her hands on some butter. She's lifting another piece to her mouth when she hears a horse plod towards them. Nearer. A crumb hits the base of her hand, falls to the floor. She leans a little into the throbbing in her pelvis. The rider calls out, and she thinks that perhaps it's Petersen who shouts back from his lodging house.

When Meriem's sure the horse has passed them by altogether, she sticks the rest of the bread into her mouth, ignoring the nervous clench of her stomach. A familiar, acrid smell reaches her nostrils, and she whisks the pot from the stovetop. Scraping the wooden spoon through the stew, she stirs up the blackened mess where it has burnt to the base.

'Merri, you never spoilt our supper, did you?' Sophie's smiling though, as she tops up her mug. 'Tinker will be happy.'

'It'll be fine,' Meriem grumbles, hands on hips, staring into the pot. 'Do you want some now or later?'

'Perhaps a bit later,' Sophie says.

Meriem can't face the stew either. Instead she lowers herself carefully onto a stool, the pain in her pelvis heavy. She takes the paper bag of dried berries from her apron pocket and lifts out one of the tiny wrinkled things and tries to imagine its appearance when fresh. Impossibly red, and probably quite plump, she thinks. She places one between her teeth, bites it in half. It's sweet, with a late, bitter note. But mostly sweet. Her tongue edges the berry's flesh from the grooves in her molars.

Dropping two more onto her tongue, she wonders if Ying is correct, and her eyesight will improve if she eats them. She closes her good eye, and scans the scullery. Perhaps her vision past the biscuit stain is better; sharper, less dull. Yes, perhaps it is improving a little.

She startles at a clatter of hooves. Slumps lower onto the stool, shoves the paper bag back into her pocket and strains to hear the horses over the ringing in her ears. But all is silent again. No footsteps approach their doorway.

Meriem can't go on like this. She glares in at Sophie's thin shadow, the moon-glow of her cheek by the light of the lamp. She just can't. The constant unease she feels around Clem, and now Dermot, like a sickening poison gushing through her body.

She thinks of the money she's saved, hidden in a twist of bonnet at the bottom of her scratchy portmanteau. Eleven pounds, nine shillings and a few pence. Enough to travel to Cooktown with the next lot of teamsters.

Sophie picks up the lamp and takes it into her bedroom. Light flickers through the doorway as Sophie moves about, cutting through the darkness.

Meriem retrieves the brown paper bag and places another berry in her mouth. She'll have to wait for the rains to ease, though. The roads aren't yet passable for buggies.

And what of Ying? Her friend. She'll be sorry to leave him, will miss his little pranks, but also his company. Meriem sits straighter. Perhaps – warm with the thought of it – perhaps he can come with her. They can go to Cooktown together. There are plenty of Chinese businesses there. She can clean, and he can be a shop boy. And then, who knows? She'll save enough to head south, and maybe Ying will want to return to China. Meriem feels a slight crease of pain at the thought.

Tinker stands up from where he's resting by the back door. Stares towards the front of the house. That's when Meriem thinks she hears a wheezing whistle. She gets up, steps closer to listen. Yes. That's surely Ying's whistle. But it's dark already, far later than they would normally meet in the grove.

Meriem snatches up her shawl. 'Sophie, I need to go out for a little while.'

'Going out? But it's late.' Sophie looks up from where she's seated on her bed. Her papier-mâché box lies open in her lap. Her eyes are shiny, her cheeks feverish. There's a plaintive lilt to her voice as she says, 'You're always disappearing. Where are you off to this time? It's too late for prayer, surely, and you've already bought supper. There's been rain aplenty to fill the pails so you don't need to visit the river …'

'There's a special meeting,' Meriem says. 'With the other women.'

Sophie casts her eyes to the ceiling.

'About a fete to raise money for a new church.' There's always talk of such things, although nothing ever eventuates. But Sophie won't know that.

'Well, go on then.' Sophie turns her shoulder slightly, peering back into the box.

Meriem carries the kitchen lantern with her but turns it low as she treads along the dirt road, the scrape of grit beneath her shoes. Five or six men mill about a fire heap out the back of Petersen's lodging house, and two men sway against each other in the open doorway of the closest beer shanty. Meriem creeps past, looking over her shoulder, glad she hasn't caught anyone's attention.

Not until she reaches the gloom of deserted road and forest does she turn up her lantern, watching her steps by its bobbing glimmer. Something brushes her elbow and she gasps, lifts the light, only for the bird to whoosh past from behind. The boobook owls continue to swoop her as she hurries along, chasing the moths that are attracted by the lantern's glow.

She wades through damp leaves to reach their grove, her lantern's aura melding with Ying's. Once there she settles down next to him on the canvas matting, and rubs her lower belly, willing the ache to lift.

'What have you brought for me this time, Mei Ying?' she asks.

Ying grins and digs around in his shirt pocket. He unfolds a handkerchief to reveal a crescent of golden pastry. He breaks off a piece, which crumbles a little as he passes it to her. She takes a bite. Soft like cake, but crisp like a biscuit too. And it's filled with a paste of some sort; not too sweet, with a slightly coarse texture. She shoves the rest into her mouth before the pastry disintegrates through her fingers.

'You like cake?'

'It's delicious, Mei Ying.' She draws her knees in tight against a cramp. Not unlike the painful twinges she felt in the days after having Pattie.

Ying douses his lamp and lies down on the canvas, fingers intertwined across his stomach. Meriem dims her own lantern and closes her eyes. A frog croaks a stuttered rhythm close by.

An accordion wheezes out faint notes in a distant camp. A sense of calm steals over her body, despite the heaviness. To think, if she leaves Sophie's household, perhaps finds another life in Cooktown, this serenity could be hers all the time. But could she be truly happy again? Like when she was small, and her pa tickled her until her ribs hurt, or brought home a sweetmeat from the store next to the flour mill. Or that time Ned gave her that bunch of cabbage roses; handed them to her, bold as brass, in front of her friends as they walked home from the dance.

She lies down on her side, facing Ying. 'Can I tell you something?'

Ying turns his head to look at her. 'You tell me, Miss Merri.'

'I have a baby.'

'Bay-beee?'

Perhaps Ying doesn't know that word yet. Why would he learn that word here, in this faraway township full of menfolk and fallen women?

'Yes, a baby.'

And even though she knows he can't understand all of her words – or perhaps it is because she knows he cannot – she tells him of water gushing between her thighs when she struggled up from the kitchen chair; of the torrential pain that rolled in and out; how her pa had to hold her steady, arms pressed about her chest and shoulders as she keeled with the agony of it. She manages to smile, though, at how indignant she felt when her ma and the midwife chatted about the best sponge cake at the church fair while she was submerged in such black anguish. She describes the tremendous force to Ying, the slipping out.

She grows quiet when she comes to the part with Pattie. A bunched-up little thing, she was. Hardly any hair, and eyes swollen shut like she'd been in a pub brawl. Meriem laughs, only realising she's crying when she wipes her nose between her fingertips.

Ying sits up suddenly, dousing the lantern. Meriem lifts herself onto an elbow, the better to hear the footsteps that crash through the undergrowth towards them. They remain very still as two dark figures blunder past them in the thicket, settling on the tree bough not fifteen feet ahead.

'Come 'ere, you tasty morsel,' a man says.

A woman laughs, tells him to mind his hands.

Meriem remains frozen in an awkward half-raised position. She can just see the shine of Ying's eyes. They're trapped. They can't move or make a sound, or they will surely give themselves away.

The couple face the river and, although she can't place the man's voice, Meriem's sure the woman is Kitty O'Halloran. She'd recognise that fluting, foolish voice anywhere. Not that the couple talk much. It's not long before their silhouettes leach into one, and all Meriem hears is the smacking of lips, an occasional groan.

She grins in the dark, sorry that there is no one she can tell this story to. How to explain her own presence in the bush so late at night? But, certainly, it will feel good to have this knowledge tucked away in the shallows of her mind when she sees Kitty and her family so hoity-toity each Sunday.

Her left hip grows numb, and she very carefully rearranges herself, so that she rests on her right. Lowers herself to the canvas.

The woman murmurs something.

'No, darlin'. It's only a bird or somethin'.'

Meriem pillows her head against her outstretched arm. Ying silently lies down behind her, his presence a lick of morning sun on her back.

28

Ying can just make out Merri's pale hair. She reaches out and, with her fingertips, gently brushes the loose strands that drape the canvas mat. She can't help but think of Ah Kee and his missing queue. She's seen him several times since that night, amazed at his cheer. Seemingly unfazed by both his inability to return home and the tong's simmering malice. But then, he has taken to wearing holstered revolvers at his hip, hidden beneath his tunic.

Tonight, he's dragged Jimmy along to watch an opera singer perform at Yip Sow Kwai's restaurant, to be followed by a banquet and fantan. Jimmy locked the store early, leaving Ying with a number of chores to finish by the time he returned. She could tell, as he counted each task off on his fingers, that he was compiling a list long enough to keep her occupied, with little room for an evening outing. As soon as the two men left, though, she tidied the shop, poured pound bags of flour, set poison down near the altar to catch the filching rat, and cleaned Jimmy's pipe, but decided to put off sweeping the floors and making up the beds until later. She paid Yeeh's servant in ginger to watch the shop and hurried towards the edge of town to seek out Merri.

And now, contentedly dished together, Ying wonders again if she could think like Ah Kee, if she could contemplate the idea of staying. Each day rolling into the next; the same, yet with fresh possibilities. But perhaps the very comfort in the thought lies in the knowledge that it's temporary. And what of the men, the women, who glance at her askance? Or the few, like those troublesome men in Jimmy's shop, who toss nasty words their way? Would she be able to live with that too? Ying turns her head to gaze up at the black sky, undecided.

'Enough, Toby,' the woman says to her companion from where they embrace in the dark. 'I must get back.' They rustle down from the tree branch and clump through the thicket, leaving the same way they arrived.

Once they hear the last of the couple, Merri rolls over. Ying shifts a little to make room.

'I thought they'd never leave.' With a soft grunt Merri turns to face Ying. 'Could you hear them kissing?'

'Kissing?'

Merri leans in, her lips pressing Ying's. She pauses, her mouth resting against Ying's, her eyelashes tickling her brow. Ying doesn't pull away. Feels like worms till the soil of her stomach, but in a nice way. In a warm way.

Merri kisses her again and this time Ying responds. Tastes the young woman's mouth, breathes in the fragrance of her skin, draws nearer. When Merri hooks a leg over her side, Ying reaches her hand under Merri's skirts and massages her thigh. Merri loosens her bodice with a sigh, revealing creamy flesh. Her nipple has the texture of a raspberry. Ying presses the heart of her tongue to its peak. Desire burns through her, a firecracker alight, the paper curling, smouldering with the heat. She pushes in closer. Pulls Merri's hips to hers.

Merri grows still in Ying's arms. She takes Ying's hand and

squeezes it between hers. 'No, Ying. No. Please. We must stop. I'm sorry. I know where this ends.'

Ying isn't exactly sure what she means, but she hears the finality, the beseeching note, in her voice. She nods, still holding Merri's fingers between hers. The tip of her tongue flicks out, cups the tear that glistens on Merri's cheek, wondering if Merri's tears taste like her own.

29

The rain starts again, seeping up through the dirt floor. Everything so damp Lai Yue can't light the fire. And even here, concealed in the hut by night's skulking shadows, he can feel their eyes seeking him out between the gaps in the bark walls, from where they hide deep in the scrub. The sheep, the men, the crow.

His hands tremble as he turns the lamp low. He prepares himself a cup of cold tea, dashing the black tea-leaves straight into his pannikin. He sips the rough, briny tea, wishing for the fine clear tea of home. His father's favourite with the hint of jasmine, or his mother's, with the fragrant green leaves that dance to the bottom of her ceramic cup. He gulps more of the brew, imagining that it burns his tongue, sears the back of his throat.

The first interminable day he spent here, Lai Yue wandered among the sheep. He clutched the rifle close to his breast, tied the machete to his waist. Mostly the sheep skittered away from him, only a few feet, before they settled in to tear up the tough grass again. One large ewe, thick with matted wool, allowed him close. Lai Yue ran his fingers over her greasy wool but was repulsed by her marbly gaze, her pale eyes with the oblong pupils. Two other sheep caught his attention, staring at him – chew, stare, chew. Watching. Always watching him. He scanned the fields; the trees;

the thin, vanishing horizon. Watching him. He swung around, trudging off in the other direction, careful to only look upon the woollen hides of the sheep, never into their eyes.

The two workmen returned on horseback towards evening to help Lai Yue herd the sheep into their large pen with the section of tin roofing. They didn't say anything to him, just pointed where they wanted him to stand, where to chase. Within half an hour the biddable creatures were swept inside and the two men had cantered off.

From the hut Lai Yue watched them disappear into the dusk. He felt a lingering unease.

Hide your money, Lai Yue. They will steal it away from you one day and we will never reach home.

'Where? Where can I hide it?'

Dig a hole, stupid.

He glanced outside.

Inside, stupid man. Where no one can see you. No wonder you have so much bad luck. You don't think straight. You need me, a girl, to do all your thinking!

Lai Yue assessed the cramped space. Under the fireplace looked unstable, beneath the bed too obvious, and the food crate might be moved. He decided that the dark corner, where the shovels and poles and wire were piled, was a perfect place. He thrust the tools and produce to the side, and dug a shallow hole in the soft, damp soil.

Lifting his shirt, he stared at the welted skin that outlined his belt – an angry rind of rubbed flesh, oily and pus-yellow in spots. He unbuckled the belt, peeling away the softened leather. Sharp breath in, clenched teeth, held tight through each stinging moment. It almost felt worse once the circumference of the wound was exposed, no longer clamped warm in the belt's grip. Excruciating when he turned or bent over and his shirt grazed the lacerated skin.

He laid the purse from his belt into its earthen haven and quickly covered it with soil. He patted the ground flat. As he replaced the hardware above his hiding spot, the metal of the tools and wire clanked so loudly he fretted that someone might hear.

And, even now, he worries. Wonders if he should move his purse to another hiding place. He peers through the doorway. The forest is a dark stain against the sky, and he reaches for his stool like a blind man, sits down to watch.

He imagines the dark specks in the distance are Pennington's homestead and the bachelors' huts, but he knows that, actually, the homestead is sunk out of his sight's range. He thinks of Mrs Pennington's garden – the passionfruit vine across the chickens' wire enclosure, the citrus trees, the creeper with the blue and white flowers that cast a sweet scent at night. And the one mulberry tree several yards from the house. Not large enough yet to throw shade over the homestead, but healthy, already bearing fruit. Lai Yue rubs his eyes, thinks of the barren trees at home.

I bet Ying isn't sitting alone. In the dark. Sore.

'She'll be working hard, Shan. Working to help get us home.'

Shan huffs. *She might even be gone when we get back. She might return home without you. It would be easy for her to leave you here to pay both your debts.*

'Don't be ridiculous! She wouldn't leave me.' But he remembers how Ah Kee got rid of him. Perhaps it was at her prompting. Shan is right. It'd be easier for her to escape their poverty here without him. Ying could go home to the farm that is rightfully his. That might no longer belong to him. Where his mother lives. Where she might not live anymore. How will they find her? His brother? Su?

The red dog scratches behind its ear; the sheep bleat and rustle against each other for room in their pen. Raindrops steal through holes in the roof, tapping an uneven beat on the food box, the bedding, Lai Yue's thigh. But Lai Yue remains still, until his rump is numb and his back aches.

He stares into the gloom of the bare hut until he is no longer alone. Shan sits on a hay bale close by. She's the only one who speaks to him. Not like Chee Fatt, their neighbour from the diggings, who's seated quietly by the bed. Lai Yue can't work out why he's here. Perhaps he is dead and this is his spirit. Perhaps it is Lai Yue's fault he has died. When he asks Chee Fatt, he merely shakes his head, says nothing, glares ahead.

Lai Yue feels he can accept Chee Fatt's silence, and Shan's nagging, but his other companions churn his stomach cold. They keep behind him, to the left, huddled in the corner. The dark woman who tumbled from the tree. She rocks, the tip of her head teetering in and out of the corner of Lai Yue's vision. He knows that next to her, upright, scowling, is the native. The native he finished off. Lai Yue twists around. Nothing. Shadows waver across the bark wall. When Lai Yue turns towards the barren fireplace again, he senses them settling back into the corner. Their presence, their stony gaze, strokes the side of his neck, feathers up his spine. He cannot sleep. He will never sleep.

30

The house is in darkness when Meriem returns. She watches Ying's shadow as he scurries down the road towards Jimmy's shop.

Stepping into the scullery, she hesitates, angling her head to glance around. No Tinker. He's not in the house or on his mat outside the back door. She closes the door and brings down the latch. Turning up the lantern, she frowns down into the pot of stew. The bowls she left stacked close by are still clean and none of the stew appears to have been eaten. She crosses to the front door and latches it as well. Lingering, she stares at the screen across Sophie's doorway, wondering why Sophie has taken herself off to bed so early. Wondering if Clem is with her. But after a few moments of silence, Meriem gives up and douses the light.

After removing her outer clothing, she lies down on her bedding, allowing her thoughts to return to the grove. How bold she was to kiss Ying, but it had seemed right. As she lay beside him she'd felt desire rising. She remembers the touch of his mouth and her blood rushes, its current strong. She feels his soft skin beneath her fingertips again. The nutty scent of him, when she pressed her face into the folds between his jaw and throat. Meriem's skin thrums. She is a bright sea anemone, shivery and fragile, seeking, sucking for more.

She covers her face with her hands. Curls her fingers through her hairline. She must stop thinking of such things. She knows the consequences of thoughts – of actions – such as this. The pain of childbirth and, far worse, the pain of loss.

But need there be the pain of loss anymore? Meriem rolls to the side and stares into the gloom. Sophie spends some of her time with Chinese men and even spoke once of a girl she worked with who married a Chinese fellow, which had appalled Meriem, but now makes her ponder. A life by Ying's side. Perhaps they could run a grocery store together. Down south where nobody knows them. Or perhaps he will want to return to his own country. She knows nothing of the place, but fancies it is like the picture on her mother's china saucers of willows and joss houses and farmers in those pointy straw hats. Her mind is drawn back to Jimmy's odd little shop. Perhaps she will grow used to the smells and colour, and won't even notice them after a while.

Rain patters on the tin roof, and she imagines the cool drops splattering her chest, her arms, her legs. Her mind drifts from bleached memories of her home in Queanbeyan to the feel of Ying's warm fingers in hers. Twice she wakes in the night, disturbed by a kitten's mewling. Falls asleep again, wondering if Tinker has found somewhere dry to sleep.

When dawn's pewter light peeks through the cracks in the wall, Meriem rises, shuffling her way across the scullery to light the stove, still wrapped in comfortable dreams of the night before. She glances towards Sophie's room, thinking of how she won't be up for hours, but pauses. The screen doesn't completely cover the doorway, which is unusual. Meriem can't recall if it was like that the night before – she hadn't noticed in the darkness. Perhaps Sophie is awake after all, would be thankful for a cup of tea. Meriem tiptoes across the floorboards, hoping Clem has left. She knocks lightly on the screen, then peeps into the room.

One of Sophie's feet is tangled in her blanket, the other one – slender, lovely arch – exposed. Meriem's eyes travel along her pale leg until hitching on a red smear that mars her thigh. Higher still, her nightgown ruched about her hips.

It's then that Meriem notes the sickly smell, butcher sweet. And something more tannic, on the turn. She steps forward, craning to see by the dim light. A wash of blood, treacle dark. Pooled in the creases of Sophie's throat. A jagged fissure above what's left of her lip. Meriem squeezes her eyes shut, concentrates on the burnt-biscuit shape of her damaged vision.

Searing heat roars through her body; her legs weaken. She doesn't know what to do but grasp Sophie's toe.

No, no, no, no, no.

31

Besides the mould that creeps stealthily across every surface, Ying can't stand the dingy odour that the rain leaves in its wake. Of clothing that won't dry, of soggy earth, of damp hide. She crushes her spare shirt to her nose, inhaling its scent, trying to discern any dank trace. Worried that she'll smell bad for Merri, but smiling at the same time, thinking of the previous evening. Pressing her face into the fabric long enough to recall how Merri caught her bottom lip between hers, feeling a loosening with it.

The barber tips a little oil into the palm of his hand and, lathering his hands together, runs his fingers through Jimmy's hair. He touches up a spot at Jimmy's temple, shaving away two or three strands, and then, still raking his fingers in Jimmy's hair until it shines, he finally divides it up to plait.

'You hear about the prostitute on the edge of town?' he asks.

'What prostitute, Ah Wong? One of Mrs Maggie's girls?' Jimmy says, eyes shut, head bobbing with the barber's tugs.

'No. One of the girls down by the river. The pale one. I don't know her name.'

Ying's hand drops to her side, still grasping the shirt. 'Which girl?' Perhaps he means the wretched women who dole out their favours by the Chinese camp.

'Pale girl, I told you. Lives with the fat girl. Next to Lo Pak's.'

'Miss Sophie?'

'Yes. Maybe that is her name.' Ah Wong shrugs as his deft fingers continue to wind Jimmy's long hair.

'What about her?' Ying asks. Too loudly. She steps back with it.

'Someone killed her. In the night.'

'Killed her?'

The barber nods. 'Yes. Last night.' He ties string about the end of Jimmy's plait. 'What did she expect? Living out there without protection? Silly.' He glances at Ying and chuckles. 'What do you look so scared about? Nobody will get you here.' He nudges Jimmy, who laughs too.

'How did she die?' Ying asks.

The barber pulls his forefinger across his throat. 'Silly,' he says again.

Ying gapes at him, feels smothered by the fragrance of hair oil and incense. What of poor Merri? She must go to her. She must find a way.

Jimmy snaps, 'Ying, serve the customer.'

She hadn't even heard the two men walk into the store, stomping fresh manure into the floor. She bites her top lip, wills herself not to heave, as she bags flour, cured meat and tea for them.

When she turns back to Jimmy and Ah Wong, she can't even be sure she took their payment. 'Who killed her?'

The barber shrugs. 'Don't know. But I'd say to be careful.' He aims a slender metal instrument into Jimmy's ear and gently scrapes. 'I heard they're looking for someone Chinese.'

Jimmy can't move with Ah Wong poking about in his ear, but his eyes swivel towards Ying. 'Why is that?'

Ah Wong wipes the tiny spoon on a rag and moves around to Jimmy's other ear. 'Someone saw a Chinese man running away from her house last night. Very late.'

32

A beautiful morning of golden light shining through the mist; of sheep hidden among the pasture grass, sometimes craning their pretty heads to look about; of feathery blossoms that diffuse to the touch and lift into the air. Lai Yue takes a deep breath, counting the posts of the distant fence again – twenty-two, twenty-three, twenty-four – relishing the calm that steals over him at such constancy. He returns his gaze to his carving. It's no longer a secret from Shan – how could it be? The carving is so obviously of her. He's captured her nose perfectly, but she's unhappy with her mouth.

The lips are too straight. I look angry. I should be smiling. I am always smiling, even when I have to put up with so much.

Lai Yue nicks another flower into her robe. 'I will, Shan.' He tries to make his words soothing, reassuring. 'I will. I will return to it last. When I am more skilled.'

He shifts his buttocks on the rock, looks about, eyes widening when he notices a plume of smoke rising in the air. Near his hut.

He squints.

The smoke comes from inside his hut.

He jumps to his feet, clutches the rifle to his side. Could it be natives, raiding his provisions, his tools, setting light to what they don't want; or is it just Pennington or one of his men, checking up on him? But why light the fire? The fire pit that remains blackly barren. His heart hammers; he feels like vomiting up the lump of dry dough he chewed on earlier with his cup of tea. His eyes roam over the sheep: one, two, three … at the fourteenth sheep he breaks into a trot. He wants to crawl through the long grass, hide behind trees, but the best he can do is crouch a little as he runs.

When he's closer he notices the horses, tethered to a red gum behind the hut. Pennington's men, then.

'What the hell does he eat?'

'Cats, so I heard. Lucky the missus hasn't lost any of hers.'

The three men in the shepherd's hut laugh. Two of them stop when they notice Lai Yue in the doorway, but the other keeps talking as he pokes around the back of the room.

'We needn't have brought the stinky bastard any more food.' The man stands with his back to the others, arms akimbo, staring down at the sacks of flour and sugar that sag by the food box.

'Rod, shut up.'

Rod turns, his grin widening when he sees Lai Yue. 'Hello there, mate. Larry, is it?'

Lai Yue nods. The words echo between his ears.

'Boss wants us to take the sheep to the dam to have a drink.'

Lai Yue nods again, stands aside for the men to file outside. Rod glances back over his shoulder as he leaves the hut.

Lai Yue has already carried pail after pail of water from the stream to replenish the troughs, but he's pleased to help the men muster the sheep, herd them to the larger body of water. He hopes he will have less water to fetch come the late afternoon. The men canter ahead, Lai Yue taking up the rear on foot. Some of the sheep drink, most stand by, a few just bleat.

On the return trip he keeps an eye on the stragglers, and by the time he reaches the hut, the three men are ready to leave.

'Eat something, man,' Rod calls out to him, grinning. Dirt cakes the wrinkles that line his face. 'You're as thin as a reed. No use to the boss if you're too weak, or dead.'

Lai Yue watches them gallop off, relieved to be alone again.

The fire has petered out but, despite the smoke that still hangs heavy in the air, Lai Yue knows something is amiss. Through the haze his nose picks up on wet dog, damp canvas – usual smells – but he can also smell the men, their body odour, their pipes.

A step further in and he sees a dirt footprint on the side of the mattress, and his pannikin has rolled over on the floor. His eyes snag on the tools stacked in the corner. They've been moved. The shovel stands to the right of the roll of wire, not the left. The hoe has fallen to the ground, the tool box almost in the same position, but not quite.

Lai Yue scrambles into the corner, shoving the tools aside, so that the spade falls with a crack against his wrist. The ground doesn't lie flat, but instead there is a tell-tale groove. He digs his fingernails into the soil, where his burial ground has been disturbed. The earth has been ploughed by others' hands. He rakes out handful after handful of earth, far deeper than he dug the first time round, knowing his purse is gone.

'I will kill them. I will kill them,' he bellows.

Shan dances around him, her green silk slippers kicking up loose soil.

Yes. Yes. Yes.

33

The house is full of men, standing about, staring towards Sophie's room. They're murmuring to each other, the mood different from usual. No ribaldry, no shouts of laughter.

'Finally,' someone mutters. 'The doctor's here.'

Meriem lurches out the back, shielding her eyes from the harsh sunlight. She retches, feels the vomit come up the back of her nose, stinging her eyes. The Chinese gardener whites in and out – she can't remember his name. Ying told her, but she just can't remember. A cup of cold tea is pressed to her lips. 'What happen?' asks the gardener, but then he's gone.

A man grabs her by the elbow, draws her to her feet. Petersen. He says something about the police. She tries to wrench her arm free as he leads her into the scullery.

'It's fine, girl. The doctor is with her now.'

Is she dead?

Her lips can't form the words.

Dr Hamer steps out from Sophie's room, shaking his head. He's paler than Meriem's ever seen him. He wipes the sweat from his brow with a handkerchief; his lips are set in a straight, hard line.

'Where's the bloody sub-inspector? Tell me he's not in Laura this week.'

'Saw Campbell last night, Doctor. He'll be about soon,' Petersen says, pushing Meriem down onto the stool against the scullery wall, before pulling a chair out from the table for himself.

'Has anyone seen Tinker?' It comes to her suddenly. Where's the dog?

'That black mongrel of yours?' Petersen says. 'No, lass, haven't seen him.'

She twists around to stare out the back door. Allows her mind to fill with concern for the dog, stupid Tinker, anything to crowd out thoughts of Sophie, her slender toes, her bare leg, her ...

'Here he is,' Petersen says, as a horse canters up to the house.

The crowd takes a step back as the policeman strides through the front door. Campbell gestures for the doctor to follow him, and they disappear into the bedroom. A moment later, Campbell pokes his head out and says, 'Petersen, clear this lot out for me, would you? It's not the blasted circus.'

Petersen nods, ushering the others out. 'You heard the man. Move on.'

The men grumble, but there's no real quibbling.

Meriem strains to hear what Dr Hamer and Campbell say to each other in the bedroom, but they're too quiet. She turns to gaze outside, wondering where the dratted dog could be. She mashes her mouth between her fingers, savouring the sting of strained skin. Wondering if he's done to the dog what he's done to poor Sophie.

She jumps when a hand grips her shoulder.

'Come to the table, miss,' Petersen says.

The doctor and Campbell are already seated as she sinks into the fourth chair.

'Is she dead?' Her mouth feels stiff, as though she's trying to pronounce foreign words.

The doctor says something, but she can't hear for the buzzing in her ears. As though a swarm of flies has taken up residence in her skull.

Petersen clasps her fingers about a mug of gin and water, tells her to drink. She's trembling so hard she needs both hands to grip the mug. She brings it to her lips and gulps down the gin, and her eyes water, bringing on tears.

'Is she dead?' she says again.

Dr Hamer leans across the table and places his hand over hers. Very slowly, he says, 'No, Meriem. But she's not conscious. She's in a bad way and I can't be certain she's going to make it.'

'Did he … Did he cut her throat?' she asks, thinking of the ring of blood around her neck.

'No, Meriem. No. Whoever did this used his fists.'

She sits back in her chair. Glares down at her own hands, at her taut knuckles that gleam white. So much damage with only his bare hands. Sophie's poor face. Blood-blackened to tar.

'Did you see who did this, miss?' Campbell asks. His sweaty hair remains pressed to his head when he removes his hat to place it on the table.

She shakes her head.

'Where were you then?'

She looks from one to the other. Shrugs her shoulders. 'I don't know. When did it happen?'

Campbell turns to the doctor, who says, 'Probably last night some time. From what I can tell from the wounds.'

Campbell stares at her, and she thinks of Ying. Of their grove. Her mind recoiling from the glint of dusky pleasure.

'I was out for a walk.'

'A walk? With your sweetheart?'

She shakes her head again. But then thinks that perhaps it's best if they think she was, so she nods yes.

'Well, who is he then?'

'I can't say.'

Campbell is stern. 'Of course you have to. If this woman dies there'll be an inquiry. Better to tell me about it now.'

'He's married.'

The sub-inspector's face relaxes into a knowing look, and she feels a prick of humiliation. But it'll have to do.

'Sooner or later, you'll have to tell me his name, you know,' he says. 'Notice anything strange when you got home?'

She thinks of the uneaten stew, the darkness, Tinker's absence. 'Where's Tinker?'

'Miss, keep your mind on this business, would you?'

'It's the shock,' murmurs Dr Hamer.

'Miss, did you notice anything unusual when you got home?'

'Nothing. I went to bed.'

'No noises? You didn't hear her call out?'

A flare of light behind her eyes. The cat mewling in the night. Was that Sophie? Calling out for her? Meriem's shoulders quake, and her upper body caves forward.

'No time for howling, miss. That's not going to help her.'

Meriem dries her eyes in the crook of her arm.

'You got any idea who might've done this?'

She looks up at him. 'Clem. Of course it were Clem.'

Dr Hamer pushes his chair back and leans his elbows on his knees, drops his head.

Campbell stares at her, disbelieving. 'Clem who?'

She searches her mind, but she can't think of his surname. 'Clement. Clement something. I can't remember. Scottish fellow.

He's a teamster or some such. Just returned.'

'Clement Morrison?' Campbell asks. 'You see him here last night?'

'No.'

'Well, miss, I think you have that wrong then. Surely.' He has an incredulous smile on his face. 'Why would he do that?'

'He's always leaving bruises on her,' she says, stung at his tone. 'Maybe he …' She thinks of his threatening manner the last time he visited. His demands on Sophie to stop seeing Chinese men. Perhaps he heard that she continued to entertain them when he was away.

'Maybe he what?'

'He wanted her all to himself. Maybe he found out …'

The sub-inspector sits back in his chair, his gaze still on her. 'No. I just don't think he'd do it. Why would he be jealous of a …' He glances across to Sophie's room. 'Jealous enough to bash her that badly?'

'No, miss,' Petersen pipes up. 'Don't believe it, either. And in any case, saw him myself last night at the new beer house on Palmer Street. He seemed in fine fettle.'

'What about robbery?' Campbell continues. 'Anything missing?'

Meriem's eyes move slowly around the room, brushing over the oak cabinet, the shoebox that contains gaming matter, Sophie's book bound in green leather.

She stands so abruptly that Petersen has to catch hold of her chair, and hurries over to Sophie's hidey-hole beneath the roofing. She steps onto the scullery stool and lifts the tin sheet. She can just make out the scratched lid of the coffee tin. Reaching in, she shakes it a little.

'Sophie's money is still here,' she says, and goes to check that her own savings remain at the bottom of her portmanteau. 'And mine too.'

The sub-inspector rubs his hair back from his forehead. 'Very strange.'

'Campbell.' Two men stand in the doorway, outlined by sunlight.

Meriem squints against the brightness, recognises Dermot, imagines she can smell the oil of him.

Campbell joins them outside, and Dr Hamer returns to Sophie's room. Petersen's stomach gurgles. He pulls out his watch, says, 'Better get back to business', but remains seated.

Meriem rises to her feet, steadying herself against the table. Through the doorway she notices two of Campbell's native police lounging against the ironwood. A dray rolls by, and the steady drum of hammer on tin can be heard not too far away.

She stands at the entrance to Sophie's room and watches the doctor kneel by Sophie's bedside, next to a basin of crimson water. The blanket has been pulled to her chin. Her face is swollen with dark shadows.

'She's lost at least one tooth, and I'm almost sure her jaw is fractured,' Dr Hamer says, without looking around at Meriem. 'You really think Clem did this?'

'Sure of it.'

His hand clenches on the mattress. 'Are you up to caring for her?' he asks.

'Yes.'

He resumes daubing away dry blood with a damp cloth. 'You'll need to keep the wounds clean. I'll fashion something or other to hold her jaw in place. I've already given her something for the pain. Now we'll just have to wait and see.'

Meriem turns as Campbell's voice reaches her. The three men have moved closer to the doorway, and she hears Campbell say, 'Would you recognise him?'

The pair glance at each other. 'Yeah, I reckon,' Dermot says.

'He were short,' says the other one.

'Well, that's not much to go on, is it?' Campbell says, his voice testy.

Meriem peers at Dermot's face, but he doesn't look her way.

'I'll have some likely fellows rounded up; see if you can identify any of 'em. And I'll look into that shop boy you mentioned, Dermot.' He waves them off before returning to the table.

Campbell nods for Meriem to join him and Petersen. 'It seems we have a couple of witnesses who saw someone running from here last night.'

'Not Clem?'

'No. You need to forget about Clem. Those two say he was with them. They say they saw a Chinaman, though. Late. You know anything about this?'

She opens her mouth to say no, but words won't come. Thinks of Ying's wood-duck shadow tripping along the road for home. Tugs on her bodice as though a corset draws tight about her chest.

'Sophie have Chinese customers?'

Meriem nods.

'Regulars?'

'Yes.'

'Well, come on, tell me who they are and I can get started on rounding them up.' He rummages in his coat pocket for a pencil stub and a folded newspaper.

'I don't know their names,' she says.

'Where can I find them?'

'I don't know.'

He pushes his chair back. Striding to the door, he looks outside to the right. 'What about that Chinese man next door? I heard he was snooping around this morning.'

'He was helping me.' The cool tea he brought. His silent help around the yard. The round, firm cabbages he sometimes left at the door.

Campbell's mouth screws to the side, unconvinced. 'It's worth talking to him. Could've been him, for all we know. Gave her a good thrashing and then ran home.'

'It wasn't.'

He stares across at her. 'You sound mighty sure of yourself. How do you know?'

'It couldn't have been him.' Wonders if she should simply admit to being with Ying. She could explain that he left her at the door, that he didn't enter the house. There was no possibility he could've hurt Sophie. That the men – Dermot and his mate – saw an innocent man run by. Dermot and his mate who are, in any case, almost certainly covering for Clem.

She looks from the sub-inspector to Petersen.

And knows she could never – never – admit her sweetheart is a Chinese man. Can already feel the potential shame of it heat her ears.

'I just know it were Clem. I know it,' she says.

'Now, listen, Miss – what is your name again?'

'Meriem. Meriem Hartley.'

'Now listen, Meriem. I wouldn't go spreading gossip about Clem if I were you. Could land you in a lot of trouble,' he says, nodding towards Sophie's room.

34

Ying huddles in the corner, where the stench of rat and sawdust is strong. She's out the back of the shop, hidden behind the crates Jimmy has arranged around her.

Her eyes have almost closed when someone says, 'Can I look around in here, Jimmy?'

'Of course, Mr Campbell, sir.'

Ying can't hear Jimmy's next words over the sound of a box being dragged across the ground.

'And you don't know where he's gone?'

'No, Mr Campbell.' Jimmy's voice is as calm as usual. 'He say he selling rice to diggers at the river, but he not returned yet.'

'And what's his name again?'

'Mr Ying.'

A crate teeters to her left, but then stills.

'Why police want Mr Ying?'

'We've got some questions about last night, Jimmy.'

'Last night? Mr Ying played mah-jong here with me, Mr Campbell.'

Campbell's voice is further away when he says, 'Is that right? Anyone else see him?'

'Yes, Mr Campbell. Our friend, Ah Kee. He play mah-jong too.'

Ying can tell by the scrape of his shoes that the policeman has returned from the yard.

'That's all right, Jimmy. You just send him along to confirm all that with me when he gets in.'

'Yes, Mr Campbell.'

They step up into the shop, but Ying daren't move. An ache steals over her thighs, locking her knees. She can't be sure how much time passes, but when a crate and then a barrel are pulled away from her hiding spot, she clamps her hands over her mouth. Tries to squeeze a bit further into her corner.

Ah Kee looks through into the space, grinning. 'It is only me. Jimmy wanted me to check on you.' He hands through a bowl of peanuts.

'Was the policeman looking for me?'

Ah Kee settles on a chair where she can see him, and lights his pipe. 'Yes. But I don't think he'll return. They rounded up five of Yip Sow Kwai's men and chained them to a tree by the Mayweather,' he says, sucking on his pipe. 'They had to let them go when the witnesses said they didn't recognise any of them.'

'What about Lo Pak? Have they let him go yet?'

Ah Kee shakes his head, tendrils of smoke billowing from his wide nostrils.

'But why?'

'I don't know.' He puffs some more, eyes narrowed as he stares at her through the smoke. 'Jimmy thinks you were the one seen by the prostitute's house last night?'

Ying thinks of the disappointment in Jimmy's face when she admitted she sneaked out to visit Merri; that it was most probably Ying that the witness had caught sight of. 'I'm friends with Miss Merri. We went for a walk,' she says, scuttling forward a little.

'Ah Kee. I've been thinking. What if I tell the police it was me? That I was out for a walk. That it wasn't Lo Pak who they saw.'

Thinking – hoping – that Merri will confirm her story.

Ah Kee laughs. But not in a joyful way. 'Ying. Has a ghost covered your eyes? You tell the police that and you will be hanging from the nearest tree within the day.'

Ying moves back against the wall, feeling sick.

'Don't fret, boy. Lo Pak will be fine. How could the witness have recognised anyone when it was so dark? They don't want to point fingers at each other, so they blame the Celestial.'

The store is busy. Ying can hear boots clomping across the floorboards, the intermittent clink of coins. She feels bad that she can't help Jimmy, but he insisted that she stay hidden away in case anyone does indeed recognise her from the night before. The air is stuffy, suffocating almost, where she crouches. She rests her head on her knees, drowsy.

But when she hears Merri, she springs to her feet, dizzy with standing so quickly.

'But I must talk to him,' Merri's voice rises as she speaks to Jimmy.

Ying darts through the gap and tries to head into the shop, but Ah Kee's grip on her wrist is firm.

'You must stay here,' he hisses, pulling her back so they can't be seen.

'He no here, Miss Merri,' Jimmy says. 'I don't know where.'

'Tell Ying ... tell him that someone saw him last night.' Merri lowers her voice and says some more that Ying can't catch. And then, 'Tell him, Jimmy. He will understand.' The loud click-click of her heels recedes as she hurries from the store.

35

Fifty-two ... fifty-three ...

Lai Yue counts the fence posts as he rushes across the paddock in the direction of Pennington's homestead. The red dog yaps excitedly, bumping into the side of Lai Yue's leg to nip at his elbow. Lai Yue shouts at it, waving it away, and bends to adjust his right shoe. His big toe has worn a hole in the fabric, and he has to shuffle his foot towards the heel to keep it in place. Straightening up, he resumes his stride through the long grass.

Fifty-four ...

How will you kill them?

In those first moments of rage, his mind blazed with candescent images of maiming those white devils with swings of his shovel or, better, the intimate plunge of a knife. Yielding flesh, nicking bone. Eye to eye. Inhaling their startled gasps.

But how swiftly the heat has burned itself out as he walks.

'Perhaps it would be best to go straight to Pennington, Shan. Tell him what happened.'

Bleating like a lamb.

He ignores her, thinking that, yes, he will tell Pennington about those red-haired devils stealing from him. Lai Yue will make sure he gets his money back. He needs that money.

Fifty-five … The fifty-sixth post hidden behind an ironbark's scaly trunk.

Lai Yue pauses, holds out his trembling hands. He can't think clearly. His rifle is slung about his shoulder, but perhaps he should have brought an axe too, or the machete he uses to cut back the spear grass.

It would be best to first tell Pennington what happened.

His steps are slower as he walks on.

Fifty-seven … fifty-eight … fifty-nine …

He's coming to the edge of the sheep's paddock, exhausted to think of how far he still is from the homestead. To the side, the dam is a turbid eye set deep in the earth. The strangled trumpeting of a bull reaches his ears from over the rise. He halts again and stares about until the sprawling fields and forest begin to spin. Now that his anger has abated, fear returns to stiffen his muscles, clack up and down his vertebrae. His eyes search the branches of distant trees. He gapes at the shadows beyond. Is someone, something, watching him? Thinks of dark men, the dark bird.

What are you waiting for?

Lai Yue shakes his head and resumes walking. When, not much further on, he catches sight of the three men squatted around a fire, drinking their afternoon tea in the shade of a clump of trees, he becomes uneasy. Here is his opportunity to confront them – all is lost, lost, if he doesn't reclaim his savings – but seeing them together, he's certain he should simply march past and continue to find Pennington.

However, he's no longer sure if his shaky legs, his jittery heart, will carry him all the way to the homestead. It takes some time for him to reach the men, and in those awkward moments he keeps his gaze low, watches where he treads. He senses their eyes on him, and his gait becomes ungainly, as though his joints have loosened from their sockets.

The red dog bounds ahead, reaching the men before Lai Yue does. He's now quite sure he would prefer to wait for Pennington but knows that if he doesn't say something, Shan will berate him.

'Well, lookee here, lads,' says one, emptying the dregs from his cup onto the grass. 'Look what the dog dragged over.'

Lai Yue works hard to conjure anger's prickle across his skin, its unyielding nature. Instead, a dreaded tide of foreboding rises through him. Faced with these men again, he already knows how it will end.

At least try, Lai Yue. An exasperated edge to her voice.

Planting his feet apart, he glares at the one they call Rod.

'Where my money?'

'Don't know what you're talking 'bout,' Rod says, rubbing the red dog's ear.

'Where my money,' Lai Yue repeats.

'What money?' Rod winks to the man opposite, who's wiping the sweat from his neck with a blue kerchief. 'You know anything about any money, Goodwin?'

'Nah, mate. You've made a mistake, Larry.'

'I tell Pennington. You take my money.'

Goodwin tucks the kerchief into his trouser pocket. 'You'll have no luck there, my friend. Pennington's away.'

'Away?'

'Away. Not at home,' Rod explains. He grins up at Lai Yue, revealing a missing canine.

Kill them.

Lai Yue remembers his rifle, lifts his shoulder to feel its hard angles. Licks his dry lips.

You kill them. Take your money back. You have time to hide their bodies so that Pennington never finds out.

Could he? There's a tremor in his fingers as he touches the strap. Wonders if he has time to swing it into his grip, draw the cock, pull the trigger. Three times.

Wonders if he dares. Panting, his heart beats so fast.

You must! Or all is lost, Lai Yue.

Rod's eyes narrow as he watches Lai Yue, and he slowly climbs to his feet. He steps close and, standing over Lai Yue, says, 'You wouldn't be that foolish, would you, Larry?' He tosses a piece of bread into the air and the red dog catches it with a snap of his teeth.

The other two men also stand. Goodwin's hand lightly clasps the Colt at his belt, while the third fellow stamps out the fire. Nobody's smiling anymore.

Lai Yue drops his gaze. Feels as though he might choke on the shame.

'Jesus, I think he's going to cry,' Goodwin says.

'Nah, no call for that, Larry,' Rod says, not unkindly. 'Why don't you scarper off home? There'll be more money one day.'

Lai Yue turns from them. His steps are swift, but he can hear their laughter as they mount their horses and canter away.

The sun is low, its last glimmer fringing the peaks of the mountain range. Soon he will be trapped by darkness, halfway home, without a lantern to guide his way. He looks to his left. His right. Turns full circle, sickened by the pace of his tripping heartbeat. Where's the red dog?

Why are you running away? Why do you always run away?

221

'I'm not, Shan. I will tell Pennington when he returns. He will surely make them pay back what they have stolen.'

You were scared. Scared of those men.

'I wasn't scared.'

He wants to count the fence posts but doesn't remember where he's up to. Something flickers behind the gums and he quickens his stride.

You are scared.

He catches his foot on a tussock and stumbles to his knees. He hears Shan's sharp intake of breath. At first he thinks she is sorry for him but, when she doesn't say anything, he realises she's ashamed of how low he has fallen. He closes his eyes and allows his head to hang, revelling in his sorry state for several drowning moments. Opening his eyes, he stares at the crease down the middle of a blade of grass and how his little finger rests near a dried-out pebble of sheep dung. The fine fur of a thistle. An ant scaling a clump of fresh kangaroo droppings. The skeletal remains of a desiccated leaf.

He hauls himself up and grunts *fifty-six* as he spies the lone ironbark. As he walks, he counts backward, out loud, hoping to drown out Shan's muttering. Although he can still hear *weak-willed* and *disappointing* and *if only* breathed in his ear.

The last of the light bleeds into the evening sky as he arrives at his hut. The sheep linger by the pen, waiting to be ushered in. But it's too late. He's tired. He makes up the fire, placing an iron pot of water over the flames to brew tea, and avoids looking at the plundered earth that once held his meagre savings.

Slumping down onto his stool, he thinks of Shan's words. *Scared. Bleating lamb.* She is right. He has always been fearful. Lai Yue remembers when he was sleepless as a boy, cold and rigid with it, and he would seek out his mother, who was still seated at the loom late into the night.

'I'm frightened.'

'Tell me what you are frightened of,' she'd say, threading a length of silk.

'I'm scared of thieves, and murderers, and ghosts, and monsters, and fox-fairies, and wolves, and ...'

'Lai Yue, nothing can harm you,' she'd always say, gesturing for him to join her. Her strong arm about his shoulders, fingers digging into his arm reassuringly. 'Nothing can harm you.'

But that was before.

The sheep fuss by the pen, scuffling the dirt. The water in the pot begins to purr.

Lai Yue leans forward and drops his head into his hands. He doesn't know if he will be able to start over. He realises he was actually better off when he first arrived in this cursed country. When he still had coin and, more importantly, hope – hope of accruing enough riches to save his siblings and restore their farm.

When did it all go so wrong? When he sought the comfort of opium? Or when Ying fell ill?

Or, before that? Perhaps when he lost Shan?

No, my love. Remember? It goes back further still. To your father.

The water bubbles, its gurgle interrupted by a sheep's treble peal.

His father. Lai Yue welcomes the familiar warmth of reproach, but Shan breaks in, warns, *Lai Yue. Remember! Beware of unfilial thoughts.*

So he searches his memory until he is returned to the father of his youth. The sombre man who recited poetry as he taught Lai Yue how to carve figurines out of the timber from fallen mulberry trees. Sometimes singing the verses, his voice vibrating over 'moonlight in the pines', and 'the plum, opening its first cold blossom'. Lai Yue closes his eyes and murmurs what lines he can recall. First the one about autumn in the mountains, but he can't remember all of it. And then the other poem, also about autumn. But this one leaves his heart heavy, with its words of loneliness and silence. He tries to match the verse to a tune his mother used to hum, and the twang of his voice rises above the hiss of the water as it boils low.

Later, when their father had succumbed to his own weaknesses, Lai Yue had tried to teach the poems to his younger siblings, and although Ying and Lai Cheng had joined in, begging to learn more, Su had sulked and whinged to be left alone. Lai Yue suspects the poems will cease with him. He thinks of Shan. He can't have children with her, and she would never allow him to marry another.

You will be the kink in the family chain.

Lai Yue nods, ignoring the stench of burning metal that hisses from the iron pot. He whispers his favourite poem but can't quite get out all the lines. He croaks the first few words, only managing 'alone in a foreign land', takes a shuddering gulp of air, and then another before 'longing for home'.

Shan draws close. *Don't cry, my love. Let me finish it for you.* And her voice is sweet as she recites, *I know far away my brothers climb the hills together; plucking prickly ash, missing the one who is not there.*

It reminds Lai Yue that nobody will be missing him. There is nothing left to miss. And in the dim hut, his thoughts shatter like porcelain – crumbling fragments of confusion, shards of lucidity. The pieces shift and tremble in the cavity of his skull. Some come together, neat, with only tell-tale fissures in the glaze, but mostly they float in the air, broken.

A sheep bleats. Lai Yue lifts his head. He rises slowly from the stool and takes the smoking pot from the fire. Lighting the lamp, he decides to go outside.

He will count the sheep. That will calm him.

36

Meriem swears as she flicks an ant from the stovetop. She forgot to dispose of the stew and a black swarm of ants spews down the sides of the pot, each one lugging a fragment of sludge. Holding the lantern low, she looks at the four dishes placed under the legs of the stove and groans when she sees that the kerosene has dried up in two of them.

Straightening, she stares at the stew some more. What to do with it? The bloody dog hasn't returned, so she can't feed it to him, and she really doesn't want to go outside so late in the evening to throw it in the bushes. Unlatching the back door, she opens it a couple of inches and peeks out. She places her lips to the gap and calls, 'Tinker. Tinker.'

Nothing. Opening the door a little wider, she turns her gaze to Lo Pak's hut, which is blanketed in darkness. Earlier in the day, she watched as two native troopers led him away. The gardener appeared his usual placid self, winding his plait about his head like a resting python before clamping on a neat bowler hat. She hasn't noticed him return, though. Wonders, shaking her head, if the sub-inspector truly believes Lo Pak is the one who hurt Sophie.

She scans the yard one last time for the dog before closing the door carefully, bringing down the latch.

Meriem checks in on Sophie, who, thankfully, has found sleep. She watches the rise and fall of Sophie's chest, how her hands are clasped lightly across her midriff, before her sight flickers to Sophie's face. Meriem hopes that, soon, Sophie will recover sufficiently to tell them who did this to her, although, of course, she is convinced the answer will be Clem.

That afternoon, once the laudanum wore off, Sophie lay motionless in bed, her blue eyes mere glimmers engulfed by the swelling. But Meriem could tell they were pleading for more relief from the pain. Thankfully, towards sunset, Dr Hamer returned. He helped Sophie swallow another dose, leaving the bottle on the side table.

Meriem returns to the scullery and eats her supper standing at the bench. She doesn't have the heart to eat at the round table, alone. She forks bits of cold potato and corned beef into her mouth, angling her ear towards the sound of a rodent or possum scrabbling its way across the roof. A tinny sound of scratching claws, and the occasional bump.

She flinches at a thumping on the front door, and drops her knife with a clatter. Frowning, she glances towards the door. Waits to see if their visitor perseveres. There's more banging, and this time she hears Clem shout, 'Sophie! Soph! Open up. I need to talk to ye.' The door rattles against the jamb.

Meriem freezes. Gapes at the door in disbelief. The hide of the man! She looks past the screen at Sophie, who, blessedly, remains submerged in her laudanum sleep.

Clem continues to call for Sophie to let him in. He slaps the timber again and again. His speech is slurred, and Meriem has been in his company enough times to know he is at his very drunkest.

'C'mon, Soph, lemme in,' he demands. 'I need to see ye, lass. Lemme in.'

Meriem waits, straining to hear voices in the beer shanties across the way, or the clip-clop of horses' hooves, but her heartbeat drums in her ears.

'Fucking let me in.' Clem pounds on the door, and Meriem is afraid that, with just a little more force, he'll break through the flimsy wall. 'Where the fuck is that fat cow of yers? Tell her to let me in.'

Meriem glares at the door. Bastard. She whisks into Sophie's room noiselessly, and rummages through her trunk, searching for that damned pistol Sophie showed her. Failing to find it there, Meriem scours the dressing table where Sophie keeps her trinkets and vanity case, careful not to upset the bottles of lotions and oils.

'I need to look on ye, lass,' Clem pleads. 'I'm worried about ye. Why don't ye let me in? They say it's bad, Soph. I need to look on yer poor face. I need to see what happened.'

It occurs to Meriem that it's possible she got Clem wrong. Maybe he is genuinely concerned about Sophie. Perhaps he wasn't the one who beat her. But Meriem doesn't want his beastly presence upsetting Sophie. Or herself, for that matter.

Hands on hips, she surveys the room once more, catches sight of the valise at the base of the bed. Rifling through Sophie's books until her fingers touch chill metal, she pulls the petite pistol from the depths. She winces as Clem resumes banging on the door, and stares down at the gun. She's not even sure that it's loaded. Is it really as simple as just pulling on the trigger?

Gingerly gripping its wooden handle, Meriem returns to the main room. She hears Clem slump against the door, slide to the ground. She tiptoes across the room and puts her ear to where a sliver of bark is missing from the wall. Listens to the slosh of liquid in a tipped bottle, the smack of his lips.

She can't quite catch all that he mumbles, but he snivels the word *sorry* often enough, and then, in a pitiful voice, as though near tears, 'I won't do it again, lass. I never meant to hurt ye like that.'

The wall shudders as he climbs to his feet, and Meriem backs away. He recommences banging on the door, kicking at it too, so that the timber buckles.

She leans against the table and aims the pistol, ready should he burst through. She yearns to scream of the damage he's done to poor Sophie. But fear holds her tongue.

He continues hollering, demanding to be let in. She bites down on her bottom lip and her neck muscles seize. The pistol wavers in her grasp.

Clem falls silent. Another voice – calm, conciliatory – murmurs close by. Petersen. Meriem is almost faint with relief. She listens as Petersen encourages Clem to leave Sophie's. To join him for a whisky.

'Come away, Clem. She's no good for you.'

Meriem hears them stumble off, gripping the pistol until the joints in her hands ache. Feels her teeth might fracture, she clenches them so tight.

It takes many minutes for her fury at both the injustice of Petersen's words and the cheek of Clem's visit to subside, and it's only when she hears Sophie whimper that she is brought back to the present. She hurries into the bedroom. Sophie still seems asleep, but her brows furrow as though she is caught in a terrible nightmare. Meriem squeezes her hand, wishing it weren't too soon to give her more laudanum.

Returning to the sitting room, Meriem pulls a chair towards the front door and sits down where she can keep an ear out in case Clem returns. The pistol rests in her lap. Her tongue runs along her bottom lip, tasting the broken skin.

37

Ying is too glum to find rest. Before leaving, Ah Kee plugged the gap of her fortress with a sack of flour atop a barrel. How long does she have to hide out like this? Crammed into the corner the whole day and half the night. Her left knee clicks as she slides up the wall to stand for a few minutes to relieve the cramps in her legs.

The bell above the front door tinkles as Jimmy closes the shop for the day. She hears him hurry past her in the back room and pull the canvas flap to the ground, shutting out the night. He drags three crates to the side so she can crawl out.

'Thank you,' she says.

Jimmy grunts but doesn't look her way. He squats to ignite the stove, and cracks five eggs into a pan. Adds chopped spinach, a little sauce. Her stomach shifts with hunger. He doesn't look angry – not like her father used to when he detected possible defiance in Lai Yue. Bulging eyes, tongue clamped between teeth. Instead, Jimmy's face appears calm, still. But she senses his displeasure in his lack of eye contact, the preoccupied crease between his brow.

She edges her way to a chair.

'Are you going out tonight, Jimmy?'

'I will not be going out tonight, Ying. You will not have the opportunity to sneak out to Miss Merri.'

'I wouldn't,' she says, deciding that she will slip out when he's asleep.

He spoons rice into a bowl. 'Miss Merri was in here earlier today.'

'Yes. I heard her.'

'She begged me to warn you that someone saw you last night, just as you thought, Ying.'

She nods, fear catching her breath. Watches as he scoops eggs onto the rice.

Passing the bowl to her, he says, 'She said something else.'

'What?'

'She said: "Tell *Mei Ying* he mustn't visit me. It isn't safe. Tell Mei Ying."'

They stare at each other. The heat of the eggs warms the bowl cupped in her hand.

He turns, serving himself from the pan. 'I have a niece at home named Mei Ying. Pretty little girl, she is.'

Her heart skips a beat. Then another. She presses the flat of her hand to her breastbone.

'I did wonder,' he continues. 'I have wondered.'

Ying lowers the bowl to her lap. 'Please don't tell anyone, Jimmy. You won't tell anyone?'

'Of course I won't tell anyone,' he says, voice tetchy, sitting opposite her. He looks troubled as he prods the rice with his chopsticks. 'We must get you out of here. I thought before that you'd be safe enough, here, under my protection, but now—'

They both turn at the sound of scrabbling at the canvas. By the time Ah Kee appears, Ying has dived among the crates, her bowl of eggs tossed in the dirt. Ah Kee laughs heartily, hand on belly.

'You thought I was the police, come to drag you away?'

'Be quiet, Ah Kee,' Jimmy says, as he ties down the canvas flap. 'Yeeh wouldn't hesitate to inform on us. On me.'

'True, my friend,' Ah Kee says, sobering.

'What did you find out?'

'A group of Chan Poon's people are heading to Cooktown in the morning.'

'Did you speak to him?'

'Yes. Paid him to include two more on the journey.'

'Two?'

'Wait,' Ying says, from where she kneels to clear up her spilt rice. A cold wash of comprehension flooding her body. 'Wait. Are you sending me away?'

'Of course, Ying. You can't stay here.'

'But I want to stay.'

Ah Kee looks to Jimmy. 'Perhaps if he hides here until—'

'Madness!' Jimmy says. 'They'll identify Ying and then what?'

Ah Kee tips his head. 'Perhaps.' Turns to Ying. 'It is your safest option.'

Ying thinks of her older brother – he won't know what's become of her. And her life here in Maytown? And Merri. She cannot leave Merri. Not now.

For several wild moments, she imagines herself living in the bush, at their grove: Meriem could visit her and bring her food; or she'll hide by day in the forest, bed down by night in Lo Pak's chicken coop. Whatever it takes to stay.

But looking at Jimmy's worried face, she realises she must leave. Feels queasy with it.

'You told Chan Poon to include two more people, Ah Kee?' Jimmy asks again.

'Yes. I will go too. I will accompany the boy to Cooktown and then head south. Disappear for a while. Where Sip Yee's men have no reach.'

'Ah, yes,' Jimmy murmurs, head bowed. 'Yes. That is a good plan, friend.'

Despite feeling so sorry for herself, Ying manages a small prick of sadness for Jimmy. Left behind. Losing both his assistant and his good friend.

Ah Kee helps himself to rice and eggs. 'When I have settled somewhere, I will send for you. I will find a place that needs a good produce store. Somewhere you can bring your wife.' He grins.

'And you, Ying,' Ah Kee goes on, mouth full of egg, 'you need to look out for a ship called the *Bowen*, heading to Hong Kong via Singapore. I will help you buy a ticket when we get to Cooktown. The boy will have money?' He looks to Jimmy.

Jimmy nods.

Having finished his supper, Ah Kee dunks his bowl in a bucket of water and takes his leave, telling Ying they will set out while it's still dark. 'We will go ahead alone and wait for Chan Poon's people on the other side of the river. Hopefully we will avoid the police.'

Ying reaches into her burlap sack and draws out Lai Yue's bird carving. She gently rubs the rough grain of its wings, brings its beak up to meet her mouth. Burying her nose in the bird's nape, she tries to inhale its woody fragrance, wondering if it's simply her memory that fashions the slight scent.

'What will Lai Yue think if I'm gone?' she says, nestling the bird into the cavity of her grandmother's mortar and pestle. 'It seems unfair to leave without him. It seems heartless.'

'I will explain it to him, Ying,' Jimmy says. 'He will be relieved you escaped such danger.'

'Perhaps.'

Jimmy holds out a plump suede pouch. 'Here is some of your money. I have kept back the amount owed to Sip Yee. I will pay your debt in a few days, after you have left.'

Ying stares at the pouch. 'Jimmy, can you send it to my mother? In case ...'

She watches as Jimmy seems to weigh the pouch in his hand for a moment, contemplating it.

'Here is what we will do. I will send some money on to her, and the rest you keep for your travels.' He pours most of the coins into another purse and hands her the pouch.

'I also have this for you.' He places a folded piece of paper on top of her sack. 'As soon as you arrive in Cooktown, I want you to find Yoke Yee and her uncle. Ah Kee will take you there. In this letter I have urged her to return home on the *Bowen* with you.'

Ying thinks of the lovely woman in the photograph by Jimmy's altar. 'But I don't need her to return with me,' she says, appalled at the responsibility of accompanying a strange young lady.

Jimmy removes his spectacles and rubs his eyes. Carefully replacing them, he says, 'I have told her the truth, Ying – *Mei Ying* – and I have suggested you pose as her female servant. The police will not catch up with you then; they will be looking for a man.'

Ying slides the purse into her sack. 'And if she refuses?'

'I don't think she will,' he says. 'I have asked her to return home to arrange our impending marriage.'

Ying's eyes drop to the letter. 'Jimmy ...'

He turns away.

'Jimmy, I have been such a burden.'

'No, no.' He picks up his pipe. 'Come clean up this mess.'

Ying tucks the letter to the bottom of her sack and climbs to her feet. She collects the pan and bowls together but places them down again. Facing Jimmy, her cheeks burn. 'Jimmy. I thank you.'

'No, no,' he repeats. His tread is slow as he steps up into the shop, smoke rising about his head.

Although Jimmy remains in his bed when Ah Kee fetches her, Ying suspects he only pretends to sleep. How could he not wake when she knocks over the shovels in the darkness, or when Ah Kee rattles his way through the tub for a clean pannikin to drink from?

She joins Ah Kee out the back and, by the low light of his lantern, she settles the bamboo pole across her shoulders, her sack resting in one basket, provisions loaded into the other.

'I couldn't sleep,' she tells Ah Kee as they head off.

'Well, I will not carry you,' he teases.

Ying doesn't feel drowsy, though. She's alert enough, joyless energy jumping through her body. It makes her leaden, somehow.

'Goodbye, Wui Hing,' Ah Kee whispers into the gloom.

Goodbye, Jimmy, she says in her head.

Ah Kee holds the lantern low so they can watch where they walk.

Goodbye, Yeeh's servant.

Their slippers whisper along the dirt road. *Goodbye, Mr Butcher. Goodbye, Mayweather Hotel.* A dog rouses, and barks half-heartedly. *Goodbye, Ming Long store.* She looks to the other side of Leslie Street. *Goodbye, Mr Doctor. Goodbye, Yip Sow Kwai.* Keeping it up – turning her mind from the mounting pressure of moving closer to *her*, to her end of town. Closer to saying, *Goodbye, Merri*.

And when she finally passes by Lo Pak's garden, and reaches her house, she can't help herself. She puckers her lips and forces the air between her teeth in a high-pitched wheeze. Slows her stride, the whistle drawn out over five steps. Takes a breath, starts again. Passing the huge ironwood, blacker than the sky.

'Ying, what are you doing?' Ah Kee says, clutching her elbow, but Ying's attention is fixed on a flicker in the doorway of the house, a shift in the shadows. Her skin leaps towards the rush of air. The approach of swift footsteps. Dropping the baskets to the ground, she pulls Merri's body to hers.

'Ying, you're mad. The police are looking for you.'

'I know.' She searches Merri's face by the weak light. Her skin is pale and her eyes are red, but she isn't crying. And for once, Ying thinks that perhaps she will be the one to cry. Feels the hot stitch of it in her chest. 'I must go. Cooktown.'

'Good. That's good, Ying.' Merri runs her hand down Ying's hair, over her ear, to her chin. Dips her head so it rests against Ying's. 'That's good. You'll be safe.'

Ying grabs Merri's hand. 'You come too. With me, Merri.' Squeezes Merri's fingertips.

Merri rolls her forehead gently against Ying's. 'Oh, Ying.'

'You come?' Swelling with hope, but also uncertain of Merri's tone.

'I have to look after Sophie.'

Ying draws her head away. Strains to see into Merri's eyes. 'You not come?'

'No.'

Merri leans her head on Ying's shoulder. Her breath is warm. Smells faintly of sour tea. 'Ying?'

'Yes?'

'Thank you for being my friend.'

The soft soles of Ying's shoes buckle to each stone and root that skims the earth. Twelve of her countrymen file ahead of her, seven behind, tramping their way along the road to Cooktown. A coach lumbers past, piled high with men and trunks. Two tethered goats trot alongside. It has been several hours since Ying glimpsed the last of Maytown's stone kerb and the dilapidated beer shanties that fringe the town. The weight of the pole hasn't yet begun to pall, but the gouging pain she feels at leaving Merri is the worst she's experienced since being ruptured from her family so many moons before. She wilts beneath the fierce sun.

'Ying,' Ah Kee says quietly from where he treads behind her. 'It will become easier.'

She nods. 'Yes, Ah Kee.' She longs to pelt ahead until she doubles over, gasping for breath, her lungs burning up the ache in her chest.

'Unfortunately, Ying, sooner or later, the price of love will always be grief.'

Ying grips the pole and trudges on, puzzled. They cross a shallow river and, blinded by the sun's flash across the water, she squints, weighing Ah Kee's words against what she knows, what she's experienced, to test their heft. Wonders how it has never occurred to her to think of love in those terms – that, with time, its final demand will always be sorrow. Perhaps best avoided altogether.

But when, towards dusk, they halt for a short rest, she realises the key to Ah Kee's words lies in thinking of her mother, of Lai

Yue and her siblings, of Merri. She's sure that, like the fibrous roots of the lotus flower, even if a single tuber is severed, her capacity for love will continue to grow and coil, threading tender connections. She pokes some rice into her mouth with shaky fingers.

'Come, we have to keep moving,' Ah Kee says, bending to lift his own pole. 'Won't be too long before you are safely on a ship home.'

Ying's self-control slips for a moment, and she digs her finger-nails into her palms until the scorching leaves her. She uncurls her fingers and stares at the crescents in her skin.

38

Rain and rain and rain and rain.

Every day, Lai Yue counts the sheep, counts the sheep. 121, 122. Counts the sheep. 123.

The men no longer help him herd the sheep into their pen, but the sheep know the ritual. 121, 122, 123. Biddable creatures.

Rain and rain.

47, 48, 49, 50 ...

Trim the cud from hooves, Sullivan says. Flick the mud, the manure, the stones.

One hundred ewes ... 122, 123.

A dragonfly swims through the air, as golden as a fish.

Sixty-five fence posts. The fences made of neat vertical bars, diagonal braces. Sixty-five posts along the west side of the field. Forty-four posts to the tree line. Count again. 42, 43, 44. Start again. Sixty-five posts to the west.

No rain. One day. Next day. Next day. Next day. No rain.

Trim the cud.

121, 122. Count the sheep. 123.

A dragonfly swims through the air, as silver as a fish.

Forty-four posts to the tree line. Perhaps more hidden behind the woods. One day he will walk there to see.

A radish tinge to the tips of the rough grass.

Biddable creatures. 123.

Natives. Zero.

Black bird. Where's the black bird?

Only 122 sheep.

Less the lamb the red dog mauled in the night. Which night? When was it that Lai Yue had to dig that hole by the dam, bury the clover-scented raw thing deep in the ground so the dog wouldn't dig it up again?

You should kill the dog.

'The boss doesn't know about the newborn lambs yet, Shan. It's the ewes he will miss. And the dog isn't taking the ewes.'

So agitated, he tried to distract Pennington with complaints of the money the others thieved from him, but the boss didn't understand.

Didn't want to understand.

118, 119, 120, 121. He must have counted wrong. Too dark to start again.

Too dizzy to make dough. Head so heavy he feels he needs to hold it up in his own hands.

118, 119, 120. The morning sun glinting bone-white in his eyes. Where? Where?

Another lamb. Red dog, red muzzle.

You must kill it, Lai Yue.

Dry mouth. Dry mouth. Bent over the stream, lapping water like a mule.

Worried that if Pennington works out the red dog is killing the lambs, Lai Yue will lose his only companion. At least, the only one that actually draws breath.

Kill it, Lai Yue.

'But it's not the dog taking the sheep, Shan.' He scans the hills for smoke, for natives, for wild dogs. He can feel their eyes on him, but he can't see them. Where? Where?

Arrk. Arrk.

118.

One sheep found drowned on the banks of the dam. Its drenched wool so heavy, Lai Yue can't pull it up onto dry ground. 117.

Aarrk.

The dog slips its rope in the night while Lai Yue listens to Shan, urges Chee Fatt to speak. Two lambs this time: one raggedy body left by the hut's door, one dragged into the scrub, chewed upon.

What will you do, Lai Yue? The boss will be so angry. He will not pay you. No money. No money. No money. No money. No home. Kill the dog. It's you or the dog, Lai Yue.

One trembling finger on the rifle's trigger.

Is it the black bird he can hear? Lifting his heavy head, still, listening.

There are better ways, Shan whispers.

Soupy head. Lettuce slopping around in soupy head. Slosh. Slosh.

Crawling to the stream.

Long afternoon staring at the rope coiled on the floor above his useless hiding hole.

115.

Arrk. Uck-uck.

Aaarrk.

Long afternoon staring into the trees.

If Pennington finds out about the sheep and the dog, he will turn you out.

Long afternoon staring.

No men. No Pennington. No money.

You will die anyway, alone, there in the hills.

No home.

You will die anyway.

He isn't frightened when he sees the black bird perched in the thatch of the hut's roof. It twitches its lacquer feathers, cocks its agate eye his way. He staggers towards the coolabah tree by the stream, carrying his stool and the heavy rope. He's already tied a loop at each end, tugged them firm, just as he prepares rope for lugging heavy loads. He hears the bird's wings swoosh as it follows, but doesn't look for where it lands. He tries, once, twice, three times to heave one end of the rope over a high branch, but its weight is too much for him. Gasping with frustration, he's too weak to cry. He tries again, heaves the rope. It catches, tips over. He draws the end down towards himself on the other side, pokes it through the other loop until the length of rope catches tight to the branch.

How will you find me?

Lai Yue takes the wooden figurine of Shan from his pocket. For once, he doesn't feel dizzy. His head is clear. His fingers are steady. He brings out his knife and gently scores one fine eye into the figurine's face, then the other. He sets her down on a stone facing the tree. 'You can see me now. Come find me.'

The black bird croaks, ends on a cackle.

Lai Yue steps onto the stool and brings the noose down over his head, feels the rough hemp rub his chin.

Thinks of the mulberry farm. Of the farmers picking the fruit and planting the seeds.

Arrk. Aarrrk.

Clad in black, crownless straw hats tilting to the sun. Tilting back to the ochre soil.

Is it Lai Cheng he can see? Younger brother? He has a birthmark: a stork in flight. But he is a grown man now. His arm around Mother.

Aaaarrrk.

Thank you, Lai Cheng. His whisper, caught on the breeze that rustles through the leaves, ripples across the stream.

AARK.

A smother of black feathers.

A shroud over his eyes.

39

'Thank you, Lord, for making it cooler,' Meriem murmurs as she sweeps dirt through the doorway. The green ribbon tied about the ironwood has faded to the colour of cucumber flesh. Two men canter past, and another fellow, dog at heel, enters the grog shanty further along the road. His dog's black too, but with white socks. So, not Tinker. She squints towards the bush, and then towards the township's centre. She likes to imagine the dog finally got up the gumption to snap at Clem's raised hand, trying to protect Sophie, and that's why Clem had to finish him. But she thinks it more likely the dog has simply loped off.

She closes the door on the daylight and lowers the wooden bar into its brackets. Crosses to the scullery to make sure the back door is latched too. It takes her eyes a few moments to adjust to how dim it is. She can just make out the shape of Wilbur lying in the corner by the lazy whoosh of his tail. Dr Hamer's spaniel, eager with both his bark and bite. On loan until the two women move on.

Meriem's been surprised at how kind people have been to them. Petersen supplied drinking straws for Sophie to sip tea and soup and, on the days without rain, Maggie Gilhooley sends over Petunia, one of her girls, to help Meriem wash and change Sophie's bedding. Even Jimmy brewed a pungent ginger concoction that Sophie seems to enjoy.

She peeps in on Sophie, but she's in the deep slumber only Dr Hamer's tincture ensures. Her papier-mâché box lies by her side, open. Meriem creeps forward and gently prises the photograph from between Sophie's slender fingers. She angles the photograph in front of her good eye, and there's Sophie, her hair dressed in flowers and a veil of white, and standing by her is a handsome man, restful hands by his sides, quizzical lift to his left brow.

The dog growls in the next room, snout sniffing along the bottom of the front door.

'What is it, Wilbur?' she says, returning the photograph to the box.

Meriem pushes in front of him and presses her left eye to the gap in the timber. Seeing that it is someone no taller than herself, she lifts the bar. Easing the door open, she peers out on Mrs Porter.

'Good afternoon,' the postmistress says, holding up a letter. 'This arrived for you, so I thought I'd bring it over myself and check in on the invalid.'

The envelope looks as though a magpie has scratched ink across its surface: her father's scrawl. It's the third letter she's received from him in a month.

'Spare a cup of tea?'

'Of course, Mrs Porter. Please come in.' Meriem seats her at the table and, hurrying into the scullery, checks the heat of the teapot with the back of her hand.

'How is Sophie?' Mrs Porter asks as Meriem sets a teacup in front of her.

'Better.' Her face no longer swollen with bruising; the tear between her lip and nose healing nicely, although the railroad of stitches will leave a nasty scar. 'Still can't move much, though, what with needing to keep her jaw still and all.'

'Poor thing.' Mrs Porter takes a sip of her tea. 'And I see that Mr Lo Pak is back in his garden where he belongs.'

'That's right. It couldn't have been him that Dermot and his friend saw. Sophie made that clear to Sub-Inspector Campbell.'

'Did she say who did attack her?'

Meriem's eyes lower to her own cup. She shakes her head.

'I saw Clement Morrison the other day. I remarked how improved the scratches on his neck were. I told him how lucky he was that his wounds hadn't festered. Could kill a man out here, what with the wet and the heat.' Mrs Porter looks meaningfully at Meriem over her teacup.

Meriem presses her lips together. If she starts now, the whole torrent of spite will spill, and she will reveal what she heard Clem say outside their house that night, and how Campbell took Clem's and Petersen's word over hers. She would probably even describe the many daydreams she has of putting a bullet into the Scottish fiend, let alone most of the other men in this dratted town. But, as nice as Mrs Porter is, Meriem's not sure of her discretion.

'And what will Sophie do once she's well?' the postmistress asks, glancing towards Sophie's room.

Meriem thinks of Sophie's dwindling coins. Her own limited money. A week before, Maggie Gilhooley sat by Sophie's side. She stroked the hair from Sophie's forehead, crooning away the tears that fell to the pillow, later informing Meriem that Sophie would move in with her girls once she was well enough. Told Meriem she was welcome too.

'I'm not sure,' she says.

'Well, that's partly why I'm here,' Mrs Porter says. 'This town is growing every day. More and more people, which means more and more letters and parcels to send. I'm quite run off my feet. Why don't you come and work with me? Once Sophie is well again, of course.'

Meriem stares at her, quite speechless at such kindness. She covers her mouth and looks away.

'I know, dear. It will be boring work compared to what you have here, but you might like the change.'

'That's very kind of you, Mrs Porter. Very kind.' She takes the glasses from her nose and wipes them on her apron. 'But I was planning on heading home. To Queanbeyan. I think my pa might be in need of me.'

'Ah, well, that's a good outcome too.' Mrs Porter drinks the last of her tea and rises to leave.

Meriem watches her stroll down the road in the direction of the post office. She calls the dog outside and they wander around to behind the house, where Wilbur piddles against a paperbark. Meriem gazes towards their grove. When she closes her eyes, she can see light wink past the leaves, can feel the damp ground rise to her buttocks. She turns her head from hovering sandflies, so distracting, nipping at her, until Ying is there too. His brown fingers, his lovely face, his wood-duck shadow. Meriem opens her eyes, reaches into her apron pocket and brings out the paper bag. She withdraws the last red berry and rolls it between her fingertips. She places it in her mouth, where it rests on her tongue. When she finally bites down, she seeks the sweet from the bitter.

40

The sun is high as Ying watches Ah Kee disappear into the crowd down on the wharf. Her thighs brace with the creaking sway of the *Bowen* as it lumbers into deeper waters. She grips the ship's rail, breathing in to allow four men to squeeze past, shuffling on the pads of their feet to shift a heavy crate. Slipping her fingers beneath her straw hat, she's reassured by the feathery hair she's grown back across her pate – it won't be much longer before she can discard the hat and arrange her hair like she used to when she was her mother's daughter. By the time she and Ah Kee arrived in Cooktown, the stubble of Ying's hair had softened, as had the sting of leaving Merri.

Their return journey to the coast didn't take as long as when she and Lai Yue first trudged to the gold fields. The track was improved and for the last portion of the trip, thanks to Ah Kee's purse and glib charm, they procured space in the back of a dray. Still so weary, though, when they finally arrived. It took most of the next morning to find Yoke Yee's uncle's shop among the many crammed along the streets near the waterfront. As they stepped into the store Ying noticed a woman seated behind the counter – the pretty woman from the photograph. Yoke Yee. Not hidden in a back room after all, as Ying had imagined. She handed over

Jimmy's letter and Yoke Yee read it, first with a frown, then once again with an amused curl to her lips. She peeped over the page at Ying, her eyes taking in her filthy tunic so that Ying dropped her gaze, tucking her hands into her pockets to hide the streaks of dirt that snaked across her palm, bedded in the creases of her fingers. But she was fortunate. Yoke Yee cheerfully complied with Jimmy's request, hiding Ying until their voyage, and helping her transform back into a girl.

Ying rubs the flat of her hand down the front of her blue smock – plain yet clearly feminine – which Yoke Yee has lent her. Aware that she looks nothing more than a quail to Yoke Yee's parrot, but smiling, nonetheless, as she remembers Ah Kee's mirth at the vision of her female 'disguise'.

They have drawn far from the port now and she feels a dip of regret to be leaving Lai Yue behind, wondering how he will react to her news when he returns to Jimmy's shop to collect her. And she already misses the freedoms she unexpectedly acquired in Maytown that might now be lost to her.

Her eyes wander over the other passengers, trying to pick out who might be disembarking in Singapore instead of travelling on to Hong Kong. A party of men have already set up a game of fantan on a rattan mat and, further along, past a row of wooden chairs and bird cages, she catches a glimpse of two white men, who punctuate their conversation with waves of their pipes. Nudging her sack with her toe, she thinks of the small pouch of money hidden at the bottom, and her shop-boy clothes, which have nuts and barky pieces of dried meat tucked into the pockets. She imagines pulling them back on and disappearing among the busy docks of Singapore. She could stay there long enough to find work. Save some more money. And then she will return to her mother, or perhaps, perhaps, she will return to this land.

She walks along the ship's deck to find Yoke Yee. A gust of wind whips her hat to the side, its warm breath shoving her along. Her gaze takes in the receding coastline, the layers of sienna and green and blue. And even the clouds flee across the wide sky, gliding towards the horizon.

Acknowledgements

First, I would like to thank Brad Grogan and the Elders of the Western Yalanji people for consulting with me on my novel.

A heartfelt thank you to my amazing publisher, Aviva Tuffield, who has been so supportive of my writing and this book for some time. Huge gratitude to my wonderful editor, Vanessa Pellatt, who I like to refer to as the author whisperer. Thank you to Madonna Duffy and all the lovely people of UQP, and thank you to Ian See.

Thank you to Dan Bidner, and Glen and Kris, who bailed us out when we became bogged in the sand by the Palmer River. Gratitude to James Sing, who shared the captivating history of his own family with me. Thank you to Dr Kate Bagnall, who graciously put up with my many questions.

I am very grateful to Asialink, Arts Queensland and the Shanghai Writers Association for the opportunity to be part of The Shanghai Writing Program and residency. Thank you so much to the Stella Prize and the Trawalla Foundation for time at the stunning Grasstrees Writing Retreat to write some of this book. *Stone Sky Gold Mountain* was written with the generous support of the Australia Council for the Arts, Queensland Literary Awards and a Griffith Review Fellowship. Thank you so much.

Huge thanks to my writer mates who helped me shape this novel – Laura Elvery, Cass Moriarty, Emma Doolan, Kathy George, Andrea Baldwin, Sally Piper, Krissy Kneen, Eleanor Goodman, Sarah Holland-Batt, Trudie Murrell, Clare Wright, John Tague, Mindy Gill and Frances Edmond. Thanks, Mum, for always wading through those dreaded early drafts, and Papa, for your loving support. Thank you to Stephen Yip, Pat Shears and the Stantons – Peter, Karen, John and Jill – for your interest and suggestions.

As always, thank you, thank you, to my amazing family for taking this long march with me. Dave, thank you for all your insight, love and forestry knowledge. All tree errors are my own.